THE GIRL IS MURDER

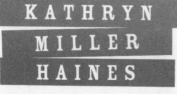

KATHRYN MILLER HAINES

SQUARE
FISH

ROARING BROOK PRESS

New York

For G & G and all the fathers

SQUARE FISH

An Imprint of Macmillan

THE GIRL IS MURDER. Copyright © 2011 by Kathryn Miller Haines.
All rights reserved. Printed in the United States of America by
R. R. Donnelley & Sons Company, Harrisonburg, Virginia.
For information, address Square Fish, 175 Fifth Avenue,
New York, NY 10010.

Square Fish and the Square Fish logo are trademarks of Macmillan and
are used by Roaring Brook Press under license from Macmillan.

Library of Congress Cataloging-in-Publication Data
Haines, Kathryn Miller.
The girl is murder / Kathryn Miller Haines.
p. cm.
Summary: In 1942 New York City, fifteen-year-old Iris grieves for her
mother who committed suicide and for the loss of her life of privilege, and
secretly helps her father with his detective business since he, having lost
a leg at Pearl Harbor, struggles to make ends meet.
ISBN 978-1-250-00639-4
[1. Interpersonal relations—Fiction.   2. Fathers and daughters—Fiction.
3. Private investigators—Fiction.   4. Missing persons—Fiction.
5. Social   classes—Fiction.   6. New York (N.Y.)—History—
20th century—Fiction.]   I. Title.

PZ7.H128123Gir 2011   [Fic]—dc22   2010032935

Originally published in the United States by Roaring Brook Press
First Square Fish Edition: May 2012
Square Fish logo designed by Filomena Tuosto
Book designed by Alexander Garkusha
macteenbooks.com

1 3 5 7 9 10 8 6 4 2

AR: 4.8 / LEXILE: HL700L

POP'S LEG WAS ACROSS THE ROOM when I came downstairs. I didn't ask him how it got there. Its location made it clear that the prosthetic had been hurled at some point, with enough force to bring down the photo of Mama that used to sit on the Philco radio.

"Morning, Pop," I said as I came into the room just off the parlor that he used as an office. He flashed me an index finger and pointed at the telephone receiver cradled against his ear. I got it; he was busy. He was always busy. This was how it was with him and me; he tried to be a private detective, I tried to pretend like I no longer existed. So far, I was the more successful of the two of us.

The minute passed and it was clear he wasn't going to be getting off the phone anytime soon. He covered the mouthpiece with his hand. "If you're going out, you might want to see if Mrs. Mrozenski needs anything at the grocer's."

He returned to his call before I could correct him. I wasn't going *out*, I was going to school, my first day of public school, which he would've known if he ever listened to anything I said. I trudged across the parlor and out the front door. Mrs. Mrozenski was sitting on the stoop drinking coffee from a dented tin cup. Beside her head hung a small sign that read AA INVESTIGATIONS.

"Good morning, Mrs. Mrozenski," I said.

"Good morning, Iris. Don't you look nice today?"

I smiled halfheartedly. I'd worried half the night about what to wear to school. Gone was my private school uniform. In its place was a uniform of my own making: my mother's pearls, a Peter Pan blouse, a plaid skirt, bobby socks, and saddle shoes.

"You have breakfast?" she asked. Mrs. Mrozenski was technically our landlady. She owned the whole house, but usually limited herself to two rooms: the kitchen and her bedroom. The rest she had given over to Pop and me, only interfering when one of us committed the unforgivable sin of moving one of her knickknacks from a table to a bookshelf or entering the house from the kitchen door.

"Not exactly."

"You cannot start school on an empty stomach." She got up like she was going back into the house. I could see what was coming: pots and pans, eggs and toast, a feast that on any other day I might've welcomed. But this was my first day at a new school. I would be lucky if I could stomach water.

"I'm all right," I told her.

She gave me a look that told me she knew what I was going through even if she was kind enough not to say it aloud. "What about lunch? You pack food?"

It hadn't occurred to me to do so. I never carried a lunch at Chapin. "I'll get something there."

"With what money?" She didn't wait for me to answer. She dug into her pocket and produced a handful of change. "You get something at the cafeteria. Promise?"

I slipped the money into my pocketbook. "I promise."

"Your father, he is good?"

I shrugged in response. Who knew how Pop was?

"He's trying to do the right thing by you, Iris. It is hard." Again, I didn't respond. What was the point? "I make pierogi tonight. Maybe some pork, too."

"Thank you. That sounds delicious."

Mrs. Mrozenski cooked dinner for us every night, asking nothing in return except for clean plates and our ration tickets. Pop was always reminding me to say thank you to her, as though Mama hadn't drilled common decency into me. But then how was he to know what I did and didn't learn in those years he was gone?

"Maybe I invite my daughter," she said.

"I don't know if Pop's going to be home tonight," I said. She was always trying to pair her daughter, Betty, with Pop. In her mind, my mother was nine months dead and it was time for Pop to move on. It was funny how nine months could seem like an eternity to one person and the blink of an eye to another. I don't need to tell you which one was my experience.

"Another time maybe. Have a good day, Iris," she said.

"You, too." As I started down the walk, I turned and waved at her. Mrs. Mrozenski waved back, and from the front window a flag with a single star waved along with her. It commemorated her son, a marine who'd been at sea since February.

It was drizzling as I trudged down the street from our house to Public School 110. The scenery matched the dull gray sky: garbage cans awaiting pickup lined the road, filling the air with the sweet scent of rotting vegetables. A pile of steaming manure lay in the cobblestone street where one of the horse-drawn delivery trucks that still operated in this area had paused in its mission.

Pop had tried to sell our move to Orchard Street as an adventure. With everything else that had happened, a fresh start would be good for us. At first I tried to be cheerful about the whole thing, but as weeks turned to months, I could no longer see the move as a change for the better. To my eyes the Lower East Side wasn't just a different neighborhood from the one we'd come from. Its name and its surroundings made it clear that we had experienced a downfall, slipping from the good end of town to the bad, descending from the top of the mountain to somewhere near its bottom. Not *the* bottom. After all, we were on the Lower East

Side, not the *last* of the East Side. That, I thought, was yet to come.

FROM THE MOMENT I entered the doors of P.S. 110, I was dodging, ducking, and holding my breath, hoping that whatever I just saw would pass by without doing me harm. The kids were rough in the way that feral cats were rough; it was like they were fighting to survive and didn't give a damn what it took to make that happen. Public school was exactly what I imagined trench warfare was like. More than once one of them locked eyes with me and I got the feeling that if I didn't move NOW they would pounce on me and eat me for lunch. I stayed close to the tan-colored walls, my hand always on the plaster, like a mouse looking for a hole I could disappear into.

"Outta the way, meat." A girl in a too-tight cardigan cut across my path, sending me toward a row of lockers. Two boys holding each other in a headlock forced me in the other direction, until I bumped into a box set aside to collect tin cans. I pictured myself tumbling headfirst into the metal scraps, but I was lucky. Not only did I stay on my feet, but the box was empty. Apparently, nobody here had time to collect aluminum and tin for the war.

I backed away from the box and checked to see who had witnessed my stumble. Only the poster above the empty collection bin acknowledged my presence. WANTED FOR VICTORY, it announced in bold type. WASTE PAPER, OLD RAGS,

SCRAP METAL, OLD RUBBER. GET IN THE SCRAP! Only someone had altered the last line with a pencil, so that the wanted items now included bloody rags. Conveniently, they'd also drawn a picture indicating what part of the female anatomy those rags might come from, just in case you were confused.

I tried to hide my shock and ducked into the girls' bathroom, hoping to catch my breath in the privacy of a stall. The doors were missing, though. A blonde in a sloppy joe sweater sat on the radiator by the window, smoking a cigarette. She didn't even shift her position when I came in. If anything, she seemed annoyed that I had interrupted her.

"What?" she said as I stared dumbly at the sight of someone smoking—*smoking*—on school property.

"Nothing," I said. "I have to . . . use the facilities."

"The *facilities*? You in the wrong place, meat?"

At first I misunderstood her—was she saying that the bathroom was not in fact the place where one relieved herself? But then I realized that her question had a different purpose: why was I in this school to begin with?

"No," I said. "I'm new."

Her eyes tracked me from the top of my pin-curled head to the toes of my scuffed saddle shoes. They lingered at my gored plaid skirt, the one I'd made after seeing the pattern in *McCall's* (years of wearing uniforms and a sudden summertime growth spurt hadn't left me with much of a wardrobe). She condemned my homemade sense of fashion with a shake of her head.

"Why did you call me *meat*?" I asked.

She crossed her legs and pointed a spectator pump toward the ceiling. "It's meat as in *fresh*. Fresh meat."

Oh. "But I'm a sophomore."

"Doesn't matter. Fresh is fresh."

"I'm Iris, by the way."

"And I'm busy. You're here to pee? So pee," she said.

Her gaze didn't leave me. I wanted to turn around and go, but those brown eyes issued a challenge that I knew in my heart I had to take. So I entered a stall, hiked up my skirt, and sat on the toilet even though it was the last thing I wanted to do.

She kept watching me. I offered the toilet a trickle and then continued sitting there, hoping to die.

"I'm Suze," she said.

"Nice to meet you," I said from my perch.

"You want a gasper?"

It must've been clear that I didn't know what she was offering me, because she produced a pack of Lucky Strikes and wiggled them my way.

"No, thanks."

Her Indian bracelets rattled as she returned the pack to her purse. "Why you want to leave the Upper East Side and come here?"

"How do you know where I'm from?"

"You got your glasses on." What was she talking about? I didn't wear glasses. "Those pearls real?"

7

They were, but I wasn't sure I'd win any favors by telling her so. "I don't know."

She huffed at my answer. "So what's your story, morning glory?"

"Excuse me?"

"Why you want to come here?"

I almost laughed at the question. Did she honestly think I was here by choice?

She seemed to recognize that she'd made an error. "Your pop overseas?"

"Something like that." I wiped, flushed, reassembled myself. I was going to be late for my first class. Not that I knew where it was.

"What branch?"

"Navy," I said.

"Bet he's an officer."

"He was."

"My man's in the Air Corps."

Did she mean her father? I didn't think so. With the paint and the clothes, Suze could pass for eighteen easy. It wasn't hard to imagine that she had a boyfriend who'd joined up.

I went to the sink and washed my hands. What should I say now? Usually, I had a gift for gab, but in this new place, with all these new people, my former self didn't have enough air to breathe.

"You think he's going to make it home safe?" she asked.

"Sure." And he had. Pop, who had never expected to fight in a war but got caught in the beginnings of one anyway, had made it home safe and sound. Except for the leg.

"Your mama must be scared."

"She's dead," I said.

"Ouch, baby," said Suze. "How?"

I answered without thinking. "She killed herself." I'd never said the words out loud before. You didn't talk about suicide. Not in a normal voice, anyway. You whispered euphemisms for it, trying to pretty-up an awful thing by calling it something else. *She took her own life. She died by her own hand. She couldn't bear to carry on.* Even the newspaper obituary had taken the stark awfulness out of what she'd done by reducing the act to a single adverb: *suddenly.*

Ingrid Anderson, *suddenly*, December 31, 1941.

And now here I was talking about it like it was no big deal. All my fear about P.S. 110 suddenly disappeared. A new school was nothing compared to what I'd already been through.

Suze stared at me for a long, silent moment. It wasn't the kind of story that she thought a girl like me was going to tell. "They shouldn't take a man with kids when there's no woman at home," she said.

That was funny. She thought I was an orphan, or just about one. "He'll be back soon," I said.

"And so will my Bill. He's young. He's strong." Suze tipped her head back and exhaled a stream of smoke that

9

seemed to draw her name in cursive letters. As quickly as it appeared, it was gone.

Now that I was standing close to her, I could make out the sweetheart wings pinned to her sweater.

"Roosevelt says it will be over soon," I said.

In just three months the war would celebrate its first anniversary. None of us wanted to believe it would linger long enough to mark a second.

She leaned her head against the window, her cheek against the pane. Her breath fogged up the glass. "That's good," she said. "I don't think I can take much more. I'm beat to the socks." She tossed her butt into the sink, fluffed her hair in the mirror, and made sure the victory rolls in her hair were pinned firmly in place. Once she was sure her appearance was up to snuff, she turned back to me. "You better make tracks, baby girl. You don't want to be tardy on your first day."

"Thanks."

"Want a tip?" she said.

"Sure," I said, trying to be casual.

She pointed at the lower half of my body. "Burn the skirt."

I assured her I would.

FIVE MINUTES LATER it was me I wanted to destroy, not the skirt.

A bell rang its warning that we had two minutes to get

into our seats. I stashed my pocketbook in my locker and tried to read the room numbers on the schedule card I'd been given in the front office. Unfortunately, the ink had smeared after I washed my hands—pretty ironic, given that my first class of the day was something called Personal Hygiene. I searched the halls for someone to help me, but in an instant the bustling crowd had vanished.

Or so I thought. At the end of the hall stood a cluster of five boys and girls, chatting like all they had was time. Like Suze, the girls were tall and broad-shouldered, their busts jutting out in a way that showed they enhanced their bosoms with handkerchiefs. They wore heavy makeup and such elaborate hairstyles that I had to imagine they'd been up since the crack of dawn rolling and pinning them in place. As teacher after teacher closed their doors and implored their classes to stand for the Pledge of Allegiance, they said their farewells and started toward their destinations. At least most of them did. One of the boys remained behind.

"You lost?" he said. I looked over my shoulder for whoever it was he was talking to. There was no one in the hallway but us.

"Yes," I said. "I'm supposed to be in a class called Personal Hygiene, but I don't know where the room is."

"Who's the teacher?"

I looked at the card but found my eyes unwilling to focus on the print that hadn't been smeared. I'd talked to boys before—friends' brothers and fathers—but to be around them in school was just . . . weird. Especially a boy like this one. His hair was greased back with pomade, and he had a smell about him that seemed to be a combination of his morning shower, a cigarette he'd smoked before entering the building, and something else I couldn't identify. His eyes were sleepy and at half-mast, as though there was nothing on this earth that could ruffle him. Not girls. Not teachers barking for everyone to sit down and be quiet. Not even the war. How on earth were we supposed to be able to learn with people like him around?

"Hello?" he said. Plenty of time had passed for me to read the name off my schedule card, but I still stood there, silent.

"It's smeared," I finally said. "But I think it says Mr. Pinsky."

"Right. Pinsky's down that way." He pointed toward one of the hallways that branched off to the left of us. "Last door on the left. Don't sit up front if you can avoid it. He's a spitter."

"Thanks." So that was two people who'd been kind to me, and first period had barely begun. Maybe public school wouldn't be so awful after all. "I'm Iris Anderson. I'm new."

"So I guessed. Pleasure to meet you, Iris Anderson." He had a slow smile, the kind that took so long to appear that you knew that when he offered it to you, he meant it. "I'm Tom Barney."

"Shouldn't you be in class?" I said.

"Shouldn't you?"

I blushed. I couldn't help myself. There was something about the way he talked that made me think I was doing something forbidden. Or maybe he just made me wish I was.

One of the girls who'd been with him earlier reappeared at the top of the hall. She frowned when she saw me, and then cleared her throat to get Tom's attention. "Look who got a hall pass," she said when he turned and acknowledged her.

"Lucky you," he replied.

"Want a smoke?"

"Absolutely. I'll meet you out back in five," he said. "I'm helping Iris here find her class."

"I'm sure she can find it herself," said the girl.

"Cool it, Rhona. I said I'll see you in five ticks."

"I'm giving you four." She turned tail and disappeared.

"I can find it on my own," I said. "Really. It's just down that hall, right?"

"Right," he said.

"Thanks again for your help."

"Any time, Iris Anderson."

WHEN I ARRIVED in Mr. Pinsky's class, one of his students was reading the morning announcements off of a mimeographed page. Rather than letting me take my seat, Mr. Pinsky gestured for me to remain near the door until the recitation ended, putting me on display for the entire room. I spent an eternity staring at my shoes while the pug-nosed girl ended her morning spiel by reminding the students that the principal wished them to "remain vigilant about their personal possessions until such time as the person or persons responsible for the locker thefts has been apprehended."

So public school not only welcomed fights in the hallway and smoking in the girls' room, it attracted thieves, too. I made a note to retrieve my purse from my locker as soon as possible.

By the time the announcements concluded, every eye in the class was watching me. Somebody faked a cough and muttered "Fresh meat" under their breath. I took a seat as the class buzzed with two topics: the new girl and who was behind the locker robberies.

I tuned out the comments about my clothes and focused on the more interesting topic.

"I heard they actually cut the padlocks open," said one girl.

"It's one of the guys in the Rainbows," said a girl with a pinched face and a husky voice.

"Sure, but which one?" asked her red-faced friend.

"Probably one of the Eye-talians."

My eavesdropping wasn't as subtle as I hoped. The girl with the pinched face turned my way and offered me a sneer. "What are you staring at?"

"Nothing," I said. I could feel color bleed into my face. I

looked away, hoping they wouldn't see my embarrassment. It was too late.

"Hold your tongue, Myrtle," the pinch-faced girl said to her friend. "You don't want to make the square from Delaware clutch her pearls."

Sadly, that was the kindest welcome I got for the rest of the morning.

Every class I went to I was stared at. I was asked to introduce myself before the students assembled in Home Economics by announcing my favorite meal to cook. When I told them toast, I was laughed at. I didn't know how to cook. There'd never been a need for me to do it before.

My walk was mimicked, my voice was aped, and I was reminded at every turn that I didn't belong. What had Pop been thinking, sending me into the jaws of public school without any kind of warning? He hadn't been thinking: that was the point. How could he know who I was when he hadn't known who I'd been?

Finally, lunchtime arrived. I went to my locker to retrieve my lunch money, anxious the whole time that the combination I thought I remembered was incorrect. I needn't have worried; the lock was gone and the locker was empty. My purse and everything in it was missing.

That did it. For the first time that day, I let myself cry. I was beyond caring who saw me.

I didn't have the heart to report the crime—aside from my house key and the money Mrs. Mrozenski had given me, there wasn't much of value in my purse. And I certainly didn't have the strength to go to the cafeteria with nothing to eat and no one to sit with. Instead, I retreated to a girls' bathroom stall and waited out the hour.

THE AFTERNOON was more of the same, just one embarrassment after another. I longed for a friendly face to make it all go away, but Suze never reappeared. Tom did, though. Just as I left my last class of the day, I saw him in handcuffs, being led out of school by two police officers.

What on earth was going on?

A boy with a camera dangling around his neck stopped to watch the action. As Tom was guided into a squad car, the boy took a photo. That task complete, he produced a notepad and pencil and jotted something down.

"What's happening?" I asked him.

"They arrested Tom Barney for the locker thefts."

"Why?"

He half snorted, half laughed. "Because he confessed. I knew it had to be one of the Rainbows, I just didn't know which one."

My heart broke: not only had I been robbed, but one of the only two people who'd been nice to me that day was the thief.

WHEN I RETURNED HOME to the Orchard Street house, Pop had a client. There was an unspoken rule that I was to remain scarce when he was in the middle of business. In fact, I think he preferred it if I was scarce even if he wasn't. But I wanted to plop down near the radio and listen to *Kitty Foyle* to take my mind off the day. So I took a risk and stayed in the parlor, keeping the Philco's volume down low so I wouldn't clue Pop to my presence. Mama's picture had been returned to its usual place, but the glass was broken out of it and a scratch had pierced the photograph, stabbing the still image somewhere near her heart.

I closed my eyes and let the tales of scrappy Kitty trying to move up in the world soothe me. For fifteen minutes I was somewhere else, caught between Kitty's world and my own the year prior. When I came home from a bad day back then—and let's face it, they had been few and far between—Mama would sit beside me and run her fingers

17

through my hair, telling me that everything was going to be all right, peppering her English with German. *"Alles hat ein Ende, nur die Wurst hat zwei,"* she would say, trying to make me smile. "Everything has an end, except sausages, which have two." Sometimes it annoyed me, but more often than not I was lulled by her calm reassurance. It would be all right. Everything did have an end, even my minor calamities. I would be fine, just like she was. Anything I was going through she had already endured.

In fact, she'd survived much more than me. Mama was a German immigrant. She'd already made it through one war.

Maybe that was why she had killed herself—perhaps she couldn't stand the thought of going through a second one.

I closed my eyes and tried to picture her there beside me. What would she say if she was here? *It will get better, Iris. You mustn't be afraid to stand on your own.* She wasn't. There was nothing Mama wasn't willing to do by herself. I'm sure part of that came from Pop being absent for months at a time, but some of it must've been because she was German. When everyone is looking at you with suspicion because of where you came from, you couldn't depend on them to help you.

It was working. I was calming down . . . until snippets of conversation taking place in Pop's office forced their way into the room.

"I would like my money back," said a voice I didn't recognize.

"All I need is another week. You have to understand, you can't force things. The opportunity has to be right," said Pop.

"You've had plenty of time. She's going somewhere every night. For all your dillydallying, I could've taken my own pictures by now and been done with it."

"You're right," said Pop. "Of course you're right." I left my spot by the radio and approached the door. It was closed, but there was a vent near the bottom to help the radiator heat circulate from one room to another during the winter. I kneeled near the opening and watched the agitated client as he paced in front of the desk. Usually, Pop just dealt with missing persons—it was his specialty, or so he claimed in the advertisement he took out in the phone directory. But this didn't sound like a missing person case to me.

I heard Pop open his desk drawer and riffle through it. "Here's the entire retainer."

"I'm disappointed in you, Arthur. You said you could help and I believed you."

"I still can. I just need more time."

"I should've gone to your brother's agency, but I wanted to give you a chance."

Even with the door between us, I could imagine Pop's expression at the mention of Uncle Adam. Detecting is in my family's blood. My uncle's in the business, too, only he has his own agency, uptown, under the family's original name, Ackerman. At the beginning of summer, after those first rough weeks in our new home, a home they'd begged us not to take, Uncle Adam and Aunt Miriam had stopped by with a pot roast, a plant, and a plan. Pop could work with Uncle Adam at *his* agency, strictly desk work, mind you, but Adam would give him a fifty-fifty split. Pop had refused the plant and the plan. He wasn't crazy enough to turn down one of Aunt Miriam's pot roasts, though. Especially with rumors of a meat ration already on the horizon.

"I don't want your help," he'd told Uncle Adam. A rift had grown between them in the months since Pop's return. When I asked about it, Aunt Miriam dismissed it as a momentary difference of opinion.

"Come on now—it's not charity," said Uncle Adam. "I've seen you do amazing things with nothing more than a phone at your disposal."

"I'm doing this on my own, Adam."

"Art—this is foolish. You can't do this on your own. Your leg—"

"Is the least of my problems."

"I've got a name and a reputation. It will take you years to build that up."

"Your name isn't my name anymore, remember?" Pop had changed our surname years before, when he'd first joined the military and didn't want to stand out.

"You know that doesn't matter."

"God damn it—I said no!"

Everything in the room stopped. I thought Aunt Miriam's bulging brown eyes were going to launch right out of her head. Instead, she turned her gaze toward me as though focusing on the child was the balm she needed to survive this moment.

"Go to your room, Iris," she said. She wasn't a woman you said no to even if there wasn't pot roast involved. I slinked away, up the stairs and presumably out of earshot, though really I lingered just beyond the turn of the hallway wall, unseen to anyone downstairs. To increase the realism of my exit, I stomped my feet on the wooden floor, then stretched a leg across the hall and kicked a door closed to further simulate that I was safely shut in my room.

"Think of Iris," said Aunt Miriam after she was sure I was gone. "She was so happy at her school. There's no reason to uproot her now."

I fought a grin. Thank God for Aunt Miriam, I thought. There was still hope. There was no reason I had to stay with Pop. I could live with Adam and Miriam, attending classes at Chapin as though nothing had changed.

"I *am* thinking of her. She's not your child; she's mine." Pop had paused, the breath in his chest rattling. Even though he'd been in New York since January, his injury still seemed fresh in those days, the pain warranting a series of pills he kept stashed on his bedside table. He hadn't yet given in to the prosthetic leg. His pants leg hung empty and he hobbled around the house on crutches, only moving when he absolutely had to. "I want you both out of this house."

"You must be reasonable, Arthur," said Aunt Miriam. "You can't rely on Ingrid's inheritance to last forever."

Pop laughed. It wasn't a joyful sound. Like a burned marshmallow, it was so charred around the edges that you couldn't enjoy the part of it that should've been sweet. "You think there's money, Miriam? There's nothing left. But don't you worry—Iris and I will be fine on our own. We don't need your *husband's* help."

"Let's go, Miriam," said Adam. From my hiding place I could see him open the front door. Aunt Miriam didn't join him.

"Let us make this right."

"And how are you going to do that? By going back in time?"

A sob escaped me, but I don't think anyone heard me. First Mama, then Uncle Adam and Aunt Miriam. Was I going to lose everyone who mattered to me?

They left after that. For a long time I stayed in the upstairs hallway, wondering if anything would be gained by going to Pop and telling him that I wanted to stay with Adam and Miriam. I'm not sure what stopped me; maybe it was the fear that I would lose him, too. Eventually, I fell asleep on the hard wooden floor. In the morning I awoke in my own bed in my new room with no memory of how I got there. Pop never said a word about it.

Now, in his office, Pop cleared his throat until it sounded like a growl building in his chest. "If you want to hire my brother, hire my brother, Mr. Wilson. That's up to you. He might work faster, but you know as well as I do that he won't be as discreet and he'll charge you twice as much."

Someone thumped his fingers on the desktop, playing a tune of indecision. Was it Mr. Wilson, or Pop regretting his words? "Tell you what," said Mr. Wilson. "If you can get me something in two days, I'll return the money to you. Otherwise, I'm taking my business elsewhere."

Pop exhaled heavily, his lips momentarily knocking together and making the *pfft* noise that horses pulling carriages in Central Park made by way of greeting. "That's very generous of you, Mr. Wilson. Very generous. I'll be in touch."

Mr. Wilson turned and started toward the door. I leaped to my feet and jumped across the parlor, landing on the sofa with a thud. By the time he opened the door and joined me, I had a copy of *Calling All Girls* on my lap and the dull air of a fifteen-year-old who couldn't care less what the adults were up to.

Mr. Wilson saw me, tipped his hat, and left the house.

Pop joined me a few minutes later. His tie hung loose about his neck, and the furrows in his face, the ones that he'd had since he returned from Pearl Harbor, seemed deeper. His limp was exaggerated, as it often was when he'd worn the prosthetic for too long. It didn't fit him right, but he didn't want to spend the money to get it fixed. The military would've done it for him, or so Mrs. Mrozenski claimed, but Pop acted like he would rather die than ask them for anything.

He picked up my magazine and looked at the cover, shaking his head at the picture of Joan Leslie holding up a U.S. flag.

"Who's that?" he asked.

"She was in *High Sierra* with Humphrey Bogart," I said. *She played a cripple*, I almost added. I'm not sure what stopped me.

"What's a sub-deb?" he asked. He was referring to the subtitle of the magazine, *The Modern Magazine for Girls and Sub-Debs*.

"Kind of like a debutante."

That didn't seem to clarify things for him.

Pop had been only eighteen when he married Mama, nineteen when they had me. Responsibility had aged him—at least that's what Mama always claimed—but he was a handsome man. Back in our old apartment there'd been a picture of him in uniform on the fireplace mantel, and more than one of my friends had feigned a swoon at the sight of his broad shoulders and delicate features.

Where was that photo now? I hadn't seen it since we moved.

"How long have you been home?" asked Pop.

"Not long." He was wondering how much I'd heard. I turned the page of the magazine and focused on an advertisement for a powder that would take the sheen off my nose.

"What did you do today?"

"I started public school, remember?" It came out snottier than I'd intended. I tried to soften it with a smile.

"That's right. And how was it?"

Awful, I wanted to say. *I was robbed and ridiculed. I don't belong there. Don't come crying to me when I start wearing tight sweaters and smoking.* But Pop looked so defeated by what had transpired with Mr. Wilson that I couldn't bear to bring him down even further. My complaints could wait. "It was all right." I turned another page of *Calling All Girls*, trying to appear nonchalant, and landed on the beginning of "Mystery at the Lookout," a new serial by the author of Nancy Drew. "What did that guy want?"

"His money back. He wanted me to prove that his wife was cheating on him." Pop became an officer in the Navy when I was ten years old and visited us only a handful of times each year for the next five. Each time he came home, it was like I was meeting him for the very first time. If there was anything positive to come from not knowing my father for so long, it was that he never really learned to be a father. He lacked the filter that most adults possessed, the one that told them to clam up in front of the kids.

"And you couldn't prove it?" I asked.

He smiled, deepening the creases on his face. "I tried. But I'm starting to think I'm too slow for the detective business." He thumped his thigh, just above where his leg ended and the wood began.

"He's giving you a second chance, though, right?"

"You were listening."

I froze. Boy, howdy—I hadn't wanted to let him know that. "He's a loud talker."

He raised the knot on his tie. "It doesn't matter. He's right. If I can't get what he needs in two weeks, I certainly won't accomplish it in two days. He should just call Uncle Adam and be done with it."

This was the most Pop had spoken to me in weeks. Like I said, he didn't know how to be a father, and while that meant he sometimes told me things he shouldn't, it also meant he often avoided me so he wouldn't give away that he didn't know *what* to say to me. "I thought you were only doing missing persons," I said.

"Unfortunately, not enough of them are missing." His eyes twinkled at the joke. Mama used to say he had a wicked sense of humor, but I rarely saw signs of it. I just assumed it was something he'd lost along with his leg. "We need money, Iris." Just as soon as he said it, he seemed to recognize that it wasn't an appropriate thing to tell me. He approached me, put his hand on my head, and ruffled my hair. I had a feeling that it was something he used to do when I was very small, but the memory was too far away for me to be sure. I stiffened at his touch. "But don't you worry about it. Your pop's taking care of things. I've got to go out for a while tonight."

"Dinner's going to be ready soon."

"You'll have it without me. Tell Mrs. Mrozenski I'm sorry I can't join you."

Tell her yourself, I wanted to say, but my heart wasn't in being disobedient. "All right."

He tweaked my nose with his finger. "Don't forget to do your homework. You don't want to rot your brain reading romance magazines."

I waited until Pop was out the door and out of sight to break the news to Mrs. Mrozenski. She was hunched over a large pan of sizzling cabbage, alternating between stirring the food and mopping her brow with a dishcloth. As she worked she danced to a tune only she could hear. Her feet were surprisingly nimble for a woman who had to be twice Pop's size.

"You hungry, Iris?" she asked as I ducked into the kitchen.

"I'm getting there." I was still getting used to her kitchen. Gone was the electric refrigerator we'd had on the Upper East Side. In its place was an icebox that leaked so often it had warped the floor beneath it. And the stove used coal—*coal*—to make its heat, burping a thick black fog that coated the porcelain surface and turned everything white to gray, including underwear we'd hung to dry on the line behind her house. Bins of coal sat outside the back door, where Pop retrieved it each morning to make sure Mrs. Mrozenski had everything she needed to run the cooker.

"Pop can't join us tonight," I said.

"Oh." She frowned at the pan. "He leave something for me maybe?"

It was my turn to scowl. "Like what?"

"Like an envelope?"

Money. He was late on the rent. That was why he was skipping dinner.

"He must've forgot," I said.

Her face relaxed. "Of course. Is no problem. I call you when it's ready?"

"Sure."

For a while I lazed by the radio, listening to *Captain Midnight* and trying not to think about the rent. Pop had lost jobs before; I knew that. It had happened twice that I knew of right after he had started up his company that summer. He couldn't follow people quickly. He was never going to be able to chase someone down. His busted pin meant that he did his best work behind a desk and on a phone, only that wasn't the kind of work that paid well. And well-paying jobs were what we needed.

It was funny how aware I'd become of money in the past few months. We were never rich before, at least not compared to my friends, but I'd never wanted for anything, either. There was always cash for comics and candy, new dresses and new movies. I didn't wonder how tuition was paid, food bought, rent kept up to date. It just was. It was shocking to go from a world where everything was provided without effort to this constant awareness that everything I did—even the air I breathed—felt like it came at a cost. At first I resented it because I believed Pop had caused it. If he hadn't been injured, if he hadn't left the military, if he hadn't come home, things wouldn't have had to change.

And maybe Mama wouldn't have killed herself.

I shook the thought out of my head. Mrs. Mrozenski turned on her phonograph and a polka platter began to compete with the noise of the radio. The smell of frying onions signaled that dinner was minutes from being ready. I had homework to do—an essay on what it meant to be a citizen that would take me a half hour at most—and then the whole evening stretched before me with nothing to fill it. I don't know what made me do it—the boredom, the loneliness, the forced cheer of the polka music—but I got up and went into Pop's office.

It was rare that I went in there. Pop never told me I couldn't, probably because it never occurred to him that he should, but the space was so much his that merely crossing the threshold felt like a violation. He had only two rules: don't disturb the paperwork on his desk and stay out of the locked cabinet that sat to the left of his chair.

The first one was easy to disobey, provided I memorized the exact order things had been in when I'd found them. The second one I had no choice but to respect. After all, the cabinet was locked. How could I do anything but stay out of it? Besides, I was pretty sure I knew what he kept inside it: his gun. He had to have one, right? All the detectives in the movies did. It seemed like precisely the sort of thing you hid in a locked cabinet.

Mr. Wilson's file was still sitting on top of the desk. I sat in Pop's chair and opened the folder. In his chicken scratch he outlined Mr. Wilson's first visit to him and described, in detail, why the man was concerned that his wife was being unfaithful. Pop had tried to follow her on three different occasions, and while he didn't write down the results of that work, it wasn't hard to read the outcome in the description of the places he visited: Upper East Side hotels one entered by climbing long flights of stairs. Pop didn't stand a chance catching Mrs. Wilson red-handed. He probably hadn't been able to catch his breath.

The job looked pretty easy to my eyes. All the man wanted was evidence of what he was already certain was going on: a photograph, confirmation from a witness, a description of the man his wife was keeping time with. No wonder Pop had failed. Even if he had been able to follow Mr. Wilson's wife, he would've drawn attention to himself. A man with an obvious limp could expect two responses:

pity or a rude attempt to ignore him. Either way, Mrs. Wilson had to have noticed him the first time he appeared on the scene.

What Pop needed was someone who could blend in, whose age and appearance meant they were easily ignored. Someone who could sit in a hotel lobby looking like a bored little rich girl waiting for her parents, and nobody would think twice about her.

Uncle Adam was right when he told Pop he couldn't go it alone. But maybe it wasn't *his* help Pop needed—maybe it was mine.

By the time Mrs. Mrozenski called me into dinner I had a plan: I was going to help Pop.

3

TWENTY-FOUR HOURS LATER I was on my first stake-out, outside the Wilsons' Upper East Side apartment building. I'd passed it a thousand times in my former life, had even been inside it once while visiting a friend after school. Now I took up space on a bench across the street. Just as I took on the posture of a bored, privileged young woman, familiar voices rang out: Bev and Bea, or—as they were usually referred to in the halls of Chapin—the twins. Blondes with blue eyes and perfect ski-jump noses, they were identically clad in Chapin's plaid skirts and white blouses. As they headed for home they were exchanging the day's gossip, their voices rising and falling with amusement as they relayed who said what to whom. I slouched down on the bench, hoping they wouldn't notice me.

"Iris?" said Bea.

I straightened up as though it wasn't them that had

caused me to slouch, but exhaustion they'd just shaken me out of. "Bea? Bev? It's so great to see you."

If they found it strange to find me loitering on a bench at twilight, they didn't admit it out loud. Instead, they surveyed me for a moment as though they weren't certain what to say next. Compliment my clothes? Nope, no hope of that. Tell me they missed my witty comments during English Lit? Doubtful.

I decided to help them out of the tight spot. "I'm waiting for my aunt," I said. "We're having dinner."

"How lovely," said Bev. "Isn't this funny—we were just talking about you today."

"Oh, really?" I stood up. For some reason I wanted to be on the same level as the two of them. Even though we were all the same height, I felt smaller. Maybe it was their school uniforms. Strange as it seemed, I missed the brief skirt and scratchy blouse and how they magically made me one of them rather than the outsider I felt like now. Wasn't it funny how a uniform, which was designed to create conformity, could make me feel so special? I bet Pop must have felt the same way when he shed his military duds and rejoined life as a civilian.

"Yes," said Bea. "We were just asking Grace if she'd heard from you."

In the weeks after we'd moved to the Lower East Side, some of the Chapin girls had attempted to stay in contact with me, chief among them Grace Dunwitty, my former best friend. She called me every other day and invited me to spend my weekends at her apartment, where I could forget the Orchard Street house while we passed our time pasting pictures of Deanna Durbin into our scrapbooks and slept beneath Grace's pink canopy.

The visits meant I had to endure Grace's endless questions about our new life. She must have thought years of sharing lunches and sleepovers meant I owed her something: *Do you miss having money?* (I guess.) *What's it like to have a father with only one leg?* (I'm not sure I know what it's like to have a father, period.) *Do you miss your mother?* (What do you think?) They were logical questions, ones I might've asked myself if I had the courage, but—boy, howdy—I resented how easily Grace asked them, how she made no attempt to hide her curiosity, how different she made me feel from everyone else. And so eventually I stopped making an effort to ride the subway uptown, stopped responding to her invitations, rejected offers to meet me halfway between her world and mine. On the Upper East Side I was the girl whose life forever changed when her mother had killed herself. But in our new home, I could just be Iris Anderson, daughter of an injured vet, a man who'd bravely endured Pearl Harbor.

"She said she's tried calling you," said Bev.

"I've been awfully busy," I said. "New school and all that."

"You have to tell us all about the Lower East Side." She

made it sound like some exotic destination she was thinking of visiting if she ever got her passport in order.

"There's not really much to tell," I said.

"Oh, come now," said Bev. "What are the people like?"

Just like you, I almost replied. *Only without the money.* "I've kind of kept to myself," I said.

"It's probably safer that way," said Bev.

"And how is public school?" asked Bea.

"Swell." I could see they weren't buying it. And why should they? We'd spent years mocking the kids who went to public school. "It's so strange being around boys," I added. I could tell that piqued their interest.

"What's it like?" asked Bea.

"More nerve-racking, I guess."

"Could you imagine getting to eat lunch with boys every day?" Bea said to her sister.

"I don't think I'd like it," said Bev. "I like going to an all-girls school."

"Don't be such a prude," said Bea.

"I'm not. Besides, it's not just boys Iris is around, it's colored boys, right?" She lowered her voice when she said it, as though admitting I went to school with kids of other races might cause me to contaminate their neighborhood.

"There are Puerto Ricans and Italians, sure."

"Well, be careful," said Bev.

I wanted them to go on their way, but it was clear I was going to have to be the one to end the conversation.

35

I looked off into the distance, where a woman wearing a hat festooned with a peacock feather was stepping out of a cab. "There's my aunt," I said. "I better go. Tell Grace I said hello."

"We will," said Bea, and then she took her sister by the arm and left. I waited until I could no longer see them before reclaiming my seat on the bench.

A breeze ruffled the pages of the *Archie* comic I'd brought along to occupy myself. With the wind came the aroma of early fall and something else—Mama's perfume. I turned, half expecting to find her behind me, but the air was empty. In our new house there was never any fear of stumbling upon her—after all, she'd never been there in life. But here on these streets, where she used to shop and visit with her friends, my mother's voice carried on the wind, her heels click-clacked down the sidewalk, her apartment keys jingled at their peculiar frequency. Was this why Pop had moved us? Not because of money, but to escape her memory?

Stop it, I told myself. *Focus on the task at hand.*

According to Pop's notes, Louise Wilson left the house every Tuesday night at seven for a Veterans of Foreign Wars Ladies Auxiliary meeting, or so she said. Lately she'd returned late in the evening with some new excuse about organizing clothes for Bundles for Britain or losing track of the time while knitting socks for soldiers and exchanging gossip. Once Mr. Wilson had gone to the church where the group was allegedly meeting, only to find its lights turned off and no sign of the dozen or so women Mrs. Wilson claimed came to every meeting. On another occasion, he followed her all the way to the Waldorf, where she disappeared inside before he was able to determine which direction she'd turned.

He had provided a photo of her that I'd struggled to memorize in the hours when Pop wasn't home. In it she stood beside her husband, her hands meekly folded in her lap, her smile tight and toothless. Her side was glued to Mr. Wilson's, as though she only represented half of the whole the two of them formed. She could've been attractive, but the years had softened her figure in a way my own mother had constantly fought against.

I continued to feign boredom on my bench, flipping through the *Archie* comic book but not reading what was on the page. My attention was riveted to the apartment building, where the uniform-clad doorman was tipping his hat as a woman exited the revolving door.

Was it her?

She asked him something, and he replied in a strong, clear voice, "Six-forty-five, Mrs. Wilson." She paused in the light leaking from the front windows and wound her watch. Then, with a smile at the man, she continued on her way up the street.

Bingo! I followed twenty paces behind, splitting my attention between her and the shop windows. If she turned to look back, I'd pause at the nearest display and pretend to examine what it had to offer.

My ploy wasn't necessary. She seemed to be in her own little world, moving forward with single-minded purpose to get to her destination. I used the time to examine her. It was a game Mama and I used to play—she would pick a random stranger as we waited for a cab or walked in the park and make me list three things I could tell just by looking at them. *Appearances are everything*, she would tell me when we stopped playing. *Remember that.* Mrs. Wilson's nails were freshly painted. There was cat hair on her coat. Her heels were expensive, but worn. They didn't strike me as the kind of pumps you donned to see a secret lover.

But then if she had a lover, she probably wasn't planning on keeping them on for very long.

I blushed at the thought. What made me such an expert on s-e-x? I couldn't even say the word out loud without spelling it.

Mrs. Wilson turned the corner, then another one. No Waldorf this night. We were headed toward the Plaza Hotel. I held back long enough for her to enter the building. I pretended to chew a wad of gum and swung my arms with the sort of entitled boredom most visitors to this address regularly demonstrated. As I walked into the lobby, I offered the doorman a sneer for his trouble.

I surveyed the room for Mrs. Wilson. She was already gone.

How was that possible? I'd only been seconds behind her. Hardly enough time for her to make it into the Palm Court, or one of the other restaurants that fanned off from the main lobby. My gaze landed on the closed powder room door. That's where she had to be. If she was meeting someone, she would want to freshen up beforehand.

I sauntered through the door and found her standing before the long row of mirrors, a tube of bright red lip cream in her hand. We both ignored each other as I disappeared into a stall and pretended to do my business.

When enough time had passed, I flushed the toilet, left the stall, and washed my hands. She had switched from makeup to hair care. She removed her hatpin, peeled off her straw hat, and used her fingers to fluff the slightly matted mess it had left behind. My own reflection danced in the glass. There was a time when I thought I might be pretty—perhaps even on my way to beautiful. Mama had been. With her blond hair and pale eyes, she cut a striking figure no matter what she wore or whom she accompanied. I hadn't been blessed with her coloring, but I was fortunate enough to not, in the words of Grace's mother, look too Jewish. I had asked my mother what she meant and she'd laughed it off as the insensitive words of an insensitive woman. But now in the flattering lighting of the Plaza's powder room, I could see hints of ethnicity. I was growing darker with age, my features slightly coarse, as though all of Mama's delicacy had vanished when she died.

Mrs. Wilson's reflection smiled at me. I tucked my hair behind my ears and smiled back.

I left her to her work and returned to the lobby, selecting a seat that would give me a good view of her when she finally returned. Instead of reading the comic, I pulled a camera from my purse and pretended to fidget with it. This wasn't Pop's preferred instrument of surveillance, a 1930s Leica he used because he claimed there was no better camera on the market. Instead, I had the small Brownie camera I'd gotten for my fourteenth birthday, a gift from Uncle Adam that took serviceable pictures, provided you were no more than ten feet from your subject. I stared through the viewfinder and pretended I was interested in capturing the ornate ceiling, then an impressionistic landscape in a gilded frame, then the pattern in the thick Oriental rug. Just as I came up from my study of the fleur-de-lis pattern, Mrs. Wilson entered the lobby and took her seat opposite me.

I continued to click away, then frowned at the camera as though I were uncertain how to operate it. She busied herself with a copy of the newspaper that had been discarded in the lobby, dividing her attention between the headlines and the elevator bank across the room from us.

"Togo Resigns as Japanese Foreign Minister," screamed her newspaper. "Fuel Rations May Be Widened to Cover Midwest."

I decided to shift positions. If whomever she was

waiting for was coming from the elevators, I needed to be closer to them if I was going to catch them on film. I tucked the comic under my arm and shouldered my pocketbook. Then I continued clicking the camera, capturing a poodle being herded across the lobby by the concierge and a floral display that prominently featured small American flags among its more fragrant offerings. The elevators dinged open and an assortment of people exited into the lobby.

I glanced toward Mrs. Wilson, waiting to see which of the men—if any—might catch her fancy. My money was on a fellow in a blue pinstriped suit. He was about her age and looked a little like Robert Young, if Robert Young had jowls. I got ready to take his picture. Her hand dashed into the air and she waved at the exiting crowd. Instead of Robert separating from the pack and heading her way, a young serviceman did, greeting her with a wide grin while he bisected the lobby in three easy strides.

They embraced and I captured their union three times, making certain to get the man's face in every shot. After their chaste meeting, they disappeared into the Oak Room, presumably to get a drink. Would this be enough to satisfy Mr. Wilson? So far all I had was proof that his wife wasn't where she claimed to be and that she was keeping company with a member of the opposite sex, neither of which seemed like evidence that she was having an affair. After all, this could just be a friend in town on leave whom she decided to get together with. Without telling her husband. In a hotel.

On second thought, maybe this *was* bad.

I decided to stay in the lobby to see what they'd do next. An hour passed, during which I read *Archie* cover to cover, and then the two left the bar and headed toward the elevators. I watched the dial indicating which floor the car was bound for, then stepped into another car and asked the operator to take me up. I arrived too late. The hallway was empty. That meant either they had run to their room or the man was staying in one of the ones closest to the elevator. I surveyed each door in turn. On one a DO NOT DISTURB sign gently swayed to and fro.

Bingo.

I put my hand on the knob and tried to turn it. It was locked. From behind the door came a deep, feminine giggle. Surely a married woman didn't come up to a hotel room with a man who was not her husband for innocent reasons. Was this enough evidence for Mr. Wilson?

Was it enough evidence for me?

I had Pop to think about. If he was going to get paid, if he was going to keep Mr. Wilson from going to Uncle Adam, he needed a photo, something more than the chaste pictures I'd captured in the lobby. Just as I was starting to think that the situation was hopeless, a maid came down the hallway, pushing a cart filled with towels, soap, and other amenities. I frowned and widened my eyes.

"Excuse me?" I said.

She looked up at me and grinned. "Can I help you, young lady?"

Boy, howdy, could she. "Gosh, I hope so. I thought my parents would be back in our room by now, but they haven't arrived yet and I don't have a key. Could you let me in?"

Her smile widened. "Of course." She produced a ring of keys and inserted one into the door. With a click, she turned the lock and gestured me in. "Now make sure you lock it behind you," she said.

"I will. Thanks. That was awfully swell of you." I kept up the little-girl act until I was inside. Fortunately, the bedroom area wasn't immediately visible to the door—there was a sitting area that one had to pass through. I quietly shut the door and armed myself with my Brownie. Then, after taking a deep breath and begging my arms to stop their shaking, I rounded the corner and captured the couple just as Mrs. Wilson was removing her brassiere.

I was out the door before she screamed.

4

I DIDN'T WANT TO TELL POP what I'd done until I had the pictures in hand. The only problem was, I was broke. The year before, I never left the house without a little walking-around money in my pocket or purse, always placed there by Mama in case I needed anything. It wasn't essentials she was thinking of, but a trip to the subway arcade, a picture show at the Rialto, or a new 78-rpm disc or comic book I just had to have that afternoon. Pop was either unaware of the financial needs of fifteen-year-old girls or simply didn't have the money to share. Either way, it was too uncomfortable a subject to broach. I would find a way to get what I needed without bothering him.

The next morning, my Brownie in hand, I sought out the school newspaper office.

At Chapin, the newspaper had been run by everyone in rotation, the bulk of the work falling to the seniors.

The paper was a privilege we all looked forward to, the information it contained a handy way to spread gossip and anoint who was worth talking about and who wasn't. I expected something similar at P.S. 110, a sort of blind worship of the printed word, but as I neared the office, I noticed the teetering stack of untouched newspapers that remained outside the cafeteria and auditorium.

It was a shame, because what I saw as I leafed through the pages on my way to the newspaper room was a wealth of information. This wasn't insider scoop about an exclusive school and its airy alumni. The stories were commentary on the media's claims that ours was a generation of layabouts who would never contribute anything worthwhile. There were opinion pieces written for and against lowering the minimum age for the draft to eighteen, and profiles on the students who'd already signed up and shipped out.

I knocked on the newspaper door and waited for someone to invite me to enter. Through the small pane of glass set in the door I could see several desks with typewriters and a chalkboard covered with story ideas that someone had already marked up with lines and check marks to indicate which they'd keep and which they'd toss. Two people were at work in the room. A girl hunched over a typewriter, hunting and pecking her way through an assignment. And a boy stared down at a folder with such intensity you would've thought it contained Axis war plans.

The boy was familiar. He'd been the kid with the camera who'd caught me up to speed when Tom Barney was arrested.

Neither responded to my knock. I turned the knob and walked inside.

The girl continued to ignore me. Her task was so strenuous that her Coke-bottle glasses practically met the page she was trying to type. The boy looked up at my entrance and then returned to the folder he had been looking through. From my new vantage I could see that it was full of glossy photographs. He wore a hat on his head, a fedora similar to one Pop owned. The band across it held a piece of paper in place that read PRESS.

"Hi," I said to the room in general. Still nothing from the girl, though the boy removed his hat at the sound of my voice, as though he was embarrassed to be caught wearing it. I approached him and decided that he was my best bet. "Remember me?"

If he did, his face didn't show it.

"I saw you taking pictures of Tom Barney the other day. When he was being arrested." Still nothing. Was I really that unmemorable? "That's a great camera you've got." I held up the Brownie and wiggled it. "As you can see, I'm not so well outfitted."

"You new?"

"I just moved here this summer."

He nodded, then focused on cleaning his lens with a

handkerchief that had been burrowed in his pocket. Initials were embroidered in one corner: P. L. "The editor already left for class. You looking to shoot for us?"

I couldn't tell if he thought that would be a good thing or not, though I suspected, given the hint of desperation in his voice, that anyone being interested in what he and the girl with the thick glasses did would be welcome.

"Oh, I'm not good enough for that." What was the best way to get someone to do something for you? Mama believed false modesty and flattery were the keys that opened every door. Whenever someone acted like she was nothing more than a dumb immigrant, she played it up, batting her eyes and musing that if she were as smart as they were, she would be so much better off. "I want to learn," I said. "I've read the paper and it's . . . amazing. The photos are really good. Like Dorothea Lange good." Okay, so I exaggerated.

"Really?" He wasn't unattractive, but there was a paleness to his skin and a scrawniness to his body that implied he either spent every hour of the day indoors or had been a sickly child who had never quite grown out of it.

"Our paper was a joke at my old school. Nobody took it seriously. I'd love to be able to do what you do, but I can't even develop film."

"I could teach you."

"Seriously?"

"You got anything in the camera now?"

I nodded and passed him the Brownie. "I'm Iris," I said.

47

"Paul," he countered, and shook my hand. He tipped his head toward the girl in the Coke-bottle glasses. "That's Pearl."

I said hi and got a nod in response. Paul led me to a small room connected to the one we were in. Inside sat several trays of chemicals that combined to make the air virtually unbreathable. He flipped a switch, turned on a fan, and warned me that the room would be completely black when he turned out the lights.

He wasn't kidding. I couldn't see my hand in front of my face.

"I'm starting by taking the film out and putting it on a reel. Then I'm going to put it in the developing tank."

I made a noise that I hoped sounded like "That's fascinating."

"What's your last name?" asked Paul.

"Anderson."

He moved something in the dark. "You Jewish?"

"No," I said before the question had left the air.

"Oh. Sorry," said Paul. "I thought you might be."

And what? I wanted to say. *You were going to blame the war on me? Tell me that I wasn't allowed in the newspaper office? Ask me if it was true our kind made love through a hole in a sheet?*

"There's a club that meets after school for Jewish students. I belong and so does Pearl. She's my sister."

"Oh." I forgot that the Lower East Side wasn't quite so homogeneous when it came to religious beliefs. At Chapin,

I was one of the only Jews in my class. I quickly learned not to talk about my religion, an easy task since neither Pop nor Mama was particularly observant. But when I stayed with Adam and Miriam, that changed. I was expected to cover my head and attend synagogue, even if it meant drawing attention to myself.

When Pop and I moved, I went back to my old ways. After all, I was the daughter of Arthur Anderson, not Arthur Ackerman. It was so much easier to pretend not to be Jewish. That way I could fool myself into believing that what was happening overseas had nothing to do with me or my family.

The lights came back on. "I just thought, if you were Jewish, you might want to come, too," said Paul.

I felt like a creep. He was trying to help me out. And now it was too late to do anything but either admit my lie or keep pretending it was the truth. "Well, I'm not, but thanks."

He poured developer into the tank and looked at his watch. As an eternity passed, I struggled to find something to say, but nothing seemed appropriate. Paul drained the developer and poured in the stop bath. Another look at his watch. Was he timing how long the developing took, or how long he was going to be stuck with me? "You know about the Jive Hive?" he asked.

I shook my head.

"It's a club just for teens that they run out of the fire hall on East Broadway. It's open every Saturday night. You should come."

Was he asking me on a date? Is that how it happened—some boy you'd just met invited you out before you knew his last name? "What do people do there?"

He drained the stop bath and poured in the fixer. "Dance. Play cards. Just bust loose, really. A bunch of kids run it. It's a good time."

"Thanks. Maybe I'll come by sometime. If I'm not busy."

The bell rang, warning us that we had ten minutes until first period began.

Paul glanced at his watch as though he didn't believe what the bell was telling him. "Nuts. This needs at least another five minutes and then the film needs to be rinsed."

"I could do it," I said. "I'd hate for you to be late for your first class."

He looked at his watch again. "I'm responsible for making sure the room is secure."

"The doors lock from the inside, right? I can make sure they're locked before I leave."

He looked at me skeptically for a moment. "All right. Just make sure the doors are locked. After you rinse the film, it's going to need to dry for a couple of hours. If you want, we can make prints after school. I'll be back here right after last bell." He exited the tiny room and in the split second the door was open I could see Pearl watching me.

Once I was safely behind the closed door, I rinsed the negative of a naked Mrs. Wilson scrambling to hide herself behind a hotel sheet, and mused over my inability to share my own secrets.

I DIDN'T LOCK THE PHOTO LAB DOOR or the newspaper room door. Instead, I hung the film to dry and wedged enough newspaper into both doors' jambs to keep them from closing properly. There was no chance I was going to risk having Paul make prints of my photos. I'd stop by after lunch to get my film. Then I'd figure out another way to get prints made.

My hope of going back to the lab was thwarted by a schedule change. Instead of letting us out for lunch at the normal time, we were kept in our classroom while the president's Appeal to Youth was broadcast over the PA system. As President Roosevelt warned the youth of the world that the Nazis, Fascists, and Japanese had nothing to offer them but death, I pictured Paul examining my film with a shocked look on his face. As soon as the speech was over and we were released to the cafeteria, I took a detour to the newspaper office and went to retrieve the roll. Unfortunately, someone had gotten there before me. The wad of newspaper had been removed from the door jamb and once again the knob was fixed and locked.

I felt sick at the discovery. How was I going to explain having pictures like that in my possession? Paul was going to think I was weird, for sure. And what if he told someone else? Or worse—what if they wrote about it in the school paper?

I was useless in my afternoon classes. Every time someone looked my way, I was certain they knew about the photos I'd taken. I headed out of P.S. 110 with a heavy heart. I'd almost cleared the property line when Paul's sister Pearl caught my eye. With a gesture I might've missed if I hadn't been looking for it, she waved. I checked behind me to make sure I was the person she was signaling to, then crossed the distance to her, terrified that I was going to have to endure some humiliating news from this odd, silent girl.

She put a finger to her lips, passed me a folder, and then spun on her heel.

She hadn't just returned my film; she'd made prints. Each image was carefully covered with a sheet of paper to keep it from sticking to the next one on the pile.

Pearl was gone before I could thank her.

Pop wasn't home when I returned from school. I left the photos beside the typewriter on his desk and focused on my homework. At six-thirty he arrived, his tired gait making it clear he'd spent the afternoon walking the streets in pursuit of something for a case. He landed so heavily in his desk chair that I could hear him make contact with the wood. With a sigh he removed the prosthetic and tossed it aside. It landed in the doorway, spanning the distance between him and me.

"Iris?" he said after a minute had passed.

I approached his door slowly, unable to read if it was anger or pleasure coloring my name. "Yes, Pop?"

"What's this?" He limply held the stack of 8×10s, so fresh they still smelled of their chemical bath.

"It's Mrs. Wilson and the man she's been seeing. I caught them at the Plaza last night."

"You followed them there?"

I didn't respond. It still wasn't clear if he wanted to praise Caesar or bury him.

"How did you get into the hotel room?"

This was good. We'd bypassed *Why were you out so late?* and *What possessed you to go uptown alone?* "I told the maid I was staying there and got her to unlock the door for me."

He stared down at the photos. "They must've seen you."

"I got out of there pretty fast." It hadn't occurred to me that I shouldn't be seen. The goal was to take a picture, not preserve my anonymity, right? And besides, what did it matter if Mrs. Wilson saw me? She was the one doing something wrong. "I was surprised by how young he was. Do you think that was the draw—that he was younger than Mr. Wilson?"

"Maybe. Or it could be . . ." Whatever he was about to say vanished and he turned his attention back to me. "They probably called the hotel detective and reported you. Did you talk to anyone? Give them your name?"

"No, of course not." My hands danced in and out of my pockets. This wasn't going the way I'd hoped. I'd done well, hadn't I?

"It's not right, Iris."

"The pictures are clear. There's no question what's going on in them."

"That's not what I mean and you know it. This isn't your business."

"I was trying to help."

"You help by going to school. By making good grades and keeping your nose clean. This isn't a business for women."

Since when was I a woman?

He waved the photos at me. "Don't do this again."

"All right."

"I mean it, Iris. If the wrong person saw you, if this man in the photo decided to come after you to get the film, what would you have done?"

I shrugged. I saw no point in hypothetical questions. Those things hadn't happened, so what did it matter? "Run, I guess."

"And if he had a gun?"

Ducked, I thought about saying, but even I knew that was too snotty. "I don't know."

"Exactly. You're a child. Be a child." And with that he tossed the photos into the garbage can.

I was heartsick that night. I understood his point: it

could've been dangerous. If something had gone wrong, I wouldn't have known how to react. But was it really fair to ask me to sit around and do nothing when the rent was late and Uncle Adam had been invoked and I was capable of helping?

As I lay in bed, staring at the few pieces of furniture that had been moved from our uptown address, my anger grew. My old Shirley Temple doll grinned at me from the dresser, her bold blue eyes staring blankly at a space just beyond me. The framed photo I'd gotten from my Deanna Durbin fan club membership smiled from the nightstand, her upper body bisected by her signature. Why had I kept these things when we moved? They didn't belong here any more than I did. Didn't Pop see how miserable I was? Didn't he understand that for one brief twenty-four-hour period I'd felt like I had a purpose?

Didn't he know how much I missed Mama?

I pinched a blanket and rubbed the satiny edge between my fingers. It was my baby blanket, a pink knitted thing much too small to do anything more than get lost in my sheets. But ever since I was born, or so Mama claimed, it was the talisman I turned to when I needed something to help soothe me to sleep. One rub of the fraying satin edge and whatever worries I had would melt away.

It wasn't working. I was too tense for sleep. If I didn't say something to him, the hours would pass and I'd find myself too exhausted to function the next day. And—boy, howdy—the last thing I needed to do was battle P.S. 110 on too little sleep.

I stuffed the blanket under my pillow, put on my robe, and pattered down the stairs. Pop was still in his office, typing up case notes. I cleared my throat to get his attention.

The typewriter ceased its noise. "What are you still doing up, Iris?"

"I can't sleep."

He cocked his head toward the kitchen. "Why don't you make yourself some warm milk?"

I took a step backward, but my feet refused to do anything more. The time for speaking up was now. "I didn't do anything wrong. I was trying to help."

He addressed the handwritten notes he'd been transcribing. "I know that."

"No, you don't. There are all these signs around school about how we can help with the war effort by collecting clothes and cans. If the government wants my help, how come you won't accept it?"

He lifted his head, finally meeting my eyes. "This isn't a business for little girls."

Before I was a woman; now I was a little girl? What had changed in the last few hours, other than my clothes? "Pop, I know I made mistakes. But I can learn. I can be good at this. I want to be good at this."

"In four years, if you feel the same way, we'll talk. Now go back to bed."

He was being a father for the first time since he had returned home, and rather than relishing it, I resented it. He missed five years of my life, the five years when he could've sent me to my room and I'd have had to accept it. But those days were past. Who we were now didn't allow for that relationship. I couldn't go back to being Iris Anderson, privileged girl on the Upper East Side, and he couldn't be a father who sent me to my room without giving me a good reason for it.

"No," I said.

He was shocked. That much was clear.

I marched over to the wastebasket and fished out the 8 × 10s. I put them on the desk in front of him. "I know we need money. I know you can't do everything anymore. I made mistakes. I admit it. But I worked hard to get these. I studied the file. I memorized Mrs. Wilson's face. I figured out how to get the photos developed without anyone being wise." Sort of. "And I'm going to keep working at it. You can throw out the pictures. You can criticize my efforts. Or you can accept my help and teach me to do a better job the next time. It's your choice, Pop, but I'm not going away."

He sighed heavily. In the movies, if Deanna Durbin had stood up for herself like this, she would've gotten exactly what she wanted, followed by an emotional embrace that cemented the fact that, even if she was standing up for herself, she would always be Daddy's little girl.

There would be no hugs and tears for me. That's not who we were.

He picked up the photos and examined them more closely. "What camera did you use?"

"My Brownie." It felt like a betrayal. After all, Uncle Adam had given it to me.

He held a photo up to the lampshade. "These shots are grainy. The light quality isn't very good."

"It was night. There wasn't a lot of light in the room."

"They saw you. Detectives have to be invisible. No one's going to forget a child with a camera."

Child? Seriously? "I can be discreet."

"I can't use these." He dumped them back into the trash can.

I stared at him, willing the tears I knew wanted to come to wait until I left the room so I could retain a little dignity. But then why not let him see me cry? He deserved to know how much his decision had stung.

"You're making a mistake," I said between trembling lips.

He shook his head at me, and the ripples on his forehead grew four feet deep. "That's the way you see it. From where I sit, I'm finally doing the right thing."

* * *

58

THE NEXT AFTERNOON I arrived home early from school and discovered Pop's office door closed. From inside came the familiar sound of Mr. Wilson. He had come by to retrieve the photos—*my* photos—and return the money he'd taken from Pop. I waited for him to ask how Pop had finally gotten the shot after all those failed attempts, but he never did. He didn't care how Pop had done it; all he cared was that the job was done.

I could barely contain my excitement. Surely Pop had changed his mind and was ready to give me a chance to show him what I could do.

Mr. Wilson tipped his hat at me as he exited the office. I feigned interest in *Ten Cent Love Story Magazine*, a romance slick that Mrs. Mrozenski had brought home with the groceries.

When Pop returned from walking Mr. Wilson out, I was waiting for him with my arms crossed, shoulders squared. "I thought you threw the photos away."

"I didn't think you'd be home yet."

"We had early dismissal today."

Pop unfurled a ten-dollar bill from his pocket and passed it my way. "Here."

"So does this mean you've changed your mind?"

"No." He put the money on the coffee table in front of me. "Take the money. I don't want you to think I'm taking advantage of you. Buy yourself something for school." He turned to head back into the office. In another thirty seconds his door would be closed, and then who knew how many hours would pass before he'd talk to me again.

"He said the photos were good, right?"

He froze and his back turned rigid. His left shoulder was higher than his right one. "That's not the point, Iris."

"Then what is?"

He sighed heavily—had he always relied on sighs to convey emotion?—and spun back toward me. "Do you know why that man wanted me to follow his wife?"

"Because she was having an affair."

"No. Because he wants out of his marriage. His mistress wants him to get a divorce and he doesn't want to lose her, but he doesn't want to lose his money, either. So he's held out until he has something on his wife that will make the separation go a little more smoothly. Those photos you took just guaranteed that his wife won't get one red cent in the divorce settlement."

I was having a hard time connecting the dots. "So he was cheating on her first? That doesn't seem fair."

Pop suddenly looked uncomfortable, and not just because his leg was bothering him. "It's the way the law works, Iris. They don't care who behaved badly first. All they care about is who can prove it. These people I work for, they aren't all good people. They aren't always asking me to help them do good things. A lot of them are like

Mr. Wilson; they want proof that someone else is doing something wrong so that they can justify their own bad actions. I don't want you around that."

Poor Mrs. Wilson, with her under-eye bags and her desperate smile, was going to have her goose cooked because of me. A knot tightened in my stomach. "If you knew that was what he was up to, why did you take his money?"

"Because there are bills to pay and no one but me to pay them." He looked tired. I wasn't the only one who'd spent half the night awake. "It can be ugly, the things I'm asked to do. But I'm not being paid to make judgments, understand? And it's a good thing, too, because sometimes who's right and who's wrong isn't always so cut-and-dried. When I'm hired by a client, I'm only privy to a small part of the story."

So that's how he justified dealing with the Mr. Wilsons of the world.

"Many of the people I'm hired to look into don't want me to find out what I'm trying to find out. Often there's money at stake for them—sometimes something that's even more valuable. This job can be dangerous. That's what I was trying to explain to you last night. If you're seen, if they know where to find you, some of them will do whatever they can to make sure you don't do your job. Understand?"

I wasn't the only one at risk; he was in danger, too. That had never occurred to me before. I may not have known Pop very well, but I certainly wasn't prepared to lose him. Ever since he'd come home, I'd just assumed he was safe.

But he was more vulnerable than ever. He might've had the experience to know what to do when, but I was the only one of us with two good legs.

"So what are you going to do the next time someone hires you to follow his wife?" I asked.

"Do what I did this time, I imagine."

"But you couldn't do it this time." *I had to do it for you*, I almost said. *And I can run. At least I stand a chance at getting away.* "What happens if they take the job to Uncle Adam instead? Mrs. Mrozenski isn't always going to be willing to take the rent late, you know."

He looked at me like he was seeing me for the first time. Had I said too much? Would he disappear into his office and never come out again? "How do you know all that?"

"I just do."

He rubbed at his upper thigh, just above the prosthetic. His face took on an ashen hue and his features momentarily pinched. He was late taking his pills.

The pain he felt wasn't just the chafing and discomfort from the prosthetic. When he first came home, Aunt Miriam had warned me about something called phantom pain. *It only happens to amputees*, she'd said. *The severed nerves go haywire and sometimes the person missing a limb swears they can feel pain in the arm or leg that's not there anymore.* I'd seen it with my own eyes, how Pop would move to scratch the calf that wasn't, his hand brushing the air beneath his knee the way Roland Young's hand passed through Cary Grant's ghostly body in *Topper*.

But Aunt Miriam was wrong about one thing: phantom pain didn't just happen to amputees. Anyone who'd experienced a sudden loss could fall victim to it. I felt it every time I entered a room and expected to see Mama, only instead of clusters of severed nerves going haywire, it was my heart that seized in agony.

"Do you want me to get your pills?" I asked Pop.

"No. Not yet." He continued rubbing. "Not every job is going to be like this one. I'm still a good detective."

"I'm not saying you're not."

He held up his finger to signal that he wasn't done talking. "I can't do what I need to do if I'm worrying about your safety. I appreciate that you want to help, but you can do a lot more good staying at home where I know where you are and where Mrs. Mrozenski can keep an eye on you."

Tears crested at the corners of my eyes. I was supposed to be the dutiful daughter who did her homework, ate her vegetables, and went to bed with a smile on her face. Why did I have to be a girl? Maybe if he'd had a son, he would've been more willing to trust me.

I sniffled, more loudly than I'd intended. "Maybe I could—"

His face hardened into a slab of granite. "This isn't open for discussion, Iris. Hate me if you want, but this is my decision to make, not a fifteen-year-old girl's. Now go to your room."

I threw the ten-dollar bill beside his good leg and did as he said.

5

I DIDN'T LEAVE MY ROOM again that day. Instead, I lay on the bed, trying to figure out how things had gone so wrong. Didn't he see how much I could help? I couldn't fathom that it wasn't obvious to him.

I didn't sleep at all that night. Not even my baby blanket helped.

What did I think would happen? That he'd embrace me and thank me for helping him. Then he'd school me in the detecting business and we'd become close—better than close—not just sharing everything with each other, but comfortable enough in each other's presence that when there were silences they wouldn't cause my stomach to churn with anxiety.

I would tell him everything. Stories about the boys I was interested in. How mad I was at Mama. And he'd do the same, opening up about that awful day at Pearl Harbor and his own grief when he found out Mama was dead.

Everything would change between us because of this one little photograph.

And maybe it still could.

I wasn't going to go away without a fight. I knew he needed me, and if he was too stubborn to see it because of whatever danger he thought I was at risk for, that was his choice. I'd become the best detective I could be on my own, and then I'd show him exactly what he was missing out on.

"Do you want to go see a movie tonight?" Pop asked two days after he'd sold my photos and ended my detecting career.

"No, thank you."

"It's the new Ginger Rogers film."

"I have homework."

"I thought you already did it."

"Then I guess you thought wrong."

I could see the hurt in his eyes. And the truth was, I did want to go to the movies. But I thought my rejection of him would get me what I wanted, so I was determined to stand firm.

In the meantime I spent every waking moment learning to be a detective. When I wasn't at school, I read detective comics, listened to the spy serials, and made sure I was always in earshot of Pop's door during those times when clients came to meet with him. When he wasn't home, I sneaked into the office and studied his notes from earlier cases, not just the ones he'd taken since coming home from

Hawaii, but those he'd worked on with Uncle Adam years before, when they used to have an agency together. He filled folders with carefully typed descriptions of his environment and the people he observed. Like Mama, he found volumes of useful information in the clothes people wore, their behavior, and the places they chose to go. He could read guilt and suspicion in the choice of a hat or a misplaced verb. It was amazing stuff.

I went through his collection of props and tools: hats that hid his face in shadows, street and phone directories, city maps, picklocks, counterfeit IDs, and uniforms used by utility workers. Other things were more unusual and, I suspected, had come from his time in the Navy. For his camera, he had dozens of different parts that could improve an image under the worst of circumstances. He had tiny recorders that he could leave anywhere to capture a conversation. And there were other gadgets that I couldn't even guess at the purpose of.

But you could only learn so much by observing fictional detectives and Pop's collection of props. The best education would only come from watching Pop at work. The catch was, I had to do it without him knowing.

I'd already mastered the art of eavesdropping on him. Instead of just doing it when clients came by, I began to do it when he was the only one in the office. Much of his job was done by telephone. I had no idea what a good actor he was, how he seamlessly donned a new identity, complete with a new voice, and confidently asked for information that should've been denied him. He could be shockingly personable when he needed something.

"Good afternoon," he began one call as I huddled on the other side of the door vent. "Is this Gloria Armour? I'm so glad I reached you. I know you probably don't remember me, but this is Jack Gaviston. I met you through Bill." There was a pause. "I'm flattered that I made such an impression on you. I ran into Bill the other day and he was telling me that you knew the best way to get in touch with Randall Smythe."

There was a lot to learn from this brief exchange, even if I didn't know the details of the Smythe case. Pop knew that by implying that Gloria wouldn't remember his fictional alter ego, she would insist that she did just to get out of a potentially embarrassing situation. Hoping to cover up her own lie, she was then eager to tell Pop whatever she knew. After all, if she didn't, he might suspect she was bluffing.

It was a brilliant scheme, and from what I could tell, it worked almost every time.

There were real connections that Pop relied on, too. He had friends at the phone company, the Department of Motor Vehicles, and the utility offices who could call up phone extensions, addresses, and other information in a matter of hours. He always opened his requests with questions about how their families were doing, displaying a remarkable skill for remembering spouses' names and the pursuits of various children he'd probably never met. He seemed to understand that the best way to get people to want to help you was to show them that you were interested in them.

I tried to put what I had learned from Pop to practical use during my time at school. I trained myself to sit in a classroom and take in every detail about the students around me: what did they wear, who was sitting where, what could I tell about them from the choices they made? I studied those who seemed to be looked up to by everyone else, those who could get away with things, and those who could not. I began to know the people around me intimately. It almost made up for the fact that I had no real friends.

The person I watched the most was Tom Barney. He'd returned to school a week after his arrest, appearing no worse for wear. When he came back, so did his bounty, or at least part of it. The purses and wallets he'd stolen, including my own, were turned over to the front office, where those of us who'd been victimized were invited to retrieve them. I did so, though, like everyone else, I found my purse empty and my money long gone.

From the little I was able to pick up in the halls, Tom had been sent to a juvenile detention center for the duration of his absence and was let back into P.S. 110 on a probationary basis. I was fascinated by someone who could rob his peers and so easily slip back into the school without showing a hint of remorse for what he'd done. Maybe everyone else was willing to let bygones be bygones, but I wanted him to know how much he'd upset me. I didn't have the courage to just go up to him and confront him, though. Instead, I watched him from afar, biding my time in the same way I was biding it with Pop. Someday Tom might talk to me again, and when he did I'd give him a piece of my mind.

In the middle of September, as I sat in the lunchroom longing for the clock to move faster, I was greeted by Suze. "Hey, baby girl. Long time no see." I hadn't seen her since that first day in the girls' bathroom, and I responded to her reappearance with a mixture of relief and fear. Here, after weeks of being ignored, was a somewhat friendly face. At least I hoped she was friendly.

"Hi," I said.

She peeked under the table and took in my skirt. It was pencil cut, conforming closely to the curve of my hips. Pop had bought it for me as a peace offering. "Nice rags."

"Thanks."

"So what's tickin', chicken?"

In front of me was the notebook I was using to write down all the details I was trying to recall after giving myself one minute to look around the room. It was a way of testing my memory, and I believed that after two weeks of doing it, I was already becoming much better at analyzing my environment.

But it wasn't the kind of thing that you could share with someone. Even I knew it was kind of weird.

"Just homework," I said.

"You do a lot of homework, don't you, baby?"

I nodded, uncertain if I'd just damned myself by agreeing with her.

"How come you were staring at my friends?"

Had I been? I followed her gaze to a table near the back wall, where a group of girls in tight sweaters and heavy makeup were conversing with dark-skinned Italian boys with slick ducktails and chains that joined their pocket watches to their waists. How had I missed that Suze was there? What kind of detective doesn't make note of the one person she knows by name?

"I wasn't staring at anyone," I said.

"You sure about that? Rhona said you've been watching Tom since he sat down." She cocked her head toward the table, where Tom Barney sat with the blonde.

"I didn't mean to stare," I said. "I was just thinking and that's where my eyes landed."

"It's okay, baby. No harm. You were just making Rhona nervous, you dig? I told her you were copacetic."

I thought about telling her what Tom had done to me, but it occurred to me that telling her he'd robbed me wasn't going to help me stay in her good graces. I mean, she knew he was a thief, right?

"Heard from your pop?" she asked.

That's right—I'd led her to believe he was off being a soldier. "Not a word. What about you? You heard from Bill?"

She beamed, my earlier infraction completely forgotten. "Got a letter yesterday. Course most of it's blacked out." She pulled a note from her cleavage and unfurled it. Thick black lines crossed out much of what Bill had written to her. Either he was too free with his information or the war censor was still trying to get a handle on what should be considered sensitive information. "He couldn't even tell me where he is."

"It's to protect them," I said. "Just in case the wrong person gets ahold of the mail."

"Who's going to be reading my mail?"

"You never know," I said.

She looked back toward her friends. Despite their tough exteriors, they looked like they were having fun.

She knocked on the table with a closed fist, bidding me farewell. "I better evaporate, baby. Be good. Remember: no staring."

"I will," I said.

DESPITE MY PROMISE, I couldn't give up watching Tom. Now that I knew he was part of Suze's crew, I found myself watching all of them whenever the chance arose. There was no one at P.S. 110 more alive than them, no one more fascinating. The boys were strangely feminine, almost not

72

boys at all. They paid attention to what they wore and moved liked cats, their long graceful limbs working at a pace that seemed slower than everyone else around them. And the girls seemed so old and wise, as though they'd lived a hundred lives before this one and somehow managed to retain the knowledge from those previous lifetimes.

They were a different species than the kids I'd known at the Chapin School. But they were also a different species than most of the students at P.S. 110. In fact, the rest of the school seemed to view them as outsiders, but they didn't seem to care. They were outsiders by choice, not because someone else had put them in that position. I envied that they didn't need to belong. I suppose that's how it was when you had a group. You didn't need to be accepted by anyone else; you had already found your people.

I had to face it: there would be no group for me. The groups I might've been welcomed in—like the one for Jewish students—I didn't want to join, and the ones I used to belong to were no longer available.

"You had another phone call," said Mrs. Mrozenski one afternoon just after I'd arrived home from school. "Grace wants you to telephone her."

It was the third time Grace had called since I'd run into the twins uptown the night I'd followed Mrs. Wilson. Each time I took the message and pretended like I was going to do it right away.

"She say you no call her back before."

"I have, she's just never home."

"She just called, so she must be home now." Mrs. Mrozenski glanced toward the party-line phone that sat on a table just outside the kitchen. There was a second phone in Pop's office—a private line intended for business only.

"I'll call her from Pop's office," I told Mrs. M. She raised an eyebrow. "It's about a boy, so I think she wants a little privacy. Pop won't mind."

I shut myself into the room and sat at Pop's desk, but I never lifted the receiver. What would I say to her? *I go to a school I hate filled with people who only ever talk to me to tell me to stop staring at them. Pop and I barely speak because he thinks my wanting to be a detective is some childish fantasy. Oh, and we're so broke he frequently ducks our landlady so she won't ask him for the rent money. How are you?*

No, there'd be no telephoning Grace.

I couldn't deny how lonely I was, though. I needed friends before I permanently became that strange girl whose name no one remembered.

The next day I decided to do something about it. I arrived at school early and went straight to the newspaper office. Just like the first time I visited there, Paul and Pearl were working alone. They didn't seem surprised to see me. At least Paul didn't. Pearl was so wrapped up in her work that I couldn't tell if she was even aware of my presence.

She was the one I wanted to talk to, but it was clear that

as long as her brother was there, that wasn't going to happen. So instead I directed what I'd come to say to him.

"Remember me?" I asked him as I entered the room.

"Sure. I was wondering if I'd ever see you again. What happened? I thought I was going to show you how to make prints."

"Something came up." I looked toward Pearl. She licked the end of her pencil and pushed up her glasses. "Is the Jive Hive still around?"

"Every Saturday," said Paul. "Has your schedule opened up?" His tone didn't escape me.

"I'm sorry if I seemed rude that day. It's just when you're new . . ."

"You're not sure who's shrewd and who's square. It's all right." He tossed a look Pearl's way. She was still looking at everything but us. "If you do want to go, you're welcome to join us. There are some potent people I could introduce you to." Us? Did that mean Pearl would be there? "How 'bout you join us this weekend?"

"That would be swell," I said. "I'll see you on Saturday."

BY THE TIME SATURDAY rolled around, I was having second thoughts. What if Paul thought this was a date? What if Pearl wasn't part of the "we" he was talking about? I considered not showing up, but the rudeness of the act outweighed my discomfort. If private school had taught me

75

nothing else, it had made it clear that it was better to be uncomfortable than impolite.

Pop was thrilled that I had plans with people from school. "I'm glad you're keeping busy tonight," he said.

What did that mean? "It's no big deal," I said, not even willing to let him feel joy at my burgeoning social life. "It'll probably be boring." No, it definitely would be. Pearl had taken a vow of silence from what I'd seen, and Paul was clearly flat.

But at least I'd be out of the house for a while and not forced to continue my stalemate with Pop.

Paul had asked me to meet him at their house at eight. Pop wasn't thrilled that a young man would expect me to escort him rather than the other way around. He insisted on walking me to the address, two blocks over, and waiting on the sidewalk while I rang the bell and waited for someone to answer. As I stood on the porch, smelling the remnants of their family dinner, I noticed a flag with a single gold star winking from the window. This was a gold star house, meaning someone in the family had been killed in the war. Before I could contemplate its significance, the front door opened and Paul greeted me with a lopsided grin.

"You made it."

"I told you I would."

I waved at Pop to let him know I was at the right place

and wasn't about to be mugged or murdered. He waved back and strolled away.

"Was that your father?"

"Yes."

He stared after him. I wondered if we had violated some code of behavior. Should Pop have come onto the porch? Met Paul's parents? But then if we were going to be strict about it, shouldn't Paul have met me at my house? "What's with the limp?" asked Paul.

So that was what drew his attention. Boy, howdy—and to think I was the one who was worried about being thought rude. "He lost his leg at Pearl Harbor."

I expected an "I'm sorry" or "Gee, that's rough," but Paul wasn't the kind of person to descend into sentimentality. Or manners. "That must've been something, being right there at the start of the war."

I was feeling disagreeable. Pop being hurt was hardly something to brag about. "The war had already been going on for years before then."

"You know what I mean." He pointed his thumb toward the window. "We lost my brother four months in."

Now it was my turn to be trite. "I'm sorry."

He shrugged. "On the bright side, I can't go." He pointed at his chest. "Asthma." He turned his head and hollered into the house at a volume that made me question how bad his lungs really were, "Pearl! Let's make tracks!"

We walked side by side, Paul in the middle, to the fire hall that the Jive Hive operated out of. Pearl was silent, her attention focused more on her feet than on the air in front of her. Paul rattled on about the Princeton-Navy game that afternoon, wrongly assuming that I cared about football. I tried to feign interest, but my mind was already counting down the minutes until I could fake a headache and go home.

We arrived at the fire hall and went down to the basement, where the Jive Hive was in full swing. Frank Sinatra, fronting the Tommy Dorsey Orchestra, sang from the phonograph as we entered the large, low-ceilinged room. To the right was a table loaded with refreshments: cookies, cupcakes, punch, and Royal Crown Cola. To the left, card tables were set up with checker and chess sets and decks of cards. In the center of the room was an impromptu dance floor, where two couples clutched each other and swayed to Frank's request to "be careful, that's my heart."

I recognized some of the faces from P.S. 110, though it was hardly a fair sampling of the crowd I encountered every day. Everyone here was white and clean-cut. Either Suze and Tom Barney and the rest of their crew hadn't arrived yet or they weren't welcome.

Before we were allowed to enter, we had to sign in. A stern girl in cat's-eye specs scrutinized my information after offering Paul a much warmer welcome. She ignored Pearl entirely. In fact, she made such a point of not looking at her that I was embarrassed at her rudeness.

And then something interesting happened: Pearl spoke.

"Iris is new. This is her first time here."

The stern girl offered me a tight smile and passed me a sheet of paper. "Welcome, Iris. These are the rules. Make sure you follow them."

I scanned the sheet. No pickups was the first rule. No gambling the second. Dates must be registered in advance. The rest were a litany of dos and don'ts related to behavior. Most everything on the list seemed designed to keep the room clean and adults at bay.

Paul was greeted by a blonde who wore her hair in tight pin curls. Without looking my way, he took her by the hand and joined her on the dance floor. I was prepared to disappear into a corner to wait out my time when Pearl spoke again.

"That's Denise Halloway. Paul's girlfriend."

"Oh."

"You didn't think you were his date, did you?"

"No," I said, too quickly.

"That's good. You could do so much better than my brother." She paused and examined her thumbnail. "So why did you come out with us? Are you hoping to use him again?"

"What?"

"Like for the photographs."

My back went rigid. "I wasn't—"

She cut me off. "Sure you weren't. Want to play checkers?"

79

It felt strangely like a threat: play checkers with me or I'll let everyone know what you were up to in the newspaper office. Was I reading her right? I couldn't be sure, so I said yes and followed her to one of the tables.

She disappeared long enough to claim two sodas and a plate of cookies for us. As she sat across from me, I noticed for the first time how pudgy she was. The top button on her skirt was left open to accommodate a roll of fat that hung over the waistband. Her blouse strained at the buttons. Either Pearl shopped for the figure she one day hoped to have or her weight gain was recent.

We started the game in silence. I couldn't tell if Pearl was terrified of people or simply preferred silence to conversation. I wondered how Grace would've dealt with her, assuming she had no choice but to spend time in Pearl's presence. She probably would've chattered away, insisting on creating conversation where there was none. Chapin girls weren't known for loving silence. It was, they believed, rude.

"Paul told me about your brother. I'm really sorry."

She tilted her head to the left, like she had water in her ear. "Thanks." She picked up a cookie and put the whole thing in her mouth. Frosting oozed out of the corner of her lips. She pressed it back inside with a practiced gesture and studied the checkerboard.

I wanted to ask more, like what was his name and where had he died and did they know how, but common sense prevailed and I kept my yap shut. What made me think this quiet girl wanted to talk about a tragedy that was so raw that the mere mention of it made her shove an entire cookie (no, make that two—she'd moved on to the second one) into her mouth?

I felt like I owed her something, a wound of my own for her to pick at. I didn't want to tell her about Mama, so I offered her the next best thing. "My pop lost his leg at Pearl Harbor."

She shook her head. What did that mean? Was it a quiet acknowledgment of Pop's loss or a way of silently saying that what I'd experienced wasn't even close to what she'd experienced, and how dare I think otherwise?

"Is he still in the military?" she said when she'd swallowed the cookie.

"No. He's a private detective now."

She nodded with more enthusiasm. While her tragedy may have trumped mine, I'd at least offered her an interesting tidbit. "Does he let you work on cases?"

"Sort of." I wasn't in the mood to explain about the disagreement between Pop and me. And I had a feeling that her thinking I worked for him made me a lot more interesting than if she thought I didn't.

She jumped one of my black checkers with one of her red and claimed the captured piece. "I've seen you watching people at school. I guess that's why you do it, huh?"

I nodded, embarrassed that I'd been caught. Hadn't I learned anything from tailing Mrs. Wilson?

"Is that what the photos were for? A case?"

Another nod.

"Thanks for that, by the way," I said. "You know—getting me the pictures."

"Paul would've flipped his lid."

"So he didn't see them?"

"Oh, no. You didn't want him to, right?"

"Right."

"So I figured." She studied the checkerboard. "Was it an affair?"

"Yeah. The husband paid us to follow the wife." *Us.* So it wasn't the complete truth, so what?

"I figured that was the case from the look on her face. What did he want?"

"A divorce."

She nodded again. The record was changed and Sammy Kaye begged us to "remember Pearl Harbor." I squirmed in the uncomfortable metal folding chair. Did they really need a song to convince us not to forget something like that?

"They call me that, you know," said Pearl.

Had I missed part of the conversation? "What?"

"Pearl Harbor. It started last year, right after."

"Why do they call you that?"

"They don't like me. They think I'm a cold cut." She cocked her head again and met my eyes, obviously daring me to disagree with their diagnosis.

"That's a terrible thing to call someone." I knew it

probably wasn't what she wanted to hear, but I also wasn't sure I was ready to tell her people were wrong about her. My eyes unconsciously circled the room, looking to see who, if anyone, was watching us talk. Weird was contagious. I knew how it worked. Just sitting next to Pearl would set me up in people's minds as someone just like her.

And yet she'd gotten me the photos.

She picked up another cookie and shoved it into her mouth. There was only one left on the plate, and I realized that she hadn't gotten them to share with me; her intention, all along, had been to eat them herself. Maybe she assumed I wouldn't stick around long enough to enjoy them. "Paul says it's my own fault," she said.

"That doesn't seem very fair."

"It's probably why he invited you out with us that first day. He thinks I need friends."

"You don't agree?"

"I had them. They're the ones who couldn't cope."

I'm not sure how I knew what had happened—maybe it was intuition, or maybe my weeks of observation were paying off—but I suddenly realized that when Pearl said they started calling her Pearl Harbor "after," she wasn't referring to December 7, 1941. Her brother's death had started all this. Her friends couldn't stand the doom and gloom that descended on her when she'd lost someone she'd loved. And she wasn't strong enough to fight the changes the grief had made in her.

I knew that change. Last year I'd been a completely different person. What did I worry about back then? A new pimple that blazed on my cheek the day class photos were taken. The way last year's waistbands strained against this year's waist. Whether or not my breasts would ever fill my brassiere.

I didn't worry about war. I didn't think about my father, serving in someplace called Pearl Harbor. In fact, I rarely thought about Pop at all. As for Mama, she flitted around the edges, always smiling, and convincing me that I would be all right as long as there was the two of us. It had been just the two of us for so long.

And then it was all gone. Mama dead. Pop returned, but different. And the house, the school, the friends—all traded for a dingy brownstone on Orchard Street that smelled of Mrs. Mrozenski's cabbage rolls. And why the change? The war, of course. It ruined everything. Including me.

We were alike, Pearl and I. And she knew it, which was why she was telling me all this.

I looked back toward the front door of the club, where the girl with cat's-eye specs had been joined by another girl, this one in pearls and a plaid blazer. They caught me looking at them and quickly turned away. Former friends of Pearl's, I'd bet, wondering how it was that she'd found a new friend to spend the evening with.

"You're interesting, though," said Pearl. "I kept hoping you'd come back to the newspaper office." She lifted the last cookie. Instead of sending it to her mouth, she extended it my way. "Want one?"

"No, thanks." I looked at the checkerboard. I was being slaughtered. It was a matter of minutes before the game was over and she was declared the victor.

"So what do you think of P.S. 110?" she asked.

"It's different."

"I always wanted to go to a private all-girls school." She knew that about me, too. How? She must've seen the question in my eyes. "I work in the office during study hall, helping with attendance. Anyhow, that's how I know you went to Chapin."

I nodded, not feeling as reassured as she thought that news might make me. "So you work for the newspaper and the office?"

"I don't really work for the paper. I just hang out there with Paul in the morning so I don't have to talk to anyone. He hates it, but he hates typing more, so he lets me stay if I agree to help type up the articles. Do you miss Chapin?"

Slowly, I nodded. Whatever I said to Pearl would be safe. She wouldn't repeat it to Paul, who clearly didn't think much of his sister. And there was no one else for her to confide in.

In some ways, it made her the perfect friend. At Chapin, I never knew what Grace might repeat to someone. This girl, on the other hand, was a locked box.

"I feel like such a square here," I said. She nodded,

encouraging me to go on. "And going to school with boys is . . . strange."

"They're better than most of the girls. Believe me. It was so much easier here before they started to enlist, and if the draft passes, it's going to be even worse. The girls gang up on you around here."

"That happened at Chapin, too."

She didn't seem convinced. But I'd witnessed it often enough to know it was true, even if I hadn't been on the receiving end of those attacks. "Have you made any friends?"

She had to know the answer was no, but I hated to admit it out loud. "There's one girl I've talked to a few times who seemed nice. Suze?" I realized I didn't know her last name. Claiming her as a friend when I didn't know that one simple fact made it seem like even more of a lie.

Her eyes grew wide. "Suze Armstrong? Really?"

I nodded. So there was only one Suze. "Why are you so surprised?"

"She's a Rainbow."

"A what?"

She leaned toward me and lowered her voice. "A Rainbow. It's what they call that gang she's in."

"You mean the people she hangs out with?"

She nodded.

"So what do the Rainbows do?"

"According to them, nothing. According to the school,

steal anything that's not nailed down. You heard about Tom Barney, right?"

"Heard about him? I was one of his victims. He robbed my locker my first day at school," I said.

Pearl's eyes grew as wide as the checkers. "Seriously? What did he take?"

"My purse. I got it back but not the cash. And the worst part is, I actually talked to Tom that morning. He seemed so nice—he even helped me find my first class. I guess I must be an idiot, huh?"

"You're not an idiot. Tom is nice. In fact, up until his freshman year Tom was tight with Paul. Worked on the newspaper, played basketball—he was a real Abercrombie. But then he fell in with the Rainbows and started doing whatever they were doing, including wearing the zoot."

"The what?"

She seemed to take pleasure in educating me.

"The zoot suit. Surely you've seen them? A lot of the colored boys wear them out on the town, and the Italians and Puerto Ricans have started, too."

I might've read something in the newspaper about them a time or two, but it's not like I'd encountered a lot of boys of different races during my time at Chapin. If you were colored and on the Upper East Side, you were either lost or somebody's chauffeur.

"What do they look like?" I asked.

"Fancy suits. Bright colors. The jackets have shoulder pads, like women's clothes, and the pants are cut close to the ankle. You've seriously never seen them?"

"Not at school."

"Ah, they don't wear them at school. The zoot's strictly after-hours attire. For jitterbugging, mostly. The zoot and dancing go hand in hand." She got a strange look on her face, almost like longing. "I think they look dapper, but my father says they make whoever's wearing them look like a gangster. Or a cream puff."

I took in the group assembled at the Jive Hive. Every boy there was wearing crisp, pressed shirts and slacks with precise pleats ironed down their centers. A sweater vest broke up the monotony here and there, but otherwise their clothes were clearly chosen to make them fit in, not stand out.

"So why do you think Tom became a Rainbow?"

"Rhona, of course. She's the blonde in the tight sweater who's always with him."

"Is she bad news, too?"

"Rumor has it she can't go into the five-and-dime without the manager patting her down. And she went away for a long time last year."

"She was sent to juvie?"

"Nothing like that. The story was she'd been sent away after *getting in trouble*. Came back when it was all taken care of."

What did she mean? My question must've shown on my

face. Pearl raised both of her eyebrows multiple times. Sex. She was talking about sex. Rhona had been pregnant.

"Was it Tom's?"

"Who knows? And I don't even know if it was true. Anytime a girl leaves school, people talk."

"How long have they been a couple?" I don't know why I was so curious about them. I think I was still trying to figure out what made someone like Tom—who could help you and rob you in one day—tick.

"At least a year. That's why everyone was so shocked that they broke up." She hesitated before continuing. "She's awful. He deserved so much better. He's actually quite smart, though you wouldn't know it from the way he ditches classes now."

Why did Pearl know so much about them? Was she this observant about everyone, or was Tom someone she kept closer tabs on? "They broke up?"

"Yeah, right after he was arrested. I mean, they're friendly to each other still, but they're no longer a couple."

By eleven o'clock I'd played four games of checkers, consumed three Royal Crown Colas, and learned everything there was to know about the student body at P.S. 110. Pearl may have been an outcast, but she was an observant one. I wasn't the only one she'd scrutinized, just the only one who bothered to talk to her.

"I probably should go home," I told her. "It's getting late."

"I'll get Paul to walk you. You shouldn't be out alone."

She returned the checkers to the board and started to go in search of her brother. Something stopped her, though, and she turned back toward me. "You don't have to talk to me at school if you don't want to. I'll understand."

What had brought this on? "Will you talk to me?" I asked.

"Sure."

"Then why wouldn't I talk to you?"

Her mouth fluttered, but she didn't have an answer for me.

Paul, Denise, and Pearl walked with me to Orchard Street and waited until I was safely in the house. Pop's office door was closed, so I figured he was working. As I crossed the parlor and headed toward the stairs, the newspaper on the table caught my attention. As I moved closer for a better look, it wasn't the headlines that drew into focus, but the date.

It was Mama's birthday.

So that was what Pop meant when he said it was good that I had plans. And what about him? What had he done to mark the occasion?

I approached the office door and knocked.

"Pop?"

"Yeah?" His voice sounded strange. I opened the door and found him seated at his desk. His face was a blotchy mess. Had he been crying? Pop never cried—not even when his leg was at its worst—and yet all the signs were there.

"I just wanted to let you know I was home."

He forced a smile on his face. "Have fun?"

"It was better than I thought it would be."

"Good, good."

"What did you do?"

He cocked his head toward his typewriter. "Just typed up some case notes. You better get to bed. It's getting late."

"All right." I felt like I should say more, but I was uncomfortable seeing him in his grief and embarrassed that I'd almost let the day pass without feeling any of my own. "Good night, Pop," I finally said when nothing else came. And then I went upstairs and cried myself to sleep.

6

I SLEPT IN THE NEXT MORNING. When I came downstairs Pop was sitting in the office writing notes in longhand.

"I was wondering how long you were going to sleep," he said.

"Sorry. I was pretty beat. Where's the typewriter?"

"Repair shop." He pushed an envelope my way. "Give this to Mrs. Mrozenski for me."

"Aren't you joining us for breakfast?"

His head tipped toward the tablet in front of him. He was looking at a row of numbers. It wasn't hard to imagine what these figures represented. Nor was it difficult to put together what the pawn ticket he'd tried to hide under the pad of paper meant. "Too much work, I'm afraid. I'll make it up at lunch."

I gave Mrs. Mrozenski the envelope just like he asked.

Now that I had a friend and found school slightly more

tolerable, money became my new obsession. Not only did I worry over what we owed, I was constantly thinking about money I used to have and how wasteful I'd been with it. Maybe if Mama hadn't been so indulgent, Pop wouldn't be struggling now.

As sore as I was at Pop, I couldn't stand the thought that he would be selling his office, little by little, to make ends meet. I wanted to help and that meant hocking the only thing I had of value: Mama's pearls.

I took them to a pawnshop I'd seen on the way to and from school, a small storefront that always sparkled with jewelry that told the sad tale of life since the war: a wedding ring had less value if the person who'd given it to you had gone away.

I lingered on the sidewalk for a long time as I tried to get up the courage to go inside. What would Mama think if she knew I'd sold her jewelry? Would she be proud of me for helping Pop out, or mad that I'd gotten rid of the one thing I had left of her?

What did it matter what she thought? If she wanted to dictate what I could and couldn't do, maybe she shouldn't have killed herself.

"How's Personal Hygiene?" said a voice just past my shoulder.

I turned to find Tom behind me. What was he doing there? Was he hoping to pawn something, or steal it? "It's fine," I said.

"You okay?"

I was crushing Mama's pearls in my hand. I eased my hold and dropped them in my pocket.

"What do you want?"

He put his hand on the display window and leaned against it. "I hear you used to go to Chapin."

My already sour mood gave me the strength to say what was on my mind for once. "Is that why you robbed me? Because you thought that if I used to go to private school it meant I had money?"

"Come again?"

"You heard me."

Before he could respond, the pawnbroker banged on the glass and gestured for us to move away. It was Tom that was the problem. He didn't want some thug scaring away his customers. "I better blow," he said.

"Yeah, you better."

He tossed a look my way but didn't say another word. If I hadn't known any better, I would've sworn he looked embarrassed.

I never got up the courage to go inside.

I told Pearl about the conversation over lunch. We sat together every day now, and walked home from school most afternoons.

"Why were you at a pawnshop?" she asked.

"I was just walking past," I said. "He didn't even have the

guts to apologize to me. I guess now I know why he talked to me on my first day of school. He was probably casing me. Did he seriously think that if I was rich I'd be going to this school?"

She mulled this over a mouthful of sandwich. "He just found out you went to Chapin."

"Huh?" I said.

"He didn't know that when he robbed you. He came into the office a few days ago and said he'd heard that someone who used to go to Chapin went here now. I told him it was you."

This was new. "Why did he want to know?"

She shrugged. "Beats me."

For the next three days I tried to linger in places where I knew Tom hung out, hoping he would appear and explain why he was so interested in Chapin, but it never happened. On the fourth day I arrived at school only to find Tom wasn't there. There was nothing new about that, of course, but his absence continued for five consecutive days.

"Have you noticed Tom Barney is missing again?" said Pearl during lunch about a week after I'd realized Tom was gone. We were in our usual spot at a table near the front of the cafeteria. She always brought her lunch, a strange concoction of sandwich, fruit, and some sort of dessert it was obvious her mother or grandmother had slaved over. I longed to try these confections—after all, sugar was becoming a scarcity—but I could tell that they were one of the only things Pearl could depend on to help her get through the day. She ate them so quickly, with such a ferocious hunger, that I had to wonder what would happen if one day she opened her plain brown bag and found they weren't there.

"What was he arrested for this time?" I asked.

"Nothing. He's actually missing. His mother met with Principal Deluca this morning."

"How do you know?"

"I saw her." Pearl studied me until her frown matched mine. "What's the matter? Are you worried about him?"

"Hardly." If anything I was irritated—I wanted to know why he'd been asking about Chapin and why he'd had the gall to rob me. "Why? Are you?"

She shifted her focus to what remained of her lunch. "No. Why would I be?"

The school that day was abuzz about the disappearance. Wild theories were tossed about wherever I went. Tom Barney had joined the Mob. He'd robbed the wrong person and paid for it with his life. He'd gone off to Hollywood. He was riding the rails. He was holed up somewhere drowning his sorrow in cheap booze over the breakup with Rhona. The only people who didn't seem to be talking about Tom were the Rainbows.

At least not in public.

The next day while I was in the cafeteria restroom doing my business, Rhona and Suze came in to touch up their makeup.

"I'll bet he went to the Jersey Shore again," said Suze. "He'll come back when he's ready. Just like last time."

At the sound of her voice, I stopped what I was doing. Unlike the restroom in the main hallway, these stalls mercifully had doors. Slowly, I pulled my feet off the floor.

"I don't know. I've got a bad feeling," said Rhona. Her voice was surprisingly gentle. I couldn't see her, but I was pretty sure I could hear tears weighing down her words. "I can't believe he hasn't called to let me know he's okay."

"Sorry, baby doll, but you aren't his to call anymore."

"Still . . ." Rhona was definitely crying. I shifted, hoping to catch a glimpse of her face through the crack in the door. The toilet seat groaned when I moved and all activity in the bathroom stopped. "Who's there?" asked Rhona. I didn't respond though I was certain they could hear my heartbeat.

"Let's make tracks," whispered Suze.

I waited ten minutes before following them out the door.

A week passed and Tom didn't reappear. Then another week, and another, until I was certain Tom Barney was gone for good.

I was just getting used to the idea that he wasn't coming back when one afternoon, a dour-faced freshman interrupted my typing class with one of the dreaded notes that directed a student to go to the office immediately.

"Iris Anderson," announced Miss Wisnieski, our instructor. She didn't need to finish her sentence, though she did anyway. "You're wanted in the front office."

There were two reasons you were called to the office: for discipline and for bad news. I wasn't the kind of girl who got into trouble. That meant, as everyone in the room probably knew, that bad news was waiting for me.

But what? Had something happened to Pop? "Should I take my things?"

She studied the note more closely, but apparently all the information it had to offer had already been communicated. "No. You may come back for them."

As thirty faces watched, I left the room with the slip clasped in my hand.

"Psst . . . Iris. Over here."

I followed the sound and found Pearl near the girls' bathroom. She waved me in and, once I was safely inside, blocked the door with her body.

"I'm supposed to go to the office," I said.

"You're kidding, right? I sent the note."

That's right. It was her study hall, when she worked in the attendance office. "You can do that?"

"Apparently so. It's my first time abusing my power." She beamed with the jolt of having done something forbidden. I would've been happy for her if I hadn't convinced myself the note meant something horrible had happened.

"So what's going on?" I asked.

"Your pop was here."

"At school?" She nodded. "How do you know?"

"Paul told me. He saw him right before lunch. He said he was trying to talk to the Rainbows."

How come I hadn't seen him? Probably because he didn't want to be seen by me.

"Do you think it has something to do with Tom Barney?" asked Pearl.

"I don't know." I was so dumbstruck that Pop had been at the school that I didn't know how to respond. Was he checking up on me? It wasn't possible. The only friends I'd mentioned to him were Paul and Pearl.

"Anyway, I thought you should know."

"How'd Paul know it was him?"

"Paul remembered seeing him the night we went to the Jive Hive." It was the prosthetic that had given him away. Try as he might to hide it, Pop's limp was the first thing you noticed about him. "Paul asked me if he was a cop, because I guess the Rainbows thought that was the case. And I told him, no, he's a private detective, and that you sometimes help him out. He was pretty impressed by that."

"What would my pop want with the Rainbows?"

"Your guess is as good as mine."

We waited out the period in the restroom, testing out theories of why Pop was there. When the bell rang, I grabbed my things and headed home. I was dying to find out what he was up to, but it looked like any fact-finding was going to have to wait. Pop was in the office with the door closed when I arrived home. And he wasn't alone.

Through the vent I eyeballed a man and woman. The woman's face was long and horselike, her eyes underscored by bags so dark I would've thought they were makeup if it wasn't clear she avoided the stuff on the rest of her face. Her husband was round, his face ruddy. They didn't look like the kind of people who could afford a detective.

"Here's the photo you asked for," said the woman. From her pocketbook she produced a small, framed picture.

Pop took it, gave it the once-over, and set it on the desk. "And this is how he looked at the time he disappeared?"

The man and woman exchanged an indecipherable look. "Not exactly," said the woman. "The photographer made him put on that getup. He was fit to be tied, I'll tell you. He wanted to wear that awful zoot suit of his, but the school was having none of it."

Zoot suit? So Pop *had* been to school because of Tom. And these must be his parents.

The man I believed to be Mr. Barney looked at Pop through lowered lids; now that I knew who he was, I saw the resemblance between him and his son. "Did you have any luck today?"

"I talked to a few of his friends and got access to his locker. Does the address 240 Houston Street mean anything to you?"

"No," said the woman. "Why?"

"Someone left a note in his locker with that address. *If you're serious, meet me at 240 Houston Street #7D at 4:00.* It's something to follow up on, anyway," said Pop.

"And how much is that going to cost me?" asked Mr. Barney.

"Frank!" said his wife.

"This is ridiculous, Louise. You know it and I know it. The no-good kid has run off."

"But he wouldn't do that. Not our Tom."

Mr. Barney shook his head. "He hasn't been our Tom for a while."

"He was always such a good boy. Never gave us trouble. And then two years ago he got these new friends and suddenly he was talking back, breaking curfew, and going to those . . . places."

Mr. Barney leaned toward Pop. "Negro clubs."

"He said they went there to dance. They liked the music. In any case, we didn't approve," said Mrs. Barney. "Those are dangerous places. We've heard stories."

"Drugs. Drinking," said Mr. Barney.

"You didn't tell me he'd been arrested for stealing," said Pop.

Mr. and Mrs. Barney exchanged another look. "It wasn't his fault. He was forced into it."

"Louise—" said Mr. Barney.

"You know it's true. Tom's not a thief."

"According to the school secretary, he admitted it," said

Pop. "And spent a week at a detention center. I'm surprised he wasn't expelled."

The Barneys exchanged a look. Even from my vantage I could read it: they'd begged the school to take him back.

"How were things at home after that?" asked Pop.

"How do you think?" said Mr. Barney. "I let him know that that was the last straw. I wasn't fixing things for him anymore. One more mistake and he was out of our house for good."

Pop's chair squeaked as he leaned back in it. "Then isn't it possible that's what happened here? He made a mistake and took off, knowing he wouldn't be welcomed home?"

"That's what I've been saying since the beginning," said Mr. Barney. "The kid screwed up and didn't want to pay the piper."

"He wouldn't run away. He wouldn't do that to me," said Mrs. Barney.

But he had run away before, if what I'd overheard Suze say was accurate.

"I think we're done here," said Mr. Barney. His chair creaked as he started to stand.

Mrs. Barney grabbed onto him and pulled him down. "Please, Frank—we need to find him. I can't take another month of this. If something's happened to him, if some-one's hurt him, we need to know that."

"Okay, okay—stop with the tears already." Mr. Barney

passed his wife his handkerchief. "What did those kids he hangs out with tell you?"

"Not much," said Pop. "They're scared. They're terrified they're going to get into trouble."

"This isn't about them!" Mrs. Barney's voice rose into a shriek. I jumped at the sound, accidentally rattling the door vent. They all looked my way. Slowly, so as not to make any other noise, I backed away from the door and prepared to bolt. "I'm sorry," said Mrs. Barney. "I forgot myself. It just seems to me that if they're his friends, they'd want to help."

"Don't give up hope," said Pop. "They have to know that Tom's disappearance is going to bring them under close scrutiny. And they'll eventually realize how much more suspicious their silence makes them seem."

Would they? It seemed to me that they'd never talk to Pop unless they trusted him, and that wasn't going to happen. He was an adult, after all.

Which was precisely why he needed my help. There was nothing dangerous about roaming the school halls and trying to find out what the scoop on Tom was. And I was bound to be loads more successful at it than Pop. I was innocuous and supposed to be there. He stood out like a lion in a den of cubs.

"I've only been on the job a week. Time has a way of working in our favor in cases like these," said Pop. "Eventually, one of them is going to make a mistake and lead us to your son. You can count on it."

"And what do we do until then?" asked Mrs. Barney.

"We wait," said Pop.

THE BARNEYS LEFT TEN MINUTES LATER. By then I'd planted myself on the sofa and was humming with so much excitement that my legs were vibrating.

Pop walked them to the door and then turned to face me. "You're home."

"Only for a few minutes." I could tell he was trying to analyze what sort of mood I was in. I decided to play it cool. Not cold, but clearly not interested in anything he might've been up to, either. If he was going to let me work on Tom's case, it needed to be his idea.

"How was your day?"

"A little strange. A boy's gone missing and it's all anyone's talking about." I picked up the radio guide and flipped through it like I was looking for something more interesting to entertain myself with. "I heard you were at school today," I said.

"How'd you hear that?"

"Paul saw you. He remembered you from the night you walked me to his house." I deliberated how to play the next part. I could mention Tom by name, or I could let Pop introduce the topic. The latter made more sense to me. "Am I in trouble or something?"

He seemed surprised at the question. And a little relieved. "No. There was some paperwork they needed. Records from Chapin. I thought it would be easier to bring it over in person."

"Oh." To say I was disappointed was like saying Frank Sinatra was okay-looking. Seriously? He expected me to believe that lie? "New clients?"

"Old clients come for a follow-up."

I ground my teeth. My previous attempt to thaw failed and I could feel the ice returning to my spine and shoulders.

He thumped his fingers on the fireplace mantel. "Are you all right?"

I offered him a tight, false smile. "Of course. Why wouldn't I be?"

He didn't join us for dinner that night.

I WAS SO STEAMED I was willing to let Pop flounder on the case. Let him hit a dead end and tell the Barneys they had to take their business elsewhere. But as the evening wore on and reality set in, I knew he couldn't afford another failure. My pride wasn't worth us missing another month's rent. He wasn't going to ask me for my help—I had to accept that. After telling me to stay out of the business before, he couldn't go back and tell me he'd changed his mind. After all, it had to have hurt his pride to need his fifteen-year-old daughter's assistance. But what if I were to do a little work on my own, just to see if there was anything worthwhile to be found?

Things looked slightly more fraught in the light of the next day. It was all well and good to say I was going to investigate Tom's disappearance, but how did I expect to pull it off? A normal girl would've just put her ear to the ground and asked her friends for the scoop, but I was an outsider. How on earth could I expect a bunch of cool cats who'd barely looked my way to confide in me? Sure, there was Suze, who'd at least talked to me, but even she was bound to get suspicious if I went up to her and started quizzing her about Tom.

Especially if she put two and two together and realized that the private eye who'd been interrogating the Rainbows was the father I claimed was still at war.

I SPENT MOST OF THAT first morning trying to come up with a plan of attack. By lunch I had . . . nothing. I was desperately unprepared.

"What's eating you?" asked Pearl.

"Tom Barney's parents came to see my pop yesterday."

Her eyes grew enormous behind her Coke-bottle lenses. She set down the cookie she was about to devour and gave me her complete attention. I let it all out then—well, most of it. I didn't tell her that I was looking into things without Pop's blessing. Or how worried I was about money. Instead, I focused on how ill-equipped Pop was to find out anything from the Rainbows. She waited until I was done before responding.

"So that's why he was here yesterday. You are so lucky."

"Lucky or not, I don't know how to find out any more than what we already know."

"Your sources are right there." She jerked her head toward where the Rainbows were sitting.

"Sure, I'll just go up to them and ask where Tom is."

"You said Suze talked to you once before, right?" I nodded. It was twice, actually, but who was counting? "So see if you can't get her to do it again."

I thought about it for a minute. Pop said that one of the reasons I screwed up the Wilson case was I didn't stay invisible. Pop knew how to charm information out of people— he did it all the time. It was all about ingratiating yourself to them. You had to make them want to tell you stuff.

Asking about Tom straight out would definitely tip my hand, but that didn't mean that Suze couldn't be a way to get information. She'd been nice to me because of our connection—both of us were suffering the agonizing uncertainty of having loved ones off to war, or so she thought. I could ask her about Bill again, but coming out of the blue that might seem strange. No, if I was going to get her to talk to me, it had to be because *I* had received some news.

It was, in many ways, the perfect setup. After all, I'd been pulled out of typing class the day before. As far as anyone knew, the news could've been delivered then.

I didn't tell Pearl my scheme. I didn't want to admit that the tenuous connection I had with Suze was built on a big fat lie. And I certainly didn't want my one friend to know that I was about to play on Suze's sympathy by claiming that I had bad news about Pop.

Fortunately, Pearl had to leave before the lunch period ended.

"I'll find out if there's any other talk in the attendance office," she told me as she packed up the cookie she still hadn't eaten. "Meet me after school on the steps."

"Sure."

As Pearl exited, Suze, Rhona, and a third girl headed for the girls' restroom. The hot lunch that day was liver and onions—the liver was cold in the middle, and the onions hadn't been cooked at all. I'd pushed the onions to the side when I ate, having no desire to eat them raw and reek of them all afternoon. When the girls made their exit, I shoved the onions into my napkin and gently blotted the gravy from them. Once they were more white than brown, I squeezed them until their juice oozed through my fingers. Just in case anyone was watching, I feigned dropping something under the table, and when I bent down to pick it up, I pressed my onion-soaked fingers against the corners of my eyes.

I hadn't been prepared for the stinging. Or for the smell.

The onions worked their magic, though. Instantly, I had a face full of tears. I picked up my things, clutched a napkin to my cheek, and entered the girls' bathroom.

All three girls were smoking. The cigarette smoke combined with the onion fumes was pure agony.

"Oh, sorry," I said between tears that had progressed from pretend to real. "Is it all right if I . . . ?"

Rhona shrugged. The girl I didn't know exhaled a plume of smoke. Suze said, "Go on, baby."

I eased myself into a stall and tried to figure out what to do next. Hadn't they noticed my tears? Or had I miscalculated and smeared liver gravy down my face?

I wiped my cheek with a tissue to check for signs of food. My face was clean. I put my fingers against my eyes again and reignited the water. I sniffed, I sighed, and when that failed to stir any reaction, I blew my nose as loudly as possible.

The warning bell rang. We had ten minutes to get back to class. "You coming, Suze?" asked the nameless girl.

"I'm right behind you," she said.

The door groaned opened and closed. My eyes longed to be flushed with water. I eased out of the stall and found Suze waiting for me.

"Everything copacetic?"

"I . . ." I squeezed my eyes tight and willed more tears. They didn't come, and so I forced my mind to wander to the saddest thought it held: Mama. That did the trick. No longer did I need onions and cigarette smoke. The emotion was real now. "No. Not really."

"Did something happen to your pop?"

I nodded to let her know that yes, that's exactly what was upsetting me. "He's been wounded."

"Oh, no."

"We got a telegram yesterday. They pulled me out of

typing class to tell me. I can't stop thinking about him." I was a terrible person. At least part of it was true. I *had* been pulled out of class and Pop *had* been injured. It had just happened ten months before.

"Are they sending him home?"

"They didn't say. I don't know how bad it is. I don't know if he can come home. I don't know if he might . . ." My voice trailed off.

"Oh, baby, you must be sick inside." She put her arm around me and I breathed in the scent of My Sin perfume and baby powder. Sick inside? She didn't know the half of it. Someone knocked on the bathroom door and with the authoritarian tone of a teacher told us to clear out and head back to class.

"You better go," I said. The onion was getting more potent, turning my waterworks into a waterfall. I tried to stop the flow, but without some water and alone time, that wasn't going to happen anytime soon.

Suze got a wad of toilet paper from the stall and passed it my way. "I can't leave you like this. You got someone you can talk to?"

I hesitated before shaking my head.

"Well, now you do. Meet me on the front steps after school. And try not to think too much between now and then. Seriously, baby—it won't help anyone." She wrinkled her nose and took in a whiff of air. "Do you smell onions?"

I mopped my eyes and shook my head.

"Must be this whole damn place. I can't stand it when they serve liver and onions. Even when I don't eat it, it follows me wherever I go."

THE CLOCK COULDN'T MOVE fast enough. I had no idea how I was going to get Suze to talk about Tom, but that didn't matter at the moment. Maybe I couldn't get everything I needed in one day. This afternoon might be about building trust. Once she and I were true friends, I could figure out how to find out everything Pop might need to know.

I worried she might've forgotten about me at the end of the day—after all, it had been four hours since we last spoke—but after school she was waiting for me just where she said she would be. And she wasn't alone—Rhona and the nameless girl who'd been with them in the restroom were with her.

"Hi," I said, feeling uncomfortable that my audience of one had grown to three. The two girls gave me the once-over, their eyes at half-mast. The idea of spending time with me was clearly not high on their list of things they wanted to do. *Don't worry*, I wanted to tell them, *I'm not looking forward to this, either.*

From the corner of my eye I saw Pearl exit the school. She had a book with her and settled down on a bench to wait for me.

"Hope you don't mind, but Rhona and Maria wanted to join us," said Suze. So that was the girl's name—Maria. I wasn't aware there was a destination for this meeting, but the group started walking and I trailed along, wondering how on earth I could ask the three of them about Tom without appearing like I was digging for information.

It was obvious I couldn't. At the very least Rhona wouldn't appreciate my interest in her ex-boyfriend.

Rhona poked a thumb over her shoulder. "Aren't you friends with that girl over there? Pearl Harbor?"

She and Maria shared a giggle.

"Not really."

"I always see you two eating lunch together."

"She's tutoring me," I said.

"In what?" asked Rhona. "How to gain fifty pounds?"

I wanted to defend Pearl, but I had a feeling that would do little to endear me to them.

"Why do you call her that?" I asked.

"Because she's gotten big enough to be a target from the air," said Rhona. "And she's the worst disaster to ever strike the U.S. on its own soil."

"Rhona's just sore because Pearl was going around telling everyone she was knocked up last year," said Maria.

Rhona shot her a look that should have struck her dead.

"Are you sure it was her?" I asked. "She doesn't strike me as a gossip."

"Trust me—your little friend is more than happy to go around talking about me and anyone else who catches her eye." Rhona stepped toward me until I could smell the cigarette still on her breath. She put her index finger into the center of my chest and pushed with so much force that I had to fight to stay upright. "You tell her that the next time she opens her mouth to say my name, she's going to find my fist in it."

"Shush," said Suze. Rhona lifted her finger and looked ready to deliver another blow to my sternum when Suze shot her a look that made her instantly step away from me.

Was Suze defending Pearl? Or me?

My chest burned where Rhona had poked it. I rubbed the spot, certain I was going to find a hole that went all the way through me. "I'm sorry she said stuff about you. Her brother was killed in the spring," I said. "I think that's why she eats so much." As soon as the words came out of my mouth, I wished I could take them back. I shouldn't be talking about Pearl, not even if I thought I was defending her. I certainly wouldn't have been happy if Pearl was going around telling everyone her theories about why I acted the way I did.

Maria rolled her eyes. "What a bringdown."

"Grief does weird things to people," said Suze.

Rhona's scowl remained fixed. Nobody in high school wanted to be talked about. Nobody.

"I'm sorry about your pops," said Maria. "What branch is he?"

"Navy," I said.

She lit a cigarette, discarding the match on the pavement beneath her.

"Rhona's got a Navy boyfriend," said Suze.

I saw my opportunity and leaped at it. "I thought you went with that boy Tom Barney."

"Not anymore. He took off and I took up with someone new." Rhona threw her head back and laughed. The other girls echoed the sound. "It's about time I found someone more mature."

"Rhona's Jim is twenty-three," said Maria.

"Wow," I said, unable to hide my surprise. Could this really be the same girl who'd been crying about Tom just a few weeks before?

I realized they were all staring at me. How long had I been musing on this in silence? "How old is Bill?" I asked Suze.

"Nineteen," she said. "He graduated last year."

"And what about you?" I asked Maria. "Do you have a boyfriend who's joined up?"

"Maria likes a little chocolate in her milk," said Rhona. "She goes with a boy from a colored school."

"But he's talking about enlisting when he graduates," said Maria. It was funny how defensive she sounded. What was so great about dating someone who had joined up? It wasn't like you could step out with them once they were overseas. Wouldn't you rather they were here, safe with you?

As though she'd heard my thoughts, Suze told Maria, "Don't wish for it. Staying home doesn't make him less of a man."

"And it won't turn him pale, either," said Rhona. "You stuck on someone?" It took me a minute to realize the question was directed at me, and even longer to figure out what she meant.

"No," I said. "I mean, I don't really know anyone."

"That'll change," said Suze.

The group turned and entered Normandie's Pharmacy on Catherine Street. Suze snagged a booth in the back and we each slid across the red leather upholstery, Maria and Rhona on one side, Suze and me on the other. "You like egg creams?" Suze asked me.

"Sure." I didn't have any money on me, and even if I did, I could hardly afford to spend it on soda. "I think I'll just have a glass of water," I said.

"Don't worry—it's my treat," said Suze. She held up four fingers and the man behind the counter caught her signal and nodded his acknowledgment. Across from him, the pharmacist worked with a mortar and pestle to crush pills into a powder.

Rhona killed her cigarette and lit a fresh one. Maria

followed suit. They both looked my way like I was a circus animal they were hoping would entertain them. Why had they come? Had Suze suggested they join her just in case spending time with me bored her to death?

Maria leaned over and whispered something to Rhona. The two women slid out of the booth, telling Suze they'd be right back.

"They don't like me," I said.

"Rhona's just sore about Pearl. And Maria doesn't like anyone Rhona doesn't like."

"So was it true?"

Suze shrugged. "About Pearl being behind the rumor? Who knows? Rhona wants to blame someone, so she blames your friend. And if Pearl gets the blame, so does anyone who knows her."

I thought about once again claiming that Pearl wasn't my friend, but I didn't want to feed Suze another lie, not when I was hoping she'd be honest with me.

"Maybe I should go." I slid toward the edge of the booth and dragged my purse after me.

Suze snagged my bag and gently pulled me back. "They don't know you, baby. That's all. When you're a senior, fresh meat seems like a thousand years ago."

"So why did they come?"

"Rhona wants to talk to me and didn't want to wait. Where Rhona goes, Maria goes." Her eyes drifted toward the ladies', where the two girls had disappeared. How many hours did they spend in public restrooms? "Don't worry about them. Let's talk about you. You feeling better?"

I shrugged, uncertain of how far to take this charade. "Just scared, I guess. I don't know whether to hope there's another telegram at home or to be terrified of the same thing. I almost didn't come to school today."

It was a telegram that had told us Pop's fate right after Pearl Harbor. I had come home from Chapin to find Mama in tears, the brief scrap of paper clenched in her hands. She never let me read it. Instead, she told me what it said, trying to frame it as potentially good news since it meant Pop finally got to come home for good.

I remember wanting to share her tears, but I couldn't find it in me to cry. Instead, I buried my head in her shoulder and pretended to sob until Mama's own tears dried up. It was the last time she ever held me.

"I was that way when all Bill was giving me was radio silence," said Suze. "But you can't sit home and suffer. It doesn't change the way things are going to turn out, you dig? Besides, they got you out of class once for news. If there was more, they would've done it again." Suze was so mature. I always assumed public school girls grew at a different rate, lacking access to knowledge those of us of privilege were exposed to. But while it was clear that I might have been more book smart than the average girl at P.S. 110, they possessed a world-weariness that made me seem like a baby in comparison.

"Right," I said. "But it's not like I have much choice. All I have is home and school." *And Pearl*, I should've said.

"Not anymore, baby—you've got me."

I raised an eyebrow. "Come on now, Suze. It's swell of you to take care of me like this, but you have to admit, you don't want to spend every afternoon babysitting someone like me."

She cocked her head to the right. "How old do you think I am?"

"Eighteen?"

"Try sixteen."

"How come—?"

"I'm hanging with the big fish? You don't choose your friends, they choose you."

Suze was sixteen, only a year older than me. And yet with all our differences, she might as well have had a hundred years on me.

"You're still thinking like a private school girl, where everyone stays in their neat little rows, wearing their pressed plaid skirts. You've got to get out and live a little, baby. It'll take your mind off your pops and it will make the day go a heck of a lot faster."

"You're right," I said. "I'd like that."

The dark-skinned soda jerk came over with a tray of glasses. He set the four egg creams on the table and offered Suze a wink. "You off today, Suze?"

"Yeah, Reggie."

"You work here?" I asked after Reggie had disappeared.

"Only three days a week." She played with one of her wooden bracelets. "It's mainly coffee and doughnuts, but it's enough to keep me in clothes and out of trouble. You got a job?"

I shook my head no.

"Must be nice," she said in a way that made me wish I'd invented something.

"I guess most everyone at P.S. 110 works, right?" I said. How could I turn the conversation around to Tom?

"Some do, some don't—just like anywhere else. You know what—you should come out with us Friday night," said Suze.

My heart skipped a beat. What did they do on Friday nights? Prowl the streets? Rob the elderly? Shoplift? "Are you sure Rhona and Maria want me to?"

"I'm asking, not them."

I tried to squelch the excitement building inside me. "What about the others? Won't they mind?"

"What others?"

"Those boys I always see you with. Tom Barney and those two Italians?"

"Tommy's AWOL. As for the other cats, they do what they want to do, just like us."

"What do you mean Tom's AWOL?"

"Absent without leave. He's been missing for weeks now."

"Missing? Is he all right?"

"Knowing Tommy, he's fine. School's not his game. He'll come back when he's ready."

The questions I wanted to ask fought for supremacy. Before I could decide which one to voice first, Rhona and Maria returned.

"When who's ready?" asked Rhona. She claimed an egg cream for herself and downed the first sip, smearing a crescent moon of bright red lip cream on the edge of the glass.

"Tommy," said Suze.

Rhona's eyes narrowed. "What are you talking about him for?"

"Iris was asking why he hasn't been around."

"Why?" asked Rhona. "You interested?"

I blushed. "I was just curious. I hadn't seen him for a while."

"Tommy goes where Tommy goes," said Rhona. "Don't hold your breath waiting for him to reappear. Pity, though; you are his type."

What did that mean?

"Thank God that crippled private eye didn't reappear," said Maria. "I thought for sure he'd be waiting for us outside the cafeteria again."

"I told you I'd take care of it," said Rhona.

I concentrated on my drink, hoping that by doing so they wouldn't notice that I'd turned as red as Rhona's lip cream.

"Tell Suze what you did," said Maria.

"I picked up the horn, made a call." Maria gave her a look that made it clear that this explanation was insufficient. Rhona rolled her eyes and pantomimed lifting a phone receiver. "Hello, Principal Deluca? This is Mrs. Randall Hyatt, Rhona Hyatt's mother. I understand that you've permitted male strangers to harass young women on campus. This is unacceptable, and if it doesn't stop immediately I will go to the school board about it."

"You didn't!" said Suze.

"She most certainly did," said Maria.

"What did he say?"

"It was hard to tell with all the stuttering and back-pedaling, but he apologized and promised my dear mother that it wouldn't happen again." She finished the egg cream in a single gulp and pulled a handful of change from her purse. With a clatter she deposited two dimes on the table, then gestured to Maria to follow suit. "We've got to blow. I'll catch up with you later, Suze." She offered me a wide smile that stopped at her eyes. "See you around, Iris."

"What did I do?" I asked as soon as they were gone.

"It's not you, baby. It's Tommy. She's worried about him and she doesn't like talking about it."

I couldn't let that pass without comment. "If she's so worried about him, why has she taken up with someone else?"

"That's her pride talking. If he's safe and avoiding her,

she wants to punish him by showing him that she's moved on. The truth is, she's sick about it."

That had certainly been corroborated by what I'd overheard. "So is that who the private eye was asking about? Tommy?"

"I wasn't there, but from what everyone else said, he was the one and only topic."

"Wow." I stirred the dregs at the bottom of my drink. It was almost solid chocolate down there. "No wonder she's upset."

"He probably just took a powder. He's done it before. Of course, those times he always told Rhona where he was going. I think that's what worries her the most."

"What could keep him away for so long?"

"It's hard to say. He could've done something bad, gotten pinched, and decided it was better to stay gone than face his pops."

"His old man's strict?"

"Tight as a girdle. It's amazing Tommy can breathe some days. He has an older brother who wound up in the joint and his pops is convinced Tommy's going to do the same."

I wished I could take notes, but there was no way that was going to happen without drawing suspicion. Maybe that was why the Rainbows hadn't wanted to talk to Pop: they believed Tom wanted to stay lost.

"But if Tom was lying low until the heat was off him, don't you think he'd try to contact one of you?" I asked.

"That's what I'm hoping. At the very least, he'd need cash."

"What about the money from the locker thefts?"

"That was used for something else."

I was dying to ask what that something else was, but I could tell I was quickly approaching the point of asking too much. Besides, there was only so much Suze was going to be able to tell me. The person who knew Tommy, who could best guess at his whereabouts, was Rhona. She was the one I needed to talk to.

"You feeling better?" asked Suze.

"Much. Haven't thought about my pop for a half hour now."

"So come out with us on Friday. See if you feel like spreading your wings a bit. If nothing else, you'll be giving your mind a rest."

"What do you on Friday nights?" I asked.

"Dance, of course. It's the only way to end the week."

"Where do you go?" I asked.

"The land of darkness. It's the best place for it, baby girl."

A thrill passed through me. She was talking about Harlem. I'd never been there before. It was forbidden territory, not because anyone had ever told me not to go there, but because I knew that it wasn't the kind of place young white girls went. And now *I* was going there.

Rhona would be there on Friday, and maybe by then in

her eyes I wouldn't be the odd little girl following her crowd. I'd think things through between now and then— what to ask and how to ask it. I'd have a plan. I'd find out why she was worried about Tom.

"All right," I said. "Just tell me where to meet you."

8

I WAS ITCHING WITH QUESTIONS by the time I got home that day. What had Tom done with the money from the locker thefts? How could Rhona be both concerned about Tom and willing to take up with someone else to teach him a lesson? Why had she said I was Tom's type?

"Hi," I told Pop as I came in the door. His own door was open, giving him a clear view of me as I arrived. I wondered if it was deliberate; perhaps he no longer wanted to be surprised by my comings and goings.

"Hello yourself," he said. He had a stack of phone directories in front of him. "How was school?"

"Fine. What are you working on?"

"Trying to track down a missing person for an attorney handling a will. If I find her, she has quite a bit of money coming her way."

I couldn't tell if it was the truth or if he was doing something to help chase down Tom.

"You had a phone call from Grace Dunwitty. I told her I'd have you call her when you got home." He pushed a piece of paper my way with Grace's exchange scrawled on it. "She said she's called before."

"I know." I waited for him to say something more, to, at the very least, ask me if I was avoiding Grace, but it wasn't in Pop's nature to pry into my life. Besides, if he did, it might give me permission to pry into his. And then what? Would I ask him what it was like to have only one leg? Or if he missed Mama as much as I did?

"You ever see those kids you went to that club with?" he asked.

"I eat lunch with Pearl almost every day." I saw my chance and grabbed at it. "In fact, she asked me to go out again this Friday."

"Where?"

"A dance." It was sort of the truth. After all, there would be dancing.

Pop nodded. "Sounds good. They seemed like nice kids."

How would he know? He hadn't even bothered to talk to them.

He didn't ask anything else. Not where the dance was, not how late I'd be. I should've been thrilled, but I was strangely disappointed. For a man who refused to let me work for him because he was worried about my safety, he was curiously nonchalant about the whole thing. Maybe it just didn't occur to him that high school kids could get themselves into trouble, despite what Tom Barney's disappearance implied.

"Here." He passed me a pile of rumpled bills he'd unearthed from his pants pocket.

"What's this?"

"What does it look like? If you're going to a dance, you need a new dress, right?"

I stared at the money, simultaneously touched and uncomfortable. Was this part of the retainer from Tom's parents? Or had he pawned something else? "Thanks, but I'm okay."

"Take it, Iris. You deserve a treat."

He turned his attention to the newspaper in front of him. War news. There were numbers on the front page, never a good sign. I knew what those digits meant: lives lost, boats sunk, planes downed. Numbers never meant anything good. Victories were reported with vague, verb-heavy language like "pushed back," "taken over," "captured," and "defeated."

"How long do you think it will last?" I asked Pop.

He looked at the front page, wondering, I'm sure, what had inspired the question. "It's hard to say. The Germans and Japanese are good fighters. It could end tomorrow." I read between the lines. They weren't just good enough to beat us; they could do it fast.

"So they're better than we are?"

"They're more prepared. They've been at this longer. We

have a lot of catching up to do. Our military wasn't ready for this."

"But we can catch up?"

"Maybe."

This was one of those moments when I hated that Pop didn't immediately think he needed to reassure me. Would it hurt him to tell one little white lie to help me sleep better at night? "Do you think the draft is a bad idea?" I asked.

"I think eighteen and nineteen is awfully young. But it won't affect me—what do you think about it?"

"I don't know."

I didn't have time to worry about it. I had other things to focus on. Things like going to a dance club in Harlem and finding out about Tom Barney.

PEARL WAS WAITING FOR ME outside the cafeteria the next day. "What happened to you yesterday? I waited for you after school."

"I'm so sorry," I told her as we entered the lunchroom and claimed our usual spot. Her lunch bag bulged with delectable offerings. What would it be today? Cake? Pie? Chocolate doughnuts? "I actually ended up going with Suze to Normandie's after school."

"Seriously?" she asked. "How did you arrange that?"

"I went into the restroom pretending I was crying. She stuck around after Rhona and Maria left and asked me what the matter was." I couldn't tell her the whole truth, but I needed to provide some sort of explanation for how I'd wrangled an invitation. "I told her I was just so lonely since starting public school. I hadn't made any friends."

"And that did it?"

I didn't blame her for her disbelief. Hollywood would've rejected that scene as too dull to be believed. "That did it."

"Wow." She let this roll about her head for a moment. I expected more questions, but she decided to let it drop. "Did she talk about Tom?"

"A little, after school. I mean, I couldn't tell her why I was asking, not if I wanted her to be open about it."

"Or honest about it. You can't trust the Rainbows. Remember that."

I don't know why, but Pearl's comment irritated me. Yes, they had a bad reputation, but the Rainbows had their good qualities.

And besides, her need to remind me that some of them were dishonest made me wonder if what Rhona said Pearl had done was true. It was hard to believe that everyone stopped talking to her just because her brother died. Being a gossip, on the other hand, might've sealed her fate.

"Do they know where he is?" she asked.

"Not yet." I chased a pea around my plate. "Did you know Tom's brother?"

She pursed her lips. They were dusted with sandwich

crumbs that I longed to tell her to wipe away. "Yeah. His name's Michael. He was in my brother's class."

Her dead brother's class. "Were they friends?"

"Not particularly. Michael was always a troublemaker. Peter was pretty straitlaced."

Peter. It was the first time she'd said her other brother's name out loud.

She pulled out a folder and slid it across the table to me. "What's this?"

She raised an eyebrow. "What do you think?"

I lifted the edge and saw Tommy's name typed on an official-looking form. "You pulled his student record?" My irritation at her instantly lifted.

Pearl put her finger to her lips, like I needed a reminder that this was on the q.t. "I need to get it back by the end of the day. Think you can do that?"

"Absolutely." The boredom I'd been expecting to face that afternoon instantly washed away. The topmost page of the file was Tom's schedule, written in Pearl's familiar sloping scrawl. "Did you do this?" I asked.

She nodded. "I thought it might be helpful for you to see what classes he was in. They keep the schedules filed separately and I couldn't get into that cabinet."

"Do you memorize everyone's schedule?"

"Of course not." She played with the lid from her milk bottle.

But she knew his, and a thousand other details about him. I couldn't believe it had taken me so long to put two and two together: Pearl liked Tom. And not just a little bit.

"So are you going to go out with Suze after school again?" she asked me.

"I'm not planning to. Actually, I'm going to go out with them on Friday to see if I can't find out more."

"Them?"

"Suze, Rhona, Maria, and those two Italian guys who are always with them."

"Oh." She unwrapped the rest of her bag's offerings. A piece of coffee cake glistening with translucent icing was among its contents. "How did that happen?"

"I don't know. She just asked if I wanted to go and I said yes."

She continued staring at her lunch. "Where are you going?"

"Dancing. At a club. In Harlem."

She looked up and her eyes grew wider than Little Orphan Annie's. "A negro club?"

"I think it's a black and tan. Otherwise, how could we get in?" I felt like an old pro, using the lingo I'd seen in the movies and read in the magazines.

She removed the cake from its waxed paper cocoon and took a bite. "That should be interesting." She licked her fingers clean and dug into the bag for a napkin. "I've always wanted to go to Harlem."

Did she expect me to invite her to go with us? I tried to ignore her fishing expedition and concentrate on my own lunch. "I'd invite you, but that might seem strange. After all, I cried about not having any friends."

"Oh, I know. I'm just saying that I'd like to go *sometime*." She took another bite of cake. I wished she'd use a fork, or at the very least stop licking her fingers after every bite. "Want some?" she asked.

"No, thanks." I needed to clear things up with her, just so if it became an issue, there wouldn't be a problem. "Were you ever friends with Rhona?"

She looked like she was about to laugh. "Um, no. You've met me, right?"

She had a point. "Did you start the rumor that Rhona was pregnant last year?"

A V formed between her eyes. "Why would you ask that?"

"She seemed to think you had."

"You talked about me?"

"She'd seen us together and asked about you."

"So you told her she's nuts, right?"

Was she? It didn't escape my notice that Pearl hadn't denied the accusation. If she had a crush on Tom and Tom had started seeing Rhona, ruining the reputation of his new girlfriend might have seemed like a great idea. "I didn't exactly know you back then, Pearl. I mean, if she was talking about something that happened last week, sure, I'd defend you. But this was a year ago."

She let the cake fall back to its wrapping. "I'm the same person I was a year ago."

That was impossible. Even if her brother hadn't died and her weight hadn't ballooned, no one was exactly the same person they were a year ago. "I just changed the subject," I told her. "But I thought you should know that Rhona thinks the story started with you. She seemed pretty upset about it."

"Well, thanks, I guess. For letting me know." She wrapped up the cake. She was done with it. Whatever appetite she'd had had been killed the minute I mentioned Rhona. "I should return the file by the end of the day. Can you meet me right after school?"

"Absolutely," I told her.

I SPENT THE AFTERNOON with Tom's file hidden inside my American History textbook. There was a lot to go through. The first pages were his attendance records, meticulously filled out in blue ink. In the past year and a half, he'd racked up almost thirty days of unexplained absences, and an equal number of tardies. Letters had been sent home, the carbon copies of which were retained for his file. After stating his concern over Tommy's extraordinary number of days away, Principal Deluca asked for an explanation and a meeting. In return he got letters that had clearly been forged. Tom's "mother" described a number of health problems plaguing her son, ranging from colds and infections to much more dire things like polio and rubella. There was also a record of at least one phone call from Mrs. Barney, though it was clear from the notes pinned to the message slip that the recipient had doubts about whom they were talking to. Whoever it was reiterated poor Tom's failing health and promised to give her son a good talking-to about the importance of completing his education.

You could almost hear the laughter those letters and that call had to cause, especially for the people writing them (Suze? Rhona? Whoever it was dotted their i's with a small circle). Eventually, the principal seemed to realize that the meetings he requested were never going to happen and the letters he sent would always be intercepted. Although he continued to write to Tom's parents, the tone in the most recent letters changed from that of one authority figure addressing another to that of a concerned administrator addressing a student whom he wasn't quite ready to give up on. "While I am sympathetic to the changes that have occurred in Thomas's life over the past year, I do hope he understands that continued absences might result in his failing to graduate with his class. I would hate for him to have to repeat a grade, especially since his work shows such promise when he does bother to step into the classroom."

He wasn't exaggerating Tom's potential. The proof was in the next several pages in the folder: Tom's report cards. Given his friends, I would've expected a slew of C's and an occasional D or F, but Tom was almost exclusively a B student. In the area that allowed for teacher commentary, instructor after instructor lauded his innate intelligence while taking him to task for not applying himself. Three years before, when he was still Paul Levine's best friend and preferred pressed pants to the zoot, his grades had been A's.

The last items in the folder were a slew of discipline reports, authored by teachers who'd broken up fights in the hall. While Tom was present at each incident, along with two other boys, he never received any disciplinary action. Why? Had his friends insisted he was an innocent bystander and saw to it that he got off?

It was impossible to tell for sure, though one teacher hinted at a possible explanation in his description of a fight Tom had been present at. "It's a shame Mr. Barney continues to associate with troublemakers and ne'er-do-wells. It's obvious that he possesses a slippery moral character that makes him fall easily under the influence and sway of others. While I have no doubt he was not a participant in the above-described activity, especially given eyewitness statements, it's clear he wishes himself to be thought a thug capable of these grievous offenses. It pains me to think what may become of him in another year or two if he continues down this path."

If that was true, maybe he had committed the locker thefts to prove he was just as tough as his friends?

It was enough to make my head spin.

So what had I learned? Tom Barney was smart, liked to skip school, and wanted to be where the action was. Even though nobody had ever seen him do anything wrong—or at least had the courage to report that they had—he wanted people to think he was as tough as the boys he associated with.

How did someone who defined himself through the opinions of others just disappear?

I MET PEARL at four o'clock on the school steps. With the kind of discretion Sherlock Holmes would've killed for, I slid the folder inside my American History book and exchanged her text for mine.

"Thanks," I said. "That was swell of you."

We fell into step together and headed toward the office. "Learn anything?" she asked.

"A lot, though I don't know that any of it has anything to do with why he disappeared. He appears in a lot of the write-ups for things two other boys were collared for, but he never got punished for any of them. Not even detention. Why do you think that is?"

"Who were the boys who got the blame?"

I checked my notes. "Benicio and Bernadino."

"Ah, Benny and Dino. They're the two Italian boys who are always with Suze and her crew." She paused near a row of lockers. Already the halls were virtually empty, but this didn't seem like the kind of conversation we should have in the vicinity of the principal's office.

"So why did they get blamed and he didn't?"

"Probably because he's pale instead of tan and his last name doesn't end in a vowel."

"Seriously?"

"That counts for a lot around here," said Pearl.

"Then why did he bother getting involved in what Benny and Dino were doing? For the thrill?"

Pearl licked her lips. "Back when Tom and Paul were pals he always seemed like he wanted to please my brother. He was that way with me, too. But then after his brother went to jail, it was like something snapped and he decided it wasn't worth trying to be perfect anymore. Paul told me Tom's father was pretty tough on him, more so after Michael was arrested. If you can't please someone no matter how hard you try, at some point it might seem easier to go ahead and become the thing they think you're going to be. Either way, you're going to disappoint them."

I knew what that was like. I'd felt that way myself a time or two. "So do you think that's why he broke into the lockers? To prove he was exactly what everyone thought he was going to be?"

"Probably." Pearl seemed distant. I got the feeling that she wanted to stop talking to me and go on her way.

"I'm sorry about what I said about Rhona," I told her. "I should've defended you."

"Why? Like you said, it wouldn't have made sense for you to stick up for me. And I couldn't care less what she thinks about me, anyway."

I doubted that was true. Pearl struck me as the kind of person who cared deeply about how others felt about her.

She thumped her chubby fingers across the top of the textbook. "Maybe on Saturday we could get together. Talk about what happened on Friday night."

"All right."

"We could sleep over at my place. You'd have to put up with Paul, but I know my mother would love to meet you."

"I'll ask my pop, but I can't imagine a reason in the world why he'd say no."

We parted ways at the office door. As she disappeared inside to return the file, I wondered if it was possible that Rhona was wrong about Pearl. Or was I being naïve because I wanted to believe that my brand-new best friend wasn't capable of lying to me like I lied to her?

CHAPTER 9

FRIDAY NIGHT WAS ALL I could think about for the next two days. My nerves were swiftly replaced by my excitement about going somewhere forbidden. What would the club be like? Would people be smoking? Drinking? Would the music be so loud that I couldn't think? Would they even let me in?

Friday at lunch, just as Pearl and I were debating whether Deanna Durbin was a better actress than Shirley Temple, Suze came over and greeted me with a wide smile. "Feeling better?" she asked.

My own smile matched hers. Was that a mistake? "Some," I said. I offered Pearl a sidelong glance. She was staring at Suze as if Rita Hayworth had just parachuted out of a plane and decided to join us.

Suze slid next to me on the bench. "No more news?"

"Not a peep." I didn't want to talk about this in front of

Pearl, so I swiftly changed the subject. "Are we still on for tonight?"

"If you're game, so are we. How about we meet at my aquarium at eight?" She gave me an address that wasn't far from where we lived.

I could sense Pearl's longing to be included. It radiated off her like heat. I think Suze sensed it, too, because she smiled Pearl's way and introduced herself.

"It's nice to meet you," said Pearl.

"Likewise," said Suze. "I better beat tracks. See you at eight." Once she left, I tried to pick up my conversation with Pearl from where we'd left off, but she wasn't having any of it.

"She wears a lot of makeup."

"Really? I hadn't noticed."

"Do you think she stuffs her bra?"

"Beats me." It didn't seem fair to talk about Suze behind her back.

"What news was she asking about?" she asked.

"What?"

"She asked if you'd had any more news."

She'd picked up on that? Boy, howdy—Pearl was a lot more perceptive than I gave her credit for. "I think it's just an expression like, 'Hey, Joe, what do you know?' "

Pearl's face made it clear she wasn't buying it, but it didn't look like she was up for pursuing it further, either. "You must be excited about tonight," she said.

I was, but it didn't seem like I should admit it. "I'm more nervous than anything."

"What are you going to wear?"

I'd spent half the night worrying over that very subject. I couldn't bring myself to spend Pop's money, not after my stripped-down tale of where I was going that night. Besides, what did girls wear to dance clubs in Harlem? "I haven't really thought about it yet."

"I can't believe your pop's letting you go." She unraveled her lunch bit by bit. Today's dessert was some sort of nut-encrusted roll that smelled of honey.

"He doesn't exactly know."

"You didn't tell him?"

"I told him we were going dancing." I didn't bother to tell her that she was part of that "we." "He didn't ask where and I didn't volunteer it."

"Oh." She looked concerned. I understood where she was coming from. Lying to a parent was a big deal, even if it wasn't lying so much as omitting important details. "I guess you didn't tell your mother, either?"

"My mother's dead."

Her sandwich fell, limply, onto its waxed paper wrapping. "Seriously? You never told me that."

"You never asked."

Her forehead furrowed. "Why would I ask something like that?"

I shrugged. "Can't we talk about something else?"

"Sure." She paused long enough to let me know that no other subject could possibly be as important as this to her. "It just seems strange. I mean, you knew about Peter. Why wouldn't you tell me about your mother?"

Because it wasn't the same? Because I thought I'd shared enough when I told her about what had happened to Pop? "I just didn't," I said.

"How did she die?"

She wasn't going to let this drop, was she? Couldn't she see how uncomfortable the topic made me? What was it going to take? "She killed herself." There. Subject closed, I hoped.

"When?"

I was reminded of Grace Dunwitty and all the other girls I used to consider my friends, circling me like sharks while they made their consolation call at our uptown apartment. After they left, Aunt Miriam had told me that they were young and didn't know any better than to ask prurient questions ("What was prurient?" I'd asked her; "Rude," she'd replied), but I knew that wasn't the case. These were good girls from good homes. They knew better. But Mama's death had devalued me in their eyes. They no longer had to be tactful to someone like me. Scandal invited inquiry.

I dropped my silverware onto my plate and gathered my things. "She did it on New Year's Eve. In a hotel room. She took a bunch of pills. I don't know why she did it. No, she didn't leave a note. She wasn't depressed that I knew of, but then after hearing that my father had lost his leg, who knows what was going through her head. I have to go." I stood to leave. Pearl put her hand on mine and gently pushed my lunch tray back onto the table.

"I'm sorry if I upset you."

"You're acting like I lied to you," I said.

"I don't think you lied. I just find it weird that you didn't tell me, that's all."

"Just like you didn't tell me that you have a crush on Tom Barney?" It felt like a low blow, but I didn't care. Her lips fluttered but she didn't respond. "There are some things I just don't want to talk about, all right?"

"All right," she said. Her voice was soft and full of regret. For a while we ate in silence, though it was obvious neither of us had any appetite left. As I sat there, trying to down the salty, greasy pasta that was that day's lunch, I felt terrible. Of course Pearl was curious. Who wouldn't be? Was it really fair to bite her head off over it? I almost said as much, but right then she looked up at me and asked, "Is that why you lied to my brother about being Jewish?"

"What?"

"It's on your school record. Suicide is forbidden by Jewish law. Were you afraid we'd judge you for that? Because those were your mother's actions, not yours."

I couldn't have been more shocked if she'd slapped me with her sandwich. I stood up from the table so quickly that my chair threatened to topple over. "You may think Suze wears too much makeup and dresses like a tramp, but at least she had the good sense to let the subject drop."

"You told Suze about your mom?"

Was she really making this a competition? I shook my head. "I've got to go."

"Wait. I didn't mean it like that." Her voice was too loud. A table of boys to the left of us caught wind of our conversation and echoed her words back at her, their own voices raised in falsetto. *Wait. I didn't mean it like that.*

I left my plate where it was and exited the cafeteria, while the table of boys exploded with laughter.

I SPENT ALL OF AMERICAN HISTORY fuming about Pearl, instead of listening to the lecture on war preparedness. To think there was a time when I felt guilty about not defending her to Rhona. No wonder Rhona thought she was the one who'd spread the rumor about her absence. Even if Pearl hadn't done it maliciously, I could see her clumsily making assumptions about Rhona's personal life and then repeating them within earshot of the wrong person.

She'd probably do the same thing to me. "Her mom committed suicide," she'd tell people. "And so now she thinks she can't be Jewish."

By the time typing class arrived, I'd spent as much energy as I could muster being mad at Pearl. I let my mind empty as we took our places at the machines and keyed *The quick brown fox jumps over the lazy dog* in time to the ticking of a metronome. When my mind wasn't tallying the number of mistakes I'd made, I let it worry over what I was going to wear that night. While my wardrobe had matured since those first, early days of school, it had by no means become fashionable. By the time class ended, I had an outfit in mind: my pencil skirt and a blouse that made me look like I had a bosom.

I half expected to find Pearl waiting for me after school, but she'd either left before me or was deliberately hanging back until she was certain I was gone. I'd overreacted and I knew it. Of course she was curious—I would be, too. In her shoes I probably would be wondering what else I was keeping from her.

I made it home and spent far too much time taming my hair. Pop was out, so I sought Mrs. Mrozenski's approval on my attire.

"You're going to a dance?" she asked.

I nodded, hoping she would have the good sense not to ask where.

"You look very grown-up. Maybe, though, something is missing." She went upstairs to her bedroom and returned a moment later, a girdle in hand. It clearly wasn't hers, but rather some castoff her daughter, Betty, had left in her possession.

I thanked her and, after a quick lesson on how to squeeze

146

into it, I put the garment on. Instantly, I achieved the smooth silhouette the skirt demanded. And a sudden, inescapable feeling that I couldn't breathe.

At seven-thirty I made the brief, anxious walk to Suze's house, arriving fifteen minutes early. If our home was a step down from the Upper East Side, hers was a leap. The apartment was one of many in a tenement building that hugged a thin, weed-choked sidewalk. Outside, bored children played jacks, hopscotch, and any other game they could think of that took less money than imagination. Row after row of laundry rippled in the evening breeze on lines strung between the close-set buildings. There was no attempt at maintaining privacy here. Brassieres and shorts were as prominently displayed as trousers and dresses, all bearing the telltale signs of wear and tear that were visible even from where I stood at street level.

I would've died of embarrassment, but no one here cared. This was poverty. In comparison, at Mrs. Mrozenski's house, Pop and I were on easy street.

I carefully made my way up the stairs and into a narrow hallway. Suze had told me they lived in number six, so I followed each labeled door until I reached one that didn't bear a numeral but, because of its proximity to number seven, had to be the apartment I was looking for. Inside, dishes clattered as someone washed up after dinner. A woman's nasal voice screeched at top volume. I couldn't tell if she was angry or deaf.

I leaned against the door and tried to verify that I was at the right place.

"You need to learn some respect, little girl. This isn't a hotel," said a voice from inside.

"I told you I had plans." That was Suze, or someone doing a pretty good imitation of her.

"You don't decide when you get to come and go."

"I'll stay with her tomorrow."

"I don't have to work tomorrow."

"You don't have to work now."

"I do if you expect food on the table. Who else is going to provide it?"

"I gave you my paycheck."

"Gee, a whole five dollars, Suze. Don't tell the Rockefellers."

"What do you want from me? I go to school. I go to work. And now I want to go out."

"That little girl in there needs someone to watch over her."

"Then you do it—you're her mother." Footsteps pounded across the floor, growing louder as they grew closer to the door.

"Don't you walk away when I'm talking to you! You're getting too big for your britches."

Suze responded, though her voice was so low that the words were indistinct. What came next wasn't so quiet though: it was the sound of flesh hitting flesh.

"You come back here right now!"

The door flew open and Suze emerged, unlit cigarette in one hand, pocketbook in the other. Her cheek was red, one eye partially closed. Behind her a woman in factory coveralls and a dark blue snood tried to grab hold of her arm and missed.

"I said come back here right now!"

Suze slammed the door behind her and took two steps before seeing that I was in the hallway.

"Sorry," I said. "I'm early."

"No, it's good. I need to truck out of here."

I followed her down the stairs and out of the building. At the stoop she paused and pulled a compact out of her purse. With a practiced hand she studied her reflection, assessed the damage, and then carefully covered the woman's handiwork with her powder puff. The red was lost beneath the makeup's sheen.

I tried to imagine what could bring Mama to hit me, but the idea that she could strike me was so absurd that I couldn't invent circumstances to support it.

But maybe if she had struck out at me instead of herself, she'd still be here.

"What happened?" I asked.

"What always happens? She doesn't like the way I dress, the way I talk, or who I hang out with. She's tired, we're poor, and my no-good father hasn't made an appearance for months." She held her eye open with one hand and stared at the red that appeared threaded through the white.

"Maybe you should stay home tonight."

"Maybe you shouldn't beat your gums off time." She instantly regretted saying it; I could see it in her eyes. "I'm sorry, baby—I didn't mean to bust a button. She has me rattled. Look, she's sore that I won't stay home and sit with my sister. The brat's old enough to take care of herself, she's almost eleven, but the truth is Ma feels guilty for taking the swing shift, so she thinks if she can goad me into staying, she can forgive herself for working."

"What does she do?"

"Munitions work. The hours are long, but the pay's nothing to sneeze at. She's right—my little paycheck isn't even a drop in the bucket."

"Where's your father?"

"I don't know and I don't care." She added lipstick and rouge to her palette, then returned everything to her purse. Now that her own appearance was taken care of, she turned her attention to me. "Oh, baby—what's this?"

"What's what?"

Her fingers indicated my pencil skirt. "We're dancing. You can't dance in a straitjacket."

What was she talking about? I could move my feet just fine.

"Are you wearing a girdle?" she said.

"Yes."

"Boy, do you have a lot to learn. Come on." She took me by the hand and pulled me around to the side of the building, where a row of windows stared across the brief alleyway at the brick wall of the building next door. What a view. At the rearmost window she paused, pushed over a coal bin, and then hoisted herself on top of it. She threw one leg over the window's ledge and then motioned for me to follow. Seconds later she was inside the building and I was left to negotiate the tight skirt and tall bin. After a few graceless attempts, I made it up to the window and over the ledge.

We had landed in a bedroom. Instead of finding Suze, I found a young girl lying belly-down on a bed, flipping through the new Nancy Drew, *The Quest of the Missing Map*. This had to be the sister.

"Hello," I said. "Where's Suze?"

She tipped her head toward a wardrobe, where Suze was rapidly flipping through rows of clothing I recognized from school. "Here," she said, flinging a navy blue skirt my way. "Try this on."

I looked around, hoping there was a screen I could duck behind to change. Apparently, I was expected to exchange skirts in front of Suze. And this child.

"I'm Iris," I said to the little girl, because it seemed to me that if she was about to see me in Betty Mrozenski's girdle, we might as well be on a first-name basis.

"This is my kid sister, Barbara," said Suze.

"Ma's going to be mad," said Barbara.

"Ma's already mad. And she won't get any madder unless you tell her I came back here, brat."

While Barbara stared down her sister, I pulled off my clothes and pulled on Suze's. Her A-line skirt was designed to lift into the air when I twirled, which I did at that moment under Suze's orders.

"Now that's a skirt you can dance in," she told me. "Here." She passed me a necklace and a pair of earrings from a box on her bureau. They were just paste, but I felt like I was being loaned the crown jewels.

"Are you sure?"

"Absolutely. Where we're going, you have to be togged to the bricks. Now hold still." She put her hands on either side of my face and pushed my head until I was looking directly at her. From her pocketbook came the powder puff, rouge, lipstick, and mascara. While I prayed she had steady hands, she painted my face until it looked just like hers. "Perfect," she said when her work was finished.

I caught sight of myself in the tarnished mirror above her dresser. I did look good. Grown-up, almost pretty. Red cheeks, red lips, eyelashes that went on forever.

Suze turned her attention to my feet. "How big are your dogs?"

I told her and she again turned to the wardrobe and pulled out a pair of well-worn pumps. "These are small, but they'll do. Can't have you ruining the effect with saddle shoes."

I slipped on the leather loafers with Cuban heels, longing to see how different my legs looked. The shoes were tight, but I didn't care.

"Now you're hotsy totsy from head to toe. All right, sunshine. We got to blow." Suze climbed out the window and instructed me to follow her.

"It was nice meeting you," I told Barbara.

She didn't bother to reply.

10

I STRUGGLED TO KEEP SUZE'S PACE out on the street. It was obvious the scene with her mother had bothered her more than she was willing to let on, but I wasn't sure how, or if, I should ask any more about it. Adults didn't act that way in my world, and I had a funny suspicion that if I condemned her mother for her behavior, Suze would defend her. And the last thing I wanted to do was to put us at odds. After all, I'd been in enough arguments that day.

"So your aunt was okay with you coming out tonight?" she asked me.

It took me a minute to remember that I lived with my fictional aunt. "Absolutely."

"No curfew?"

Pop hadn't said anything about when I needed to return. "Nope."

Suze eyed me suspiciously. "Lucky dog. If I'm not home

by twelve-thirty I get the belt." She raised an eyebrow. "Of course, sometimes it's worth it."

"My aunt doesn't have any other kids, so I don't think it occurred to her that she needed to tell me when I should come home."

Suze laughed. "Enjoy it while you can. After tonight, I'll bet she gives you all kinds of rules."

We met up with Rhona and Maria outside Normandie's Pharmacy. Rhona ignored me. Maria greeted me by saying, "Nice hardware," which I realized was a reference to the jewelry Suze had loaned me. Five minutes later, two Italian boys I recognized from the Rainbows' lunch table joined us. Benny was tall and tan, both features set off by the oversized dark blue pinstriped suit he wore. His shoes were polished to a high sheen and from his waist hung a watch on a chain that he twirled as he approached us. With him was Dino. He also wore an oversized suit, only his was a butter-yellow color that made it seem even more like a costume. Neither introduced himself to me. Instead, they talked to Rhona and Maria and periodically looked my way like they were wondering why I was still there.

I was starting to wonder, too.

The plan was to pool our money and take a cab into the heart of Harlem. As we waited for a taxi to appear, everyone searched pockets and pocketbooks for enough coin to get us there and into the club. It was obvious that everyone was broke and no one was eager to pay more than their share. By the time we found a car willing to go north of 96th Street, we still hadn't sorted out how we were going to pay the bill.

I was starting to panic. What if the entire evening was canceled? "I've got it," I said, producing Pop's small wad of bills from inside my purse.

"Are you sure?" asked Suze.

She had no idea how hard it was for Pop to come up with that dough. She probably thought it was walking-around cash my aunt and uncle gave to me. "Why not? After all, you're all being so nice about taking me with you. It's the least I can do."

After that the mood toward me drastically improved.

We piled into the cab, Suze in the front seat, Rhona and Maria on the boys' laps in the back. I was wedged into the remaining space beside them, trying not to become overwhelmed by the cigarette smoke they began to fill the car with.

The cabbie drove like a madman, obviously eager to get us into Harlem and get himself on his way. I rolled down the window and concentrated on the view as the wind whipped my hair in my face. I'm not sure what I was expecting to see—crime out in the open, maybe—but Harlem looked pretty much like the rest of New York, save the skin color of most of the people living there. There were grocers and produce stands, children out playing in the dimming twilight, and couples walking hand in hand, dressed in their best getups, many of which mirrored our own attire. When we paused at a traffic light, I could hear music coming from somewhere nearby. I thought it was the radio, until I saw a man singing on a street bench, using the wooden seat as his stage. He saw me watching him and rewarded me with a smile before launching into another song and dance.

At last we came to a stop on Lenox Avenue. Brightly lit clubs lined the block, their names identified in brilliant neon that pulsed against the darkening sky. I paid the driver, adding a tip, and we all tumbled out of the car and onto the sidewalk. Suze took me by the arm and pulled me toward what looked like a large theater marquee. It read SAVOY and a huge crowd of people lingered beneath it, clearly waiting to get inside.

"What's the holdup?" I asked.

"The band's still frisking the whiskers," said Maria. "Until they're ready, we wait." I stared at the building, trying to take it all in, an impossible feat given its size. It was a block long, stretching the distance between 140th and 141st streets. Music leaked out its windows and doors—brass instruments, drums, piano, and guitar, each sounding strangely tempered as though they were saving up their energy for the real thing.

At last the doors opened and the crowd streamed inside and up the stairs, our group among them. As I followed the flow, I saw both black and white faces itching to get on the dance floor. Many of the men were outfitted in the same strange suits Benny and Dino wore. The women, by and large, were stunning. All wore skirts like the one Suze had loaned me, reaching to the middle of their calves but capable of standing straight out at the waist. Many had flowers in their hair and heavily made-up faces that told of the hours of preparation they'd endured for this evening. The air was heavy with the scent of hairspray, perfume, cigarettes, and another smoke I couldn't identify but which I found pleasantly sweet. As we at last arrived at the entrance to the ballroom itself, I could see signs reporting that the Savoy Sultans were one of two bands taking the stage that night.

"The joint is jumping. You ready to bust loose?" Suze asked me.

"As ready as I'll ever be."

The ballroom was gorgeous. The wooden floor gleamed with wax; the chandeliers twinkled in the dim light. Two bandstands populated the room, one of which was already taken up by a group playing a song I didn't recognize. I had no idea how we were expected to dance in there. The place was wall-to-wall people, except for a small cordoned-off section where a few pairs of dancers performed such feats of gymnastics that I was terrified they were going to hit the vaulted ceiling.

"What's that?" I asked Suze.

"Cat's Corner. That's where the best of the best strut

their stuff." We found a spot near the wall where we were less likely to be trampled, and I watched as these extraordinary dancers continued their demonstration. I'd heard about swing and certainly knew much of the music that fell under that label, but I'd never seen the dancing that accompanied it before. At least not like this. The men literally threw their partners around and the women let them, demonstrating such grace, trust, and athleticism that I wanted to weep for the sheer beauty of it all. How had they learned to do that? Weren't they afraid their partners would drop them? Were they embarrassed when their skirts rose into the air, showing off their garter belts? Would they be mortified to learn that every time they flipped I could see the white flash of their panties?

But it wasn't just the dancing that grabbed my gut and held me solid. The music was different. This wasn't Benny Goodman rocking the airwaves from the parlor radio. These musicians worked their instruments like they were part of themselves—trumpets grown in place of arms, pianos where there should've been legs. Instruments didn't sound like instruments here: they were animals that growled, hooted, and barked in four beats to a measure. I don't know how the musicians got them to sound that way, but it was more alive than any music I'd heard before.

"What do you think?" Suze yelled above the roar of the band.

"It's amazing!" I wished I had a chair I could sink into so I could take it all in. I felt like I'd woken up in a foreign land. All around me people talked about scobo queens, hepcats, high steppers, trucking, and tumbling. With each word I didn't understand, I turned to Suze and asked for a translation. She patiently laid out the racket for me as best she could. "Can you dance like that?" I asked her.

"No way. Half of those hoofers are working on Broadway. You ready to get in there?"

I backed away from her, instantly afraid. "Not yet."

"Relax, baby—just watch and learn. Nobody ever died from doing the jitterbug."

Before I could respond, a man took hold of Suze's arm and pulled her into the center of the dance floor. They joined the gyrating, swinging mass of humanity while I pressed myself against the wall. So this was what people did on Friday nights. They didn't stay home reading Nancy Drew novels or biding their time learning the detective business. They lived.

I caught a glimpse of Maria in the arms of a black man whose smile was sixty watts, easy. She was one of the better dancers on the floor, so comfortable in her man's arms that I had a hard time telling where he ended and she began.

"Having fun?" Rhona joined me, a silver flask in her hand. Perspiration had plastered her hair to her head.

"I'm swell. Just swell." I'd forgotten my reason for being there. How convenient that it hadn't forgotten me.

"Want a tipple?" She passed the flask my way. Desperate to make her stay by my side, I accepted her offer and took a swallow. The booze burned down my throat, and it took everything in me not to choke and cough it back up. Is that what alcohol was like? And people drank it by choice? "Where's Suze?" she asked.

I struggled to keep myself from gagging. "Dancing. I saw Maria over that way. Is that her boyfriend?"

"If he isn't yet, he will be." She took a sip and screwed the cap back on the container.

"How come you stopped dancing?" I asked. Talking suddenly seemed easier.

"I needed a rest. How come you didn't start?"

"I needed a lesson."

She laughed at that. This was good. "You should get Benny or Dino to take you for a spin. They can cut a rug with the best of them."

"Is Tommy a good dancer?" I asked. I was surprised to hear the words come out of my mouth. Apparently, whatever was in the flask had erased my ability to deliberate before talking.

"Fantastic. One of the best. He was in Cat's Corner a time or two."

"It's a shame he's not here tonight."

She raised an eyebrow, but didn't respond right away. I was being too obvious. She had to know I was up to something. "You think I don't remember you, don't you? Talking to Tommy in the hall, hanging on his every word like God himself was speaking."

"It wasn't like that, Rhona."

"Tell me another one while that's still warm. I got my boots on, girlie. I know what I saw." She shrugged and unscrewed the flask for another drink. I decided to move away from her. If she didn't like me—and it was clear she didn't—I wasn't going to prolong my misery by forcing her to talk to me.

"Wait," she said. She put her hand on my arm to stop me. "I'm sorry. I'm being a beast, aren't I?"

"You shred it, wheat," I said.

She grinned at that. I was learning their world, bit by bit. "You just remind me of her."

"Her who?

"Tommy's Upper East Side bobby soxer."

This was new. "He has a girlfriend uptown?"

"Had. You went to private school, right?" she asked. I nodded. "So did his latest obsession. He loves those girls in their prissy little uniforms who reek of old money. Tommy thinks he's too good for public school girls. Fancies himself a real B.T.O."

"Oh." Was that why Tom had asked Pearl who it was who had gone to Chapin? "I didn't realize he was seeing someone."

"You and me both. I followed him one day. Saw her with my own eyes."

No wonder she'd gotten a new man when Tom disappeared. She wasn't being callous; she was simply doing as he'd done. "So maybe he's been with her this whole time?" I said.

"Nope. She gave him the gate back in September, but he wouldn't hear it. Kept showing up at the duchess's school and her fancy apartment, hoping to win her back. It was pathetic."

I couldn't see it. But I also couldn't see Rhona lying about it. Her story dripped with truth. And jealousy.

"He told you that?"

"Nope, but he told Benny, and that's practically the same thing."

"They could've gotten back together, though."

"If they did, she's doing a fine job covering it up. I saw her out with stars and stripes on her arm just last week."

"I'm sorry, Rhona. She sounds awful."

"She is. And check this for irony—her name is Grace. You expect more from a girl with a name like that, you know?"

A chill passed through me. "What's her last name?"

She snapped her fingers as the name came back to her. "Dimwitted. What a name, right?"

It would've been, if she'd remembered it correctly. It was actually Dunwitty. Grace Dunwitty. My former best friend at the Chapin School.

11

GRACE DUNWITTY WAS THE DEFINITION of sub-deb. The daughter of a doctor, she was the third person in her family to go to Chapin. I met her my first day there, when our big sisters for the day sat us down together at lunch and introduced us. She was a year older than me and I liked her immediately. She was everything I wanted to be: pretty, blond, outgoing. The only thing I didn't envy about her was that, like her mother, she was an unapologetic snob.

She was the last person in the world that I would've paired with someone like Tom Barney. The boys Grace went with were students at our brother school, boys who came from wealthy families, spent summers at the club, and were shoo-ins for the Ivy League. She would've seen someone like Tom as cut-rate, not worth the energy it took to cross the street to avoid talking to him.

What had changed?

"I know Grace," I told Rhona.

"For real?"

"Well, I used to know her. We went to the same school." I shook my head, trying to think a clear thought despite the one-two punch of booze and music. "I can't see her with Tom."

"Neither could I, but I've seen enough with my own peepers to know it was true."

"What did he see in her?"

She was drunk enough that my curiosity didn't seem strange. Either that or she wanted someone to talk to about this.

"If I had to guess, I'd say a way out. To him a girl like Grace was a ticket out of the Lower East Side."

It didn't escape me that she was speaking in the past tense. She passed me the flask again. Before I could take a drink, a hand extended her way and she took it, allowing the man attached to the other end of it to pull her onto the dance floor.

More hits from the flask and I was ready to take on whatever the night offered me. That meant that when Benny approached and asked me if I wanted to learn to jitterbug, I told him yes without thinking about it.

The next ten minutes were a blur as he tried to show me the basic steps and I tried to follow them without running into anyone else on the dance floor. My self-consciousness was gone. It didn't matter that I stumbled or that I was as graceful as Pinocchio taking his first wooden steps. The music and the mass of humanity around me embraced me and made me feel alive for the first time in months.

"Now you're cooking," said Benny as he swung me to the left. And—boy, howdy—I was, too. I never considered myself graceful or, for that matter, athletic, but the music and the booze gave me the courage to give it my all. The steps no longer felt frenetic and strange, but as natural as walking. I could guess what Benny would do next, and rather than waiting for him to lead me, I anticipated his moves and mirrored them. "You've done this before," he said.

"Nope."

"Well, you're going at it like gangbusters." For the first time I saw how beautiful he was. It was funny thinking of a boy like that, but there was no other way to describe him as he moved about the dance floor, his grin never leaving his face. "What are you thinking?"

"Honestly, I can't believe I haven't tripped and fallen."

He threw his head back and laughed. "You're funny," he said.

"Thanks."

"So what do you think of the Savoy?"

"It's the most amazing place I've ever been."

"You're not scared?"

"Why would I be?"

"Tough neighborhood. Tough crowd. This ain't the kind of place a girl like you should be." His voice was playful. Was he flirting with me? I'd barely heard him speak two

166

words since we'd met, so I didn't know how to gauge his sideways smile or the way he never pulled his eyes away from mine.

"Says who?"

"Me."

"You don't look so dangerous to me," I said. Pearl had to be wrong about the Rainbows. This beautiful boy with the dark eyes and the full lips couldn't be a thief.

As though he heard my thoughts, he said, "Looks can be deceiving." And then he did something very strange—he kissed me.

It was my first kiss and I was completely unprepared for it. And yet despite the fact that I hadn't had time to analyze what was about to happen, it felt like the most natural thing in the world. There I was at a Harlem dance club, a little drunk and a lot sweaty, kissing a beautiful Italian boy wearing a pinstriped suit.

He pulled away but didn't release me. I fought an urge to ask him if I'd done all right.

I didn't want our time at the Savoy to end, but eventually it did.

Suze grabbed my arm and pulled me toward the doors, freeing my hand from Benny's. "We got to make tracks, baby girl. Can you get the others, Benny?"

"I'm on it."

We entered the stairwell, where the music dropped by several decibels. "Have a good time?" she asked.

"The best ever."

"Looked like you and Benny were getting friendly."

Every part of me blushed, I was certain of it. "Is that a bad thing?"

"Not as long as you don't expect to wear his ring come Monday."

"Oh." So what happened with Benny wasn't likely to happen again. I was disappointed but not completely surprised. After all, what could he see in a girl like me?

Perhaps the same thing Tom had seen in Grace?

"You're going to be beat to the socks tomorrow." Suze leaned toward me and took a whiff. "You're lit."

"Rhona gave me something." I looked around for the flask, but it had vanished at some point during my time on the dance floor. I hoped Rhona wouldn't be mad.

"I should've warned you: never take what Rhona offers." We started down the steps, arm in arm.

A breeze greeted us outside, drying the perspiration that had turned my skin damp and clammy. As we waited for the others, we leaned against the building and took in the people still walking the streets at that late hour. Black and white, young and old, men in uniform milled about the crowd. They gave us a look that unnerved me. Didn't they know I was only fifteen years old? Or had one kiss transformed me into someone who seemed as mature as Suze?

Suze lapped up the attention and tried to get me to

return their winks and smiles. But even as looped as I was from Rhona's booze, I wasn't ready to cross that line.

"How you doing, doll?" asked a sailor as he passed us by.

"Never been better. How 'bout yourself?" asked Suze.

"Fine until it looked like you were leaving the party. Don't tell me you're cutting out."

"If I don't get home by twelve-thirty I turn into a pumpkin."

"And your friend?"

I blushed as I realized he was talking about me.

"She's my fairy godmother," said Suze. "Wherever I go, she goes."

"I ship out tomorrow. Don't you want to help me celebrate my last night?"

"What's to celebrate? You're leaving and breaking my heart."

"Maybe if you stick around I'll decide to stay."

"If you did that and we lost the war I'd never forgive myself."

He blew her a kiss and continued on his way.

"Did you know him?" I asked.

"No."

Would I ever feel comfortable talking to a stranger like that? I didn't think so. "Rhona told me Tom was seeing a Chapin School girl. Grace Dunwitty."

Suze tossed an impatient look toward the club and fished

through her pocketbook. "Is Rhona still going on about that?" She did a double take. "You like him, don't you?"

"Tom? No . . . I mean—"

"That's why you've been asking about him. Rhona warned me, but I just assumed she was overreacting."

So they'd talked about me after our chat at Normandie's. "She is overreacting. Or she was. I mean, Tom was nice to me, but I knew he had a girlfriend." She didn't look convinced. "I know Grace. That's why I brought it up just now. We went to school together. I was just surprised to hear he was dating her."

"You and Rhona both."

"So how soon after he broke up with Rhona did he start dating Grace?"

She checked the air behind us, like she was worried that Rhona was there, listening over our shoulder. "He didn't dump Rhona. She dumped him."

"Really?"

She lit a cigarette and blew smoke at the moon. "Hand to my heart. That's why she was so surprised when he hooked up with the little princess right away. Rhona thought she was worth at least a week of mourning."

"She sure seems like she regrets the breakup."

"She was hasty, for sure. But she had her reasons."

"That had to be hard, losing Rhona and then being tossed aside by Grace. Do you think maybe that's why he went away?"

She cocked her head at me. "Honestly, baby, I can't speak to what's in his mind. If it were me and my heart were broken twice, maybe I would've gone away for a while to get my head in order. It's hard to say." She narrowed her gaze. "For someone who claims not to care, you sure ask a lot of questions."

I wanted to tell Suze the truth. But there was no guarantee she'd keep quiet about what I was up to and there was no benefit in tipping your hand too soon. Besides, if I told her I was conducting an investigation, she might put two and two together and figure out my pop wasn't overseas. "Sorry," I said. "Rhona just seemed so upset tonight. I know what it's like to say something you regret and not have a chance to apologize for it."

Her face softened. "That's sweet of you, baby girl. We're not used to people giving us second chances."

The others joined us just then, their faces slick with perspiration. Benny had his coat off and slung over his shoulder. Even though we could no longer hear the band, he danced as he moved across the sidewalk, swinging his slim hips to a tune only he could hear. The motion exaggerated the strange feminine lines of the suit, and yet seemed sexual at the same time. I felt like I was watching something forbidden. And I liked it.

"You cold?" he asked me. I was all of a sudden, so I nodded. He wrapped his jacket about my shoulders. It was so large it swallowed me whole.

Maybe Suze was wrong. Maybe that kiss had meant something to Benny.

We hailed a cab and hit the road. This time, I was one of the ones seated two by two in the back—I reclined on Benny's lap while a drunk Rhona leaned out the window and tried to sober up with the fresh air. The journey was punctuated by laughter as everyone recalled the evening, describing dancers they'd seen, moves they'd made, and hot new songs the band had dragged out and filled the night with. Dino had a memory for music, and he sang snatches of the lyrics to refresh our memories when we couldn't recall the pieces that had been played. Benny joined him on the melody, my back serving as his percussion section. As he played the song's rhythm on my spine, I relaxed against him, feeling the warmth of his breath on my neck. My whole body tingled.

The trip home went much too quickly. We were dropped off in front of Normandie's, where the street was alive with other late-night partygoers. I ponied up what money I had left to cover the cab fare and relinquished the jacket to Benny, wishing I could take it home with me and sleep with it in my arms instead of my baby blanket. Rather than dispersing right away, we all continued chatting, reluctant to call it a night. Another group of soldiers and sailors passed by, and I expected them to say something to us just like the ones in Harlem. I wondered how Benny would react if one of them flirted with me. Would he tell them to back off?

Sure enough, the group paused and looked us over. Rather than addressing Rhona, Suze, Maria, or me, though, it was the men they were interested in.

"Look," said one of them. "Pachucos. Shouldn't you be back in the barrio?"

"I didn't think they had those out East," said his friend.

"They don't," said a third man. "These aren't spics, these are dagos."

"Even better," said the first guy. "We got us a bunch of fascists here."

"We don't want any trouble, man," said Dino. "There's no signifying going on here."

"You should've thought of that before you picked out your clothes for the night. Don't you know there's a war on? All that fabric, all that waste." The first guy clucked his tongue. And then he and his friends surrounded Dino. I thought they were going to beat him up, but they had something else in mind: they each grabbed ahold of his waistband and yanked down his pants.

As Dino stood on the sidewalk in his underwear, his canary pants around his ankles, the military boys turned their attention to Benny. Now that he was aware of what they were doing, he put up more of a fight. Unfortunately, he didn't stand a chance. With five of them, and Dino momentarily restrained, Benny's attempts to keep his pants on and retain his dignity only made things worse. They struck him repeatedly, the fists on his face sounding like a mallet hitting a bass drum. With his fight beaten out of him, they pulled off his pants and then, to add insult to injury, took his hat and threw it into the street.

The men howled with laughter and slapped each other on the back before turning and walking away.

I rushed to Benny's side. He looked so small and defeated, as different from the boy I'd danced with as Pop was from the handsome man in uniform whose picture used to decorate our fireplace mantel. I offered him my hand, wanting to help him to his feet, but he pushed me away, insisting on standing without my assistance.

The rejection was completely understandable, and yet it broke my heart all the same.

While Maria and Rhona tended to Dino, Suze retrieved a handkerchief from her purse and moved to mop the blood from Benny's face.

"Back off." His voice was a growl. I was secretly glad I wasn't the only one he was pushing away.

"Should we call the police?" I asked, wishing I could do something.

"No," said Rhona. "They'll only make things worse."

I didn't see how that was possible. Both boys were humiliated, and neither had done anything to deserve it. How was it fair to let the men responsible for it get away?

"Why did they do that?" I asked.

Suze met my eyes and shook her head. I got her meaning: not now. If you have to ask questions, save them for later.

Benny pulled his pants up and helped Dino to his feet. Without saying another word, they started their way up the block. I wanted to follow them, but I knew in my heart that it was the last thing Benny would want. Suze watched them for a moment, her weight shifting from one foot to another. "You okay getting back to your cubby?" she asked me.

"Sure."

"Be safe." She took off toward her tenement. Seconds later, Rhona also turned a corner, leaving Maria and me alone to find our way home.

We walked side by side in silence. But I couldn't stop the flow of questions welling up in me.

"I don't understand," I said. "Why would they do that?"

"They thought our boys were pachucos."

"What's a pachuco?" I asked her as we lumbered in the direction of Orchard Street.

"Mexican zoot-suiters out West. They don't mix with the military."

"Why?"

"Your guess is as good as mine."

"So they punished Dino and Benny for what boys out West are doing?"

"It's more than that. They think the zoots are unpatriotic because a ton of fabric is needed to make them—fabric that should be used to make uniforms. Here they are risking their lives, and boys like Dino and Benny are mocking them. And I'm sure they weren't happy to see them out on the town with pale girls like you and Suze. Brown skin stays with brown skin. Get it?"

"But Benny and Dino are Italian."

"Where you been, little girl? The Italians aren't on our side in this war. Benny and Dino are lucky they're not being locked up like the Japs."

I felt so young and stupid. How had the evening gone so wrong? Just an hour before I'd been chalking it up as the best night of my life.

"I should've gone after them," I said.

"Benny's not yours to worry about."

"He kissed me," I said.

"And if it happens again, maybe it will mean something. Or maybe it means exactly this: there wasn't anyone else around to kiss."

For the second time in so many minutes, I recoiled in pain. I willed her to turn up the next street so I could finish my walk alone.

"I'm sorry," she said. "That was evil."

I didn't respond, terrified if I did she might take back the apology or add some comment that made her earlier remark cut even deeper.

"It's just hard to trust girls like you," Maria said.

I almost laughed. Did the girl in the gang of petty thieves really just tell me that I was the one they couldn't trust? "Girls like me?" I asked.

"Come on now—we all know you're Upper East Side. I'm surprised you're willing to be seen with people like us."

And here I'd been thinking that it was amazing that Suze would agree to be seen in public with me.

"This is my turn," said Maria.

I paused beside her. "Oh. Thanks for walking with me."

"No problem." She hesitated. There was something else she wanted to say, but I wasn't sure if I wanted to hear it. "Pearl Harbor was wrong, you know. That's why Rhona was so upset."

I was thrown off guard by the mention of Pearl's nickname. "Oh?"

"Rhona wasn't pregnant then. She was sick, but it was legit. See you on Monday."

"Yeah," I said. "See you."

I WAS SOBER BY THE TIME I got home. I expected to find the house dark, but a light was on in the parlor. As I passed through the room on the way to the stairs, Pop cleared his throat.

"Iris."

I turned and found him in his office, the door wide open so he could observe my comings and goings.

"Do you know what time it is?" he asked.

His tone was icy. Above his shoulder the clock tattled that it was one-fifteen.

"Just after one."

"And what made you think that that was an appropriate time to stay out until?"

I wasn't quite sure how to take the question. Was he mad? Seriously? "You didn't tell me to be back at a specific time."

He left his roost and came around to me. He had his leg on. Had he just returned from somewhere, or was he getting ready to go someplace? "That's because I thought you knew better. I've been worried sick. I went to that boy Paul's house and neither he nor his sister knew where you were."

Had Pearl squealed on me? Seriously?

"I told you—a dance."

"With who?"

"Some other friends from school."

"And just where was this dance?"

My mouth fluttered. My impulse was to lie and I wasn't sure where that was coming from. I'd never overtly lied to Pop before. Well, except for telling him who I was with that night. "It's a club called the Savoy."

"And just where is this club located?"

I hoped by giving him part of the truth, I might squeak by. "Lenox and 141st Street."

"Harlem?" asked Pop. I shrugged, like I wasn't sure what neighborhood we'd been in. "I thought it was a school dance."

"I never told you that." He couldn't fault me for his assumptions.

"What's that on your mouth?"

My hand went to my lips. Suze's lipstick smeared my fingers red. "Just lip cream."

"You're too young for that."

For what, I wanted to ask. *Wearing makeup or having half of it kissed off me?* "A friend loaned it to me," I said. "Everyone there was wearing it."

"Have you been drinking?"

How could he know that? "I . . ."

"My God, Iris. What's come over you? Staying out to all hours, lying about who you're with, wearing makeup, drinking. And Harlem? What could've possibly possessed you to go there?"

My mouth fluttered open but no sound came out. I couldn't tell him I was searching for Tom. Not yet.

"Who gave you the booze?"

"I . . . I don't know."

"You don't know? Do you have any idea how worried I've been? I didn't know if you were alive or dead."

It was strange to hear him being so paternal and scared. About *me.* On the one hand, I was touched to find out that he cared, but on the other, it struck me as very inconvenient. "It won't happen again, Pop."

"You better believe it won't. From here on out you go to school and you come home. That's it."

"I said I wouldn't do it again. How was I supposed to know there were rules?"

"Because you live on Planet Earth. What fifteen-year-old girl is allowed to stay out until the wee hours of the morning—in a Harlem dance hall, no less—and come home reeking of booze? Why do I have to tell you that that's forbidden?"

"Because that's what parents do," I said.

We stared at each other for a moment, each challenging the other to make the next move. I thought I had won—after all, my arguments were the most logical. But Pop had finally figured out the one essential thing about parent-child relationships: age trumps all.

"Go to your room, Iris."

"But I'm not done."

"Yes, you are. Go to your room."

Whatever courage Rhona's flask had given me had disappeared. With a huff, I turned and headed upstairs.

I didn't fall asleep for at least an hour. It wasn't the scene with Pop that kept me up. His anger would fade by morning. No, what kept my mind humming was everything I'd experienced that night: the hot jazz, the gorgeous dancers, the kiss that curled my toes, the sensation of Benny's breath on the back of my neck. And of course all I'd learned about Tom Barney and his relationship with Grace Dunwitty.

Try as I might, I couldn't picture the two of them together. Maybe that was why he'd robbed my locker and everyone else's—to get the money necessary to woo a girl he had nothing in common with.

Poor Rhona. It had to be heartbreaking to learn Tom had replaced her with someone like Grace. Especially after enduring the rumors Pearl had supposedly spread about her. No, there was no *supposedly* about it. Pearl being Pearl, she was most likely jealous as all get-out of Tom and Rhona's relationship. She had started the rumor, all right.

But Rhona wasn't pregnant. She was sick, according to Maria.

No, wait—Maria had said Rhona wasn't pregnant *then*.

I was up until sunrise pondering exactly what that meant.

12

I AWOKE WITH A BLINDING headache to the sound of the radio blaring downstairs. For a moment, as I strained against the sunlight streaming in the window, I thought I was sick. But as my eyes got used to the light, the night before came flooding back. Was this what alcohol gave you: a pounding head and a failing memory? If that was the case, I was done with it.

I put on my robe and went downstairs, worried that the radio meant that there was bad news on the war front. Mrs. Mrozenski had a habit of turning the volume up so she could continue working in the kitchen while listening to the news. She said the war got her so upset that she couldn't stand to sit still and do nothing when casualty numbers were reported. But as I came down the stairs, I realized it wasn't war news I was hearing. Someone had tuned the radio to WMCA, where *The Children's Parade* was just starting.

The living room was empty. A cup half filled with Postum, a coffee substitute Pop drank because it was cheaper than the real thing, had been left behind, as had the morning papers. The front page reported that forty-six Nazi planes had been downed. I hoped that meant Pop would be in a good mood. I knocked on his office door, expecting to find that he was already at his desk working. There was no reply from inside. I tried the knob and found the door unlocked. I opened it, praying Pop was in a better mood than the night before.

My prayers were in vain. No one was there.

I DEBATED STAYING at the house that day, but it seemed foolish to keep myself under house arrest when I wasn't sure how sore Pop was. Instead, I made myself some oatmeal for breakfast, got dressed, and took the subway uptown.

After all, I was already in trouble. What was one more infraction?

Grace lived on Fifth Avenue, in an apartment that faced Central Park. I used to think her digs were no big deal, but as I approached after all those months away, I saw for the first time how fortunate she was and how grossly out of place I had become. In my scuffed saddle shoes and Suze's skirt (smelling of smoke and who knows what else from the night before) I had to look like a servant's daughter come to pay my mother a visit during lunch. Had I ever fit in here?

I must have, and yet the idea suddenly seemed preposterous.

I approached the building and greeted the doorman. He was new, not that I would've expected the old doorman to still recognize me after so much time had passed.

"How can I help you?" He had a voice like the women at the cosmetic counter at Macy's. Even though you knew they were working for their money, they still somehow managed to communicate the idea that they were better than you. He underlined his superiority by examining me with his cold, blue eyes, choosing not to linger too long on my outfit, as though just being asked to look at it was insulting to him.

"I'm here to see Grace Dunwitty," I said. I tried to match his snobbery with my own tone, but I'd fallen out of practice. Instead of sounding rich and important, I sounded vaguely British.

He didn't have the apartments memorized yet. He glanced at the list that provided extensions for each residence and located the Dunwittys' near the top. "And who may I say is here?"

"Iris Anderson."

He picked up the receiver for the internal phone, dialed the number, and paused. As he waited to be connected, he examined his recently buffed nails. "Good afternoon, Caroline, if you could please inform your mistress that there's an Iris Anderson here to see Miss Dunwitty. Yes, *Iris*—like

184

the flower." He covered the mouthpiece and sneered at me. I'd failed the first test—the maid didn't know who I was. She came back on the line before he could say anything to me. Whatever she said surprised him—I could see it in his face. "Really? Of course. Right away." He deposited the phone on its cradle and offered me a more genuine grin. "You may take the elevator to your right. Miss Dunwitty will be waiting for you."

I lifted my nose ever so slightly and sashayed to the waiting car. The elevator operator took me up to Grace's floor. I only had one foot in the hallway when the Dunwittys' apartment door burst open and Grace rushed out.

"Iris! Is it really you?"

"It really is. I hope you don't mind the surprise."

"Mind? I thought I was dreaming." She hugged me and for a moment things felt just like old times. She'd grown taller in the months since I'd seen her, and she'd started wearing makeup. Since it was Saturday, she wasn't wearing her Chapin uniform. Instead, she had on a cashmere twin-set and a skirt that captured the sweater's azure blue in a delicate plaid pattern. "Why haven't you returned my calls?"

"I'm sorry about that. I meant to, but it's been crazy since school started."

"Never mind. I'm just glad you're here." She stepped away and took me in, keeping her hands wrapped in mine. "Look at you, Iris." I wasn't sure what that meant. Look at how I'd changed, how shabby my clothes had become? "Come on." She pulled me into the apartment. "I've got so much to tell you."

But first there were formalities. Mrs. Dunwitty was sitting in the front room, enjoying an early afternoon tea with a woman I didn't recognize.

"What a lovely surprise. I'm delighted to see you, Iris," said Mrs. Dunwitty. Her words never sounded sincere to me, though I recognized early on that they contained the same artificial quality no matter whom she was speaking to. That meant, I hoped, that I shouldn't take it personally.

"Thank you, Mrs. Dunwitty. It's a pleasure to see you again."

"This is my dear friend, Mrs. Huckabee." She turned to her companion. "This is Iris Anderson. She used to attend Chapin with Grace."

"And where do you go now, dear?" asked Mrs. Huckabee, a woman so polished she gleamed brighter than the silver tea service.

"She attends public school now," said Mrs. Dunwitty. She said *public school* like it was something very different from its reality. This wasn't a generic term for schools one didn't pay to attend, but a lofty institution all its own. "You must tell us all about your new home," said Mrs. Dunwitty. There she was being careful again—there was no mention of it being on the Lower East Side. "How is your father?"

"Very well, thank you."

"Iris's father was one of the very first veterans of this war," said Mrs. Dunwitty. "He was injured at Pearl Harbor."

"Remarkable," said her friend.

"Iris has been a tremendous comfort to him during his recuperation. She has had so many challenges to face in this past year; she lost her mother right before he came home."

I wanted to laugh. There was much more to the story than that, and yet somehow Mrs. Dunwitty had just rescued me from further inquiry. I was the daughter of a war hero, bravely nursing him back to health as I tended my own wounds over my mother's tragic death. When they made the movie, would they cast Deanna Durbin or Shirley Temple in my role?

"You poor dear," said Mrs. Huckabee. "It is, of course, these times of trial that show us how strong we can be."

"Would you please excuse us, Mother?" said Grace. "I have ever so much to share with Iris."

"You will stay for lunch, won't you?" asked Mrs. Dunwitty.

"I would be delighted to," I said.

As I followed Grace down the hall and to her room, my words echoed in my head: *I would be delighted to.* What would Suze say if she heard me talking like that? Even Pearl would've found it queer.

We closed the door to Grace's room, and she launched herself onto the pink canopied bed. Little had changed in the last months, beyond the addition of cosmetics on the vanity top and a poster advertising a concert by Frank Sinatra and the Benny Goodman Orchestra at the Hotel Astor back in May.

"Sorry about that scene back there," she said, pulling a china doll into her chest. "Oh nausea! That woman is insufferable, but since she's in the Met Guild Mother has to put up with her twice a month."

"It was fine. She seemed nice."

"So tell me everything. I can't believe you're really here. It's too much!"

I claimed the end of the bed for myself, leaning my back against one of the canopy's posts. "There's not much to tell. Public school is awful. I feel like I learned everything they're teaching years ago. But I've made a few friends. What about you?"

"Oh, everyone is wrapped up in studying for the Slimy and Atrocious Torture. It's all too desperate." I'd forgotten about the SAT. No one at P.S. 110 ever talked about the test. Chapin girls were expected to go on to college; P.S. 110 girls had no such aspirations. The subject quickly shifted from academics to the goings-on of every girl I used to know—and a few I couldn't remember—at Chapin. When she was done telling me who had changed her hair, gained weight, planned her coming out, and gotten pinned, Grace finally turned to herself. "Of course, I'm positively bored to tears without you. Fortunately, I found someone new to keep me busy."

Tom. She was talking about Tom. Finally! I sat up a little straighter. "Really? Who's that?"

"Her name's Josephine O'Hara. She transferred to Chapin this fall and we've been inseparable ever since." Grace flipped her hair over her shoulder. "You'd love her if you met her. She's very mature and plays a mean game of Ping-Pong. All the boys think she's zazz. And not just the ones our age, either. She's always getting asked out by men who think she's older. She's just oolie droolie."

I was obviously supposed to be shocked, but after being around Suze and Rhona, I couldn't muster anything more than a nod. "And what about you?" I said. "Are you seeing anyone special?"

She stretched her legs, pointing her sock-clad feet. "Oh, you know. There's always someone who catches my eye, but I'm not going steady. Playing the field is much more fun."

What was it going to take to get her to talk about Tom? "Would you ever date someone who didn't go to private school?"

"You mean like an older boy? Absolutely."

"No, I mean like a public school boy."

She pondered the question a little too long. "The hell you yell! You know how my parents are." Her eyes narrowed. "Why? Are you going with someone?"

"No," I said. "I mean, not yet. There's this one boy I kind of like."

"Do tell," said Grace.

"There's nothing to tell. We kissed, that's all. Public school boys are just so strange. They seem rough and yet at the same time . . . I don't know . . . I'm curious about them." I followed the pattern on her quilt, trying to figure out the best way to get the conversation to go where I wanted it to.

"Just because you changed neighborhoods doesn't mean you should forget your value. Have you gone on a date with him?" she asked.

I nodded. "Sort of. It was him and a lot of his friends. We went out dancing last night."

"To a school dance?"

"Nope. To the Savoy Ballroom."

"In Harlem?" Her eyes threatened to fill her face. "Holy Joe! Your pop let you?"

"He didn't know. He does now, and believe me it won't be happening again anytime soon. I went with some girls from school. They go all the time."

"What was it like?"

I struggled to describe the night in a way that did it justice. I didn't hold back. Every drink, every dance, every wondrous sight I repeated, to Grace's shock and amusement.

"I can't believe you did all that."

"I can't either. I wish you'd been there, Gracie. The music was marvelous and the boys—I didn't know men could move like that."

"It sounds like absolute bliss."

Something in her seemed to be breaking away. I got the feeling she was close to telling me about Tom, but I had no idea what else it would take to get her there.

"You should come with me sometime," I said. "I just know you'd like Rhona and Suze, even if they aren't Chapin girls."

If she recognized either of their names, she didn't show it. Perhaps Tom had never mentioned them to her?

"That would be luscious. And I'd love for you to meet Josephine," said Grace. "I talk about you all the time." Her phone extension rang. She answered it with a bubbly "Hi there, playmate," and signaled to me that she'd be just a minute. "I was just talking about you."

I gestured that I was going to use the powder room and left her to her conversation. She was still talking five minutes later, and rather than being rude and lingering as they chatted, I walked back toward the parlor, thinking I might say hello again to Mrs. Dunwitty. Her company was still there, though, and they were deep into a conversation that I didn't want to interrupt.

Especially when I realized that it was about me.

"They found her mother dead in a Yorkville hotel. Suicide."

"No!" said Mrs. Huckabee.

"Naturally, everyone assumed that she was so distraught over her husband's injury that she couldn't bear to go on."

"That hardly makes sense."

"I'm just telling you what everyone else said," said Mrs. Dunwitty.

"But why Yorkville?"

"She was German."

"And she had family there?"

"In Yorkville? I don't think so, but they all stick together, don't they? Once a German, always a German."

A teacup rattled as it was returned to its saucer. "Perhaps she wanted to make sure the daughter didn't find her," said Mrs. Huckabee.

"I wish I could say she was that considerate, but I doubt it. If you ask me, she had something to feel guilty about, and rather than running the risk that her husband would come home and find out about it, she decided it would be better to die."

"But what on earth would make her feel so guilty?"

"I think she was seeing another man."

"What makes you think that?"

"Her husband was away. She was young and attractive. What else could she have been doing?"

I backed away from the two of them, my head growing increasingly heavy.

"There you are," said Grace. She stood in her doorway. "That was Josephine. I was telling her all about you. She's dying to meet you."

"I have to go," I said.

"Oh. I thought you were staying for lunch. Our new cook is simply marvelous. She makes the most delish desserts."

I felt sick. If I didn't get out of there soon, I was going to vomit all over Grace's plush pink carpeting. "I can't. I forgot I'm supposed to help Pop with something."

"Buzz me tomorrow, all right? Let's make plans to get together more often."

I promised I would, then bade her mother a polite farewell and left the apartment just in time to get sick in a potted plant positioned just outside the elevators.

MAMA KILLED HERSELF. That's what Uncle Adam told me after I demanded something more from him than the tired euphemisms he'd offered me as an explanation for why she wasn't coming home. It was two days before Pop was due back in the States, almost a month to the day since he'd lost his leg at Pearl Harbor. The year 1942 was so new that Christmas decorations still sparkled from shop windows along Fifth Avenue, so new that every time I saw a newspaper I was convinced the date was a misprint.

"I'm so sorry, Iris," said Adam. He crushed my hand in his. He was shaking with the force of his own grief.

"But why did she do it?"

"I wish I knew."

I was staying with Uncle Adam and Aunt Miriam. Mama had to go out of town, I'd been told. She'd be home before the new semester started. Wouldn't it be nice to spend some time with the aunt and uncle I'd always adored?

But she didn't come home. If her sudden trip seemed unusual, her failure to return was even more so. *Where had she gone?* I asked Adam and Miriam. Each time I was told it was a family matter, nothing to concern myself with. She'd explain everything when she returned. Nobody made allowances for what would happen if she didn't come back. Just like nobody prepared me for what would happen when Pop did.

When Pop joined the military I was only ten years old. From that point on in my life, he became an infrequent visitor: holidays, birthdays, and a surprise now and again that I greeted with less and less enthusiasm. After all, he was a stranger now—why all this fuss because he decided to disrupt what was starting to become a normal life without him? Mama, of course, didn't see it that way. Each return was a gift, each visit's end a tragedy that sent her to her bedroom for days on end. She wrote to him constantly and cherished each letter in return, reading and rereading them until the paper began to tear apart at its folds.

In Pop's absence, I became her focus. It's funny how much someone can annoy and smother us in the name of love and how much you miss those very same things when they're gone. Mama insisted on brushing my hair every night, no matter how late she came home, no matter how much I groused about how old I was and how stupid this little ritual of hers was to me. Her mother had done it for her, she explained, and someday I'd do it for my own daughter. She quizzed me every day about what I had eaten, comparing my recited lists with the USDA food charts we'd been given at school. "More milk," she'd say. "You are a growing girl." Over dinner I was interrogated about my friends. What did they wear? How much spending money were they given? Did they all walk to school, or did some take a hired car? Were any of them going with boys yet? Always she wanted me to be in the same league as everyone else. What they got, I got. I used to hate the way she measured my life against theirs like slices of pie, but eventually I learned to play the system, increasing their allowances when I wanted more money, inventing permissive parents when it better suited my purposes. But it didn't happen very often. At some point I began to realize that what Mama wanted for me wasn't what everyone else had so much as everything she hadn't been provided with when she was a girl. I was to live the life she'd been denied.

How had she felt about the war? I never asked her. Until that December, it wasn't something I thought about, beyond wishing she did a better job hiding her accent. And after that fateful day, when a tiny island in the Pacific became the focus of so much rage, when someone else's war became our war, there were too many things to think about to worry how she was feeling. Pop had lost his leg, resigned his post, and was coming home for good. Our lives were about to change forever. A father in the house meant less freedom. And a war . . . well, I had no idea what that meant.

I didn't have time to worry about what Mama was going through. And in fact until she disappeared, and all I had was time to worry, I didn't notice the dark circles that had appeared under her eyes in the days following December 7, the shaking hands with bitten nails, the late-night phone calls—always in German. These things came to me later, when I asked myself why she had done it, when I wondered what I had missed.

The biggest question of all was how I had gone from being her everything to not even being reason enough for her to stay alive.

CHAPTER

13

I HAVE NO IDEA how I made it back to the Lower East Side. Habit must've led me, or sheer luck. I wandered the streets for a while, unwilling to go back to Orchard Street until the sickness that threatened to return had passed. Could Mrs. Dunwitty be right—had Mama been having an affair? Pop didn't act like a man who'd been betrayed by his wife. But then Pop didn't necessarily know.

Mama loved Pop, though. I was certain of that. Every visit, every letter, was something she cherished. Maybe it was possible to desperately love someone and yet be so consumed by loneliness that you were willing to betray him with someone who was around more often. It happened all the time in the movies.

I paused and found myself standing before Normandie's Pharmacy. Through the window Suze was wiping down a table with a cloth. She looked up in time to see me watching her and offered me a wisp of a smile. Then she waved me in.

I didn't want to go home. Not yet.

The bell tinkled its welcome as I passed through the doors. A few customers lingered in the booths, but it was hardly crowded.

"How'd you know I was working?" said Suze.

"I didn't. In fact, I didn't even realize where I was until I looked up and saw the sign."

"You're pale as a sheet. How 'bout a milk shake? It's on me—it's the least I can do after you sprung for all that cab fare last night."

I agreed and slid into a booth while she told the soda jerk that I'd be having a chocolate milk shake. I realized that the only thing in my stomach was oatmeal and the remnants of Rhona's flask. No wonder I was shaking.

"You're not going to believe who showed up at my bedroom window during early bright," she said.

"Who?"

"Benny."

I'd forgotten about the night before's humiliation. What had seemed so important to me just a few hours ago had faded in significance. So Benny got humiliated—so what? His mother was alive. She hadn't possibly betrayed her entire family.

"Why'd he do that?" I asked.

"He couldn't take going home with a bloody nose. His

pop's got a temper, would've blown his top if Benny had shown up wearing someone else's bruises. So he slept on my bedroom floor."

I wondered how I would have responded to this story if she'd told it to me an hour before. Jealousy? Curiosity? Right now all I felt was numb.

"Anyway, neither of us could sleep, we were so wired from the Savoy, and once he got done telling me all the things he would do to those soldiers if he ran into them again, he started talking about you."

I felt like I was listening to this conversation over the radio. "Me?"

"Don't look so sad, baby girl. Our Benny thinks you're murder."

"Murder?" I asked.

"You know—marvelous. As a matter of fact, he was talking about taking you out sometime, just you and him."

"That's nice," I said.

It clearly wasn't the response she was expecting. "Are you all right?"

"Just beat to the socks, I guess. You were right about that."

"Sorry I didn't walk you home. You made it okay, though, right?"

"I got an earful for getting in so late, but otherwise it was fine."

"Your aunt was mad?"

I nodded. That's right, my aunt. Not Pop, or my lying, secretive mother, but my imaginary aunt who'd told me I had no curfew only to yell at me when I failed to return at a reasonable hour.

Apparently, I was just another liar in a family of many.

"You should've seen how angry my ma was," said Suze. "I didn't get it until this morning after Benny had left and her shift ended, but I swear people on Houston could hear her." She had another mark on her face, poorly covered by the heavy makeup she'd obviously applied that morning. "Is that how come you're upset? Because you got in trouble?"

If only it were something that simple. I shook my head. The milk shake arrived and I focused on stirring the thick liquid until it was thin enough to make it up the straw.

"Is it Benny? Have you changed your mind about being seen with a boy like him?"

That pulled me back. I wasn't Grace. Not even a little bit. "No. Of course not."

"Then what is it?"

Should I tell her? I needed to talk to someone. I couldn't imagine telling Pearl, not after the way she'd reacted to Mama's suicide. And it's not like I could talk to Pop about it. "I heard some things about my mother today. About why she killed herself."

Suze frowned. She'd forgotten I was the girl with the weight of the world on her shoulders. "What did you hear?"

"That she might've been having an affair."

"Ouch, baby." She put her hand on mine and squeezed. "Who told you that?"

"I overheard some women talking about her."

"What was your mama like?"

I was surprised by the question. What was she like? So often it was her death I thought of rather than who she'd been before it. "Beautiful. Generous. Smart. Stubborn. She wouldn't take no for an answer." Chapin had turned me down when we first applied, though I never knew why. Mama was the one who convinced them to change their minds. She'd marched into the headmaster's office, while I was left to wait with his secretary, and ten minutes later she emerged with the good news that they had made a mistake and I would be going there after all.

That was Mama. If she thought something wasn't fair, she'd fight to the death to make it right.

Suze smiled. "She loved your pop?"

"Absolutely."

"Then what those women said was just gravel. You can't go thinking something's true just because you heard it out loud. Maybe they were jealous of her. Or maybe they were trying to make sense of why she did what she did."

"She was a German," I said. I'm not sure why I told her. Maybe to prove that she was the last person anyone would be jealous of. Or maybe because I felt like I needed to be honest with Suze about something.

"That must've been hard for her," said Suze.

"And for me," I said.

"How so?"

"You know. Being an immigrant's kid is embarrassing enough, but being a German Jew? Nobody thinks that's a good thing."

Suze nodded. "I didn't realize you were Jewish."

"We changed our last name."

"Why?"

"I don't know." The one time I asked Mama about it, she'd said it was like how Deanna Durbin had changed her first name from Edna Mae—sometimes you had to have a name that better fit who people wanted you to be.

Suze pushed her hair behind her ear. "When people already think bad of you, it's pretty easy for them to assume the worst. You knew her, though. No matter what anyone says, you know the truth, right?"

It was like with Tom and how his father assumed he was headed down the wrong path. Actually, it was probably like that for all the Rainbows. Once people thought you were bad news, there was no hope of redeeming yourself. You either proved them right or made up your mind that what they thought of you didn't matter.

"You there, baby girl?"

I looked up and found Suze staring at me. She'd been talking this whole time, buzzing in my ear like a trapped

202

fly, and I hadn't heard a word of it. How long had I been lost in my own thoughts? "Sorry."

"No need for apologies. What I said was, if you're still worried, I bet your pop could clear everything up."

I almost laughed at the thought. Even my imaginary pop, the one still fighting the war, would never be able to talk to me about this. And who could expect him to? If the idea made me sick, it was a wonder he was able to get up in the morning.

I drank some of the milk shake and fixed a smile on Suze. "You're right."

"Where'd you hear these women talking, anyhow?"

"Upper East Side. I went to see a friend I went to school with and the minute I left the room, her mother started telling this other woman all about me." The words were out of my mouth before I realized that Suze might put two and two together and realize I'd gone to see Grace.

"What a bunch of vipers. What did your friend say?"

"I couldn't tell her. Sarah—that's her name—would've been mortified. I just made an excuse and left." So now there was an imaginary Sarah to remember.

"And she didn't come after you? Some friend." The door sounded its bell, warning of the arrival of more customers. "They're playing my song," she said with a smile. "I better get moving or get fired. You going to be okay?"

I nodded.

She slid out of the booth and straightened her uniform. "You want to come to my cave tonight? I'm watching the brat."

"I wish I could, but I think my aunt would have a conniption."

"All right. Then I'll see you Monday." She paused, like she wanted to say something else but couldn't think of what magical words it would take to make everything go away. Instead, she leaned toward me and planted a kiss on top of my head.

I WAS FEELING much better by the time I got home. Maybe Suze was right. These were bored society women, after all, who had nothing better to do with their time than gossip. And I knew Mama loads better than they did. She loved Pop, practically worshipped him, and if there was another man he was temporary at best. He certainly wouldn't have been the reason for her to kill herself, any more than Pop's return would've been the motivation for her to do herself in.

I let myself into the house and was about to go upstairs to take a nap when Pop's voice stopped me.

"Where have you been?" He was sitting on the sofa in the parlor with an ashtray full of half-smoked cigarettes resting in front of him.

It wasn't a friendly question. I wasn't in the mood for

combat, so I gave him the truth. "I went to the Upper East Side to visit Grace."

"And what made you think you could leave this house without telling anyone where you were going?"

"You weren't here and neither was Mrs. Mrozenski."

"I wasn't here because I went to get us this." He gestured toward a bakery box sitting beside his ashtray. Pastries that had once been fresh but had now begun to grow stale in the hours since he'd purchased them huddled together on a waxed paper sheet. How many sugar ration tickets had he used for those?

He'd intended them to be a peace offering. I could see that. After last night's run-in he was trying to call a truce by offering me sweets and hoping that *The Children's Parade* would bring me back to myself, or at least to the self I used to be before he went to Pearl Harbor.

"I'm sorry," I said.

My apology had no effect on him. Whatever anger had been bubbling inside him after he discovered I wasn't home rose to a full boil. "First Harlem, now the Upper East Side? New York's not your playpen, Iris. You don't get to pick and choose where you want to go without talking to me first."

His ire awoke something in me. Why was he being this way? "You. Weren't. Here."

"Then you write a note or, heaven forbid, wait until I come home and ask me if you can go."

I rolled my eyes.

He plucked a cruller from the box and tore it in two. "Something horrible could've happened to you last night."

"Why? Because there were negroes there?"

He looked like I'd slapped him. "This isn't about black and white. This is about you being fifteen years old. The world isn't a safe place."

I headed toward the stairs.

"I'm not done talking to you."

"I am."

"Get back here, Iris."

I mounted the first step. "No." I paused, expecting him to order my return even more loudly, but we'd reached a stalemate and he knew it. I was my mother's daughter, stubbornness and all.

"Go then," he said. I continued my climb. As I reached the top of the stairs, he spoke again, not to me, but to himself. I couldn't make out the words, at least not most of them. The only word I was certain I heard was my mother's name.

IT TOOK ME AN HOUR to fall asleep, even with the assistance of my baby blanket. As tired as I was, I was too irritated to doze right away. When I did finally sleep, I dreamed of Mama.

She and I are in the dining room of our old apartment, decorating it for a party. She sings as she works—"Alle

Meine Entchen," a silly little German song about ducklings that she used to entertain me with when I was very small. Pop's photo is on the mantel, two candles flickering on either side of it. He is dead and has been for a while. The party we are preparing for is to commemorate the anniversary of Pearl Harbor, when Pop was killed in action.

I awoke with a start just as the sun was going down. I wasn't sure what had jolted me awake until I heard the doorbell.

It had been ringing for a while.

Did Pop have a client? I crept down the stairs and saw his office door open and the room empty. He was gone again. No lights had been left on in the parlor and what little light was left in the day made the room look sleepy and sad. I clicked on a lamp, smoothed my hair, and approached the front door.

Grace was standing on the other side.

She'd never been to the Orchard Street house before. In fact, I was pretty sure she'd never been to the Lower East Side. As I watched her through the curtained glass panel that ran alongside the entryway, I could see her growing discomfort. She was most likely asking herself why she'd come here, and I was wondering the same thing. And while I was pretty sure it was fear that fueled her nervousness, mine was powered by embarrassment. What would she think of this house? Of Mrs. Mrozenski? Of the entire neighborhood that I now called home?

"Hello?" she called out. She must've seen the curtain move. It would be impossible to pretend no one was home now without appearing unforgivably rude. With no other choice, I opened the door and pretended to be surprised to see her there.

"What are you doing here?" I asked.

"I was worried. You left so fast today and you were acting so strange. Rolph said you got sick in the hallway."

Rolph? That must've been the doorman. I felt a jolt of pleasure that he was the one responsible for cleaning up my mess.

"You could've called," I said. "There was no reason to come all this way." My fingers found the molding around the door and worked it loose.

"I was afraid you wouldn't call me back. May I come in?"

I backed away in silent invitation. She entered the house, making no effort to hide her curiosity at the way the other half lived. I went into the parlor and sat on the sofa, one leg bent beneath my body, the other dangling over the cushion.

"What upset you?" asked Grace.

I played with the cushion's cord trim. "Nothing." She cocked her head at me. It was such an old familiar gesture that I instantly felt like I'd been fed a truth serum and had to respond honestly to her questions. "I overhead your mother and her friend talking about Mama."

"Oh." She didn't look surprised. "I thought as much. I

could just die. I'm so sorry, Iris. You know Mother is a terrible gossip, and Mrs. Huckabee is twice as bad."

So now I didn't need to worry just about Mrs. Dunwitty thinking these things about Mama; the entire Upper East Side would be talking about it.

"She said my mother was having an affair."

Grace sighed and took a seat on the upholstered rocker to my left. It was a comfortable chair—overstuffed and worn until its cushion was perfectly molded to fit the human form—but she sat on it stiffly, like she didn't trust that the furniture was strong enough to maintain her slight, feminine weight. In fact, everything about her seemed stiff— even the language she used in the Orchard Street house was overly formal.

How had she ever hooked up with someone like Tom? He must've hailed from a house just like this, where the furniture never got reupholstered or replaced, but instead bore the stains, scars, and burn marks it received until its working parts ceased functioning and someone put it out of its misery and left it out for the garbage collectors to retrieve.

She eyed the ashtray, still overflowing with the fruit of Pop's afternoon. "Is your father around?"

"No," I said. "He went out."

"Mind if I smoke?"

I said no only because I was so surprised by the question. What was she going to ask next? If I'd make her a cocktail?

She retrieved a cigarette from her purse and, once it was lit, inhaled it in a practiced way that made it clear that many, many cigarettes had come before it. Maybe it was an upperclassman thing. If I'd stayed at Chapin, I, too, might've learned how to blow perfect smoke rings and master the art of ashing with one hand while wielding a cheese knife with the other. "It's shameful behavior, but you must understand how your mother's death rattled everyone. Dying . . . as she did left so many questions, and I'm sure Mother was only theorizing to put her own mind at ease."

Was she really defending her mother? It didn't seem possible, and yet—

"Of course it was completely inappropriate and I'm sure she'd be mortified to learn you'd overheard her."

"Please don't tell her," I said.

"She needs to learn." She tweaked her mouth to the left, releasing a stream of smoke. "I won't allow her to upset my friends like this."

I could imagine how that conversation was going to go. Would Grace really be doing it because of me, or because of the joy she got from putting her mother in her place?

"Really, I'm fine, Grace. I know gossip is gossip. It just took me by surprise."

The front door rattled and Mrs. Mrozenski appeared, her arm filled with bags and boxes containing that week's groceries. She smiled when she saw me, then her gaze drifted over to the strange girl sitting in her chair, smoking in her house.

"Let me help you." I leaped to my feet and took two boxes from her. Grace remained sitting and smoking, completely unconcerned that an adult had arrived. "This is Grace Dunwitty, an old friend of mine from Chapin. Grace, this is Mrs. Mrozenski. She owns the house."

Grace raised an eyebrow but still didn't get up. "Nice to meet you."

"Yes, you, too," said Mrs. Mrozenski. I followed her into the kitchen and deposited the bags on the table. "Your friend is smoking," she whispered as she removed eggs, flour, and cabbage from the packages. "She is allowed to do this?"

I shrugged, uncertain how to respond. I couldn't imagine Grace doing it in her own house. But that was the point, wasn't it—she wasn't in her house.

Mrs. Mrozenski shooed me with her hand. "Go, enjoy your company. I get this."

"Are you sure?"

"Of course I'm sure."

I returned to the parlor. Grace wasn't there. She had moved into Pop's office, where she stood before his desk, examining the papers he'd left out the night before.

I cleared my throat. "That's Pop's office," I said. "It's kind of off-limits."

"Sorry. The door was open."

She gave the room another glance before returning to the parlor. Nervous energy propelled her. Instead of sitting, she approached the fireplace. On the mantel was a collection of porcelain bells, some photos, and a glass box intended for cigarettes.

"So all this stuff belongs to Mrs.—? I'm sorry, what's her name?" asked Grace.

"Mrozenski. Most of it's hers." Only the radio belonged to me and Pop, and the glassless photo of Mama sitting atop it.

"I guess she doesn't let you decorate, huh?" What she really meant was, she couldn't imagine anyone choosing to live among these cheap furnishings and belongings if they didn't have to.

"It's her house," I said.

"You know, our last cleaning lady was Polish. I don't think you met her. Mother fired her when she found out she was stealing from us." She picked up one of the bells and shook it. I half expected Mrs. Mrozenski to come running from the kitchen and demand she put it down.

When she didn't, I decided to do it myself.

"We're not really supposed to touch her stuff," I said.

"Why? It's not like it's worth anything."

I wanted her to leave. While her visit initially seemed like a kind gesture, it was starting to feel like something very different. I glanced at the mantel clock and feigned surprise. "It's getting late," I said.

"When's your pop coming home?" she asked. She put

212

down the bell and picked up a photo of Mrs. Mrozenski's family, letting the cigarette dangle as she examined it. A piece of ash fell from the tip and landed on the faded wool rug. I kept my eye on it, worried it would burn a hole right through, but it smoldered and disappeared before any damage could be done.

"Soon, I guess. Like I told you before, I got in trouble for the Harlem trip last night. I don't think he'd be too happy to know I had a friend over on top of it." She showed no sign of leaving. What was I going to have to do? Throw her purse out the door and hope she chose to follow it? "Do you want me to call a cab for you?"

"No need. I took the subway."

I didn't hide my shock. I'd counted on her and everyone else from Chapin being too afraid to journey this way. "Do you want me to walk you to the station?" I asked.

"Oh, I know the way. I've been there loads of times."

She seemed to be baiting me and I realized for the first time that her visit wasn't just about trying to get information about me; there was something she wanted to tell me. "Seriously?" I asked.

She nodded, a smile lingering on her lips. "Jo and I do it all the time. You can't spend your whole life on the Upper East Side, right?"

"So what do you do when you come here?"

"A little bit of this and that. Go to the USO dances, mostly. Jo can't get enough of the sailors."

"And you?"

"I prefer a man in an Air Corps uniform."

"And your parents don't mind?"

"Hell's bells—I'd never tell them. Could you imagine? And it's not like I'm serious with any of them. It's all about the chase."

"The what?"

She tilted her head at me the way Aunt Miriam used to when I said something precious and naïve. "You know— what you can make them do for you. How much you can make them spend. I haven't paid for a dinner out in two months."

I'm sure I wore my disgust like a masquerade mask. But Grace was in her own little world, where it was perfectly acceptable to go out with a boy just so she could later share the tale of what a goon he was. "And then that's it?" I said. "You never see them again?"

"What's to see? They're off to war and I'm off to school." She inhaled the cigarette. She was, mercifully, reaching its end.

"It just seems like you're using them."

"It's not like they're getting nothing in return."

I raised an eyebrow, as Pearl had done when she wanted me to understand that Rhona's past trouble had to do with sex.

"Not that!" said Grace. "Not from me, anyway. But a kiss or two and a few dances go a long way toward making them

214

feel like they aren't being taken advantage of. Besides, you can't use someone who doesn't want to be used." She said it like it was a pronouncement written on a holy scroll. Were these her words or her new friend Josephine's?

"It seems strange to go to all that trouble for a boy you're not planning on seeing again."

"Why? Even if I really liked them, it's not like it could ever go anywhere. I might as well date a negro." She extinguished the cigarette in the ashtray, looped her pocketbook around her arm, and fluffed her hair in the mantel mirror. "You should come out with us sometime. It's a real gas. They can't get enough of private school girls. Of course, we don't have to tell them you don't go to Chapin anymore."

Because heaven forbid we be honest with them about *something*. "That would be swell."

"Let's make a plan to get together next week. I promise you Mother won't be around. I am so embarrassed about her behavior. I could just die."

"Don't worry about it," I said. "I've practically forgotten all about it."

"That's what I love about you, Iris. You're just so . . . resilient."

Resilient. That was a new one. I opened the door and held it for her as she passed through. "Be careful out here," I said. "It's a rough neighborhood."

14

ONCE GRACE WAS OUT OF THE HOUSE and up the street, I emptied the ashtray, picked the remnants of her cigarette from the rug, and mulled over her strange visit. I just couldn't believe that her trip to the Lower East Side was motivated by concern for me. After all, she could have called me on the telephone and accomplished just as much. Something else had sent her here. But what? If she didn't know he was missing, maybe she was hoping to run into Tom. That seemed unlikely though—she'd never mentioned him. What if Rhona and Suze had it all wrong? Maybe Tom had a crush on Grace that she never returned, and he'd exaggerated the relationship to his friends as a way of breaking free of Rhona. It wasn't hard to imagine Grace paying him a little attention one night and then tossing him aside like her military boyfriends. And if she was embarrassed to have momentarily been attracted to someone like him, she certainly wasn't going to mention it to me.

But why come here?

As I finished cleaning, Mrs. Mrozenski came into the room and smiled at my efforts.

"Your friend is gone."

"No."

"She's upstairs?"

"No, I mean she's gone, but she's not my friend. Not anymore."

She touched my hair, smoothing it with her palm. "This is good, Iris. You don't need to be around people like her." How could she tell so much about Grace in so little time? I wanted to ask her. It seemed to me that despite all the hours I'd spent learning to read people, I was still a very poor judge of character.

"She's changed a lot," I said.

"You have, too. That is life." She approached the mantel and straightened the picture Grace had plopped haphazardly back into place. "Dinner will be ready soon. I make sausages tonight."

"That sounds great."

She glanced toward the office. "Your father is not here."

"Not yet."

"You two make peace?"

So she knew about how things had been between us. Was she exercising the same sixth sense that told her Grace Dunwitty was bad news, or had Pop come to her asking for advice during the hours when I was sleeping?

"Not yet."

"He worries about you, Iris. Maybe more than most fathers. He has been through a lot."

"I know."

"We don't have to agree, but we can show respect. Sometimes that's all anyone wants."

While she returned to the kitchen, I went into the office, worried that Grace might have left some evidence of her visit during her brief time in there. Pop's paperwork lay strewn around the desk and his notes about Tom's case were on top. He had been to the prison where Tom's brother, Michael, was held. So he knew about that. According to his notes, Tom hadn't been to see him in two months, a fact Michael seemed less than happy about. "He said his brother came to see him at least once a month," Pop had written in his messy, military scrawl. "He figured either his parents had put a kibosh on the trips or Tom had a Hershey Bar that was taking up his attentions." Pop had also found out about Tom's previous disappearance. He'd talked privately with Mrs. Barney, who "seemed reticent to discuss her son's previous comings and goings, but eventually admitted he had left before and returned with a face full of fading bruises. She never learned the source of his injuries but insisted he keep them hidden from his father."

There was also an inventory of what had been found in Tom's locker: gym shoes, cigarettes, textbooks, gum wrappers, and the note Pop had told the Barneys about. It read,

"If you're serious, meet me at 240 Houston Street #7D at 4:00." Pop was no slouch. He'd checked out the address and made a note of his findings: "240 Houston #7D is a private physician's office. The occupant didn't recognize the photo of T.B., but did say the area was a popular hangout for youth because of the private back alley. No one in T.B.'s alleged group of friends copped to writing the note."

I felt a mix of pride and disappointment. Pop had done all right without me. The only thing he hadn't yet learned of, or at least made note of, was Tom's relationship with Grace.

Should I tell Pop about her? I was on thin ice with him as it was; if I told him about Grace, I would have to tell him I'd been working on the case, and who knows what would happen then. Besides, I wasn't sure Grace was involved. In fact, so far I had no proof that Tom and she even had a relationship.

So that would be my first step: verify what was going on between Tom and Grace. And maybe then I could let Pop know there was a lead he'd missed that was worth following up on.

A car door shut outside the window. I spied a yellow cab out front. Pop was home. I returned the notes to their original position, left the office, closed the door, and landed on the sofa just as Pop arrived.

"Hi," he said as he came into the house.

"Hi," I replied, my voice soft and hesitant. I wanted to congratulate him on getting so far on the case and apologize for thinking he couldn't do it alone. I could tell from the stiffness in his shoulders that our argument that afternoon was still playing in his head.

"Have a nice nap?" he asked.

"It was fine."

I didn't want to become like Grace, crabby to my parents because I thought I'd earned that right. Mrs. Mrozenski was right: I didn't have to agree with Pop, any more than he had to agree with me, but he deserved my respect.

"I'm sorry about last night," I said. "You're right: common sense should've told me that I shouldn't go to Harlem and I definitely shouldn't have drunk anything. I'm not going to apologize for coming home late because, honestly, I didn't know I was breaking a rule. The others had curfews and if I thought I had one I would've followed it, but you never told me."

"Iris—"

I held up my hand to stop him. "I'm also sorry for disappearing today. I was feeling homesick and I wanted to see Grace. I knew you were angry enough that you probably wouldn't let me go, and so I did it before you had a chance to tell me not to. That was dumb of me."

Some of the tension left his shoulders. He must've been worried I was out drinking again, or doing something else he never expected from me. The desire to see an old friend was something he could relate to.

"You can trust me," I said. "I promise. But I can't be locked up here all day every day, Pop. I'm lonely."

He sat where Grace had sat earlier, sighing as his back came in contact with the overstuffed cushion. He worked his hands into a ball, the skin reddening as he squeezed them together. "This girl you went to see was someone you went to Chapin with?" I nodded. "Good girl, good family?"

If only he knew. "The best."

He wagged a finger at me. "No more Harlem. No more drinking."

I nodded my pledge.

"Maybe I was harsh before. House arrest is over. But I want you to stay in this neighborhood. No more trips uptown. Not for the time being, anyway."

I didn't see any point in arguing with him, so I nodded my agreement.

I FIGURED SUNDAY was a lost day. Grace would be busy with church and brunch, so there was no point in trying to contact her. And besides, I had a feeling that it was best to let her come to me again. In her house, surrounded by all those silent expectations for how she should behave, she hadn't been honest with me. And while I may not have liked the girl who showed up on my doorstep, at least she was free here.

I spent Sunday lolling around the house, listening to the radio and reading the papers. On Monday I arrived at school early, hoping I might see Benny. I'm not sure what I was thinking by getting there before the morning bell. Benny wasn't the kind of boy to come to school early. In fact, it was amazing he came to school at all.

"Iris?"

As I scanned the front lawn looking for any sign of the Rainbows, Pearl approached me. Her books were wedged beneath one pudgy arm, her lunch hanging limp in her other hand.

"Hi," I said.

"How was Friday night?"

It felt like a million years ago. When I thought about explaining everything that had happened since I last saw her, I felt weary. "It was fine."

The warning bell rang. We had ten minutes to get to class.

"I missed you on Saturday."

That was right; we'd made plans to get together so I could tell her about my trip to the Savoy. Of course, that was before Pearl had squealed on me when I needed her the most.

"I kind of assumed you'd know our plans would be canceled when you told my pop I wasn't with you on Friday," I said.

"I'm so sorry for that. When he came by, my father was there. There was no way I could lie and get away with it."

That softened me. A little.

"And I'm sorry about Friday afternoon. About how I acted," she said.

I tried to remember what had bothered me so much about her behavior and couldn't. Mama. That was right. She's been mad that I hadn't told her about her death.

My good mood evaporated.

"Did you find out anything about Tom?"

I should've said no and walked away, but my desire to get back at her overruled any logic coursing through me. "Sort of. I found out he had another girlfriend right before he disappeared. A girl I knew at Chapin."

Her face grew pink. It wasn't what she had wanted to hear. "Really? Did Rhona know?"

"Rhona knew, all right. In fact, she got another boyfriend as payback."

"Was it serious with the other girl?" Her lower lip quivered.

"He thought it was. He was heartbroken when she called it off."

People pushed past us as they entered the building and headed toward their homerooms.

"I better blow," I said.

"So I'll see you at lunch?"

"Maybe."

She skulked away, clearly unhappy that her apologies hadn't made everything perfect again. But lunch with Pearl meant having to pretend I hadn't changed in the last two days, or launching into a long explanation of everything that had happened, and I just didn't want to do that.

Besides, there was a chance Benny might want to sit with me.

I spent the morning trying to figure out how I could avoid Pearl in the cafeteria. Fortunately, as I arrived at lunch, the perfect distraction landed in my lap.

"Iris! Come join us," said Suze. I looked toward the table Pearl and I usually occupied and offered the waiting Pearl a shrug. Then I followed Suze to the cluster of other Rainbows. Rhona and Maria sat together. Maria had that day's hot lunch. Rhona had an apple and an orange. An empty seat had been left next to Benny and I slid into it, trying not to stare at the mass of bruises obscuring his handsome face. No wonder he'd slept on Suze's bedroom floor. Even two days out he looked gory.

Something snapped in my head.

Bruises. Tom had had bruises that made him disappear the previous spring, that were still vivid when he came home a week later. Tom also wore the zoot. Was it far-fetched to think he'd been beaten up one night after an evening on the town and decided to lay low until the bruises faded?

"How's everything?" asked Suze.

"Better," I said. "How was babysitting?"

She rolled her eyes and took a bite of sandwich. It looked

like peanut butter. Just plain peanut butter. "Fraughty. The brat's lucky she lived through the night. Ma was happy, though. You thought any more about what I said?"

She was talking about the rumors about Mama. "Yeah. I'm not going to let it bother me. Until someone confirms it, it's not worth paying it any mind."

"Don't let it get you down, baby girl." Her bruises had also faded since Saturday, but they were still there. I wondered what it was like to live in a family that used fists instead of words to make their points. As stupid as it sounds, I almost envied her. At least she knew where she stood moment to moment. There was something so uncomplicated about basing the status of your relationship with someone on whether or not they were angry enough to hit you.

Lunch passed quickly in their company. Benny never talked directly to me, but his thigh periodically made contact with mine, and after the third time it happened, I was pretty sure it wasn't an accident. Nobody talked about the run-in with the servicemen. Instead, they recounted our evening at the Savoy and how the rest of their weekends had been dreary exercises in making money and not getting yelled at by parents and bosses.

I contributed very little beyond my tale of getting in trouble for coming home late. They were fascinated that it was the first time it had ever happened to me.

"No one told you that you had a curfew?" asked Dino.

"Nope."

"Doesn't seem right that you got in trouble then. How do you know you're breaking a rule when no one told you there was a rule to begin with?"

"That's what I told him," I said. "And he actually saw the logic. I think we reached a truce."

"Him?" asked Suze. "I thought it was your aunt."

"She's the one who caught me, but my uncle's the one who lectured me." I was amazed I could think so fast on my feet.

"So you're out of the doghouse?" asked Rhona.

"Not really. He smelled your booze on my breath, so . . ."

Rhona shook her head. "You've got to learn to cover that up. Peppermints work great. And chewing gum."

"If you can get it," said Maria. "I hear they're going to start rationing gum and most everything else."

"Disappointing high school boozers everywhere," quipped Benny.

"Don't worry," said Rhona. "I'll come up with something else. You could always kill the smell with a ciggie."

I held up my hands in surrender. "Trust me, that would only make them yell louder."

The bell signaled the end of lunch, and we all got up to throw away our trash and say our farewells. As I disentangled myself from the table, I felt a hand grab mine and gently squeeze. Warmth rippled through me and I met Benny's eyes for the first time.

"How long are you in the doghouse for?" he asked.

"I don't know. A week, I guess?"

"At least it's not forever, right?" He gave me a wink, released his grip, and with long, even strides walked away.

Should I follow him? I didn't think so. He didn't look back, anyway.

As the rest of the group dispersed, I fell into step with Dino, hoping his empathizing about my getting in trouble gave us enough of a connection that I could talk to him. There were things I needed to know. Things I didn't feel comfortable asking Benny.

"You all right by the way?" I asked, my voice almost a whisper.

"You mean after Friday? Yeah. It's no big thing."

"Maybe not to you, but I couldn't believe they'd do something like that. I mean, here they are enlisting to protect our country, and they pick a fight with one of the very people they've pledged to protect."

He looked at me like I'd just laid an egg in the middle of the hall. "Huh. Never thought of it that way."

"Does it happen a lot?" I asked.

He shrugged. "More than I'd like."

"Maria said it happened to Tom, too."

"Sure, we've all taken our licks. It's about the zoot, not about being brown."

"Did any of you ever fight back?"

"We're not chicken."

"I'm not saying you are," I said. "I'm just curious 'cause it seems like if you fought back, someone would make a big deal about how that proves you're unpatriotic. I mean, you can't hit a soldier, right?"

Another look of amazement. "Yeah," he said. "I mean, yeah. It's really unfair. They've got our backs against the wall."

"So none of you ever fought back?"

"I took a swing a time or two. But it's just easier if you go limp and let them do whatever they're going to do. Makes them mad. They want you to fight back so it'll last longer, especially if there's an audience."

"You mean the other soldiers?"

"Sure, them and the skirts. Fools thought Rhona, Maria, and Suze would be impressed if they put us in our places."

"What about Benny and Tommy? Do they fight back, too?"

"Benny usually plays possum until it passes. He's no fool. Tom learned the hard way not to stand up for himself. The one time he did, he ended up with two cracked ribs and a busted schnozzle. He was out of school for a week."

"Last spring?"

"How'd you know?"

"Rhona mentioned something about it." So I was right. The life had gotten pummeled out of him and he hadn't wanted anyone to see the damage he took. If it had happened once before, it could've happened again. And maybe this time he wasn't smart enough to lie there and take it.

"I better trilly," said Dino. "See you around."

"Yeah," I said. "See you."

I ROLLED what Dino had told me around my head throughout the afternoon, barely paying attention during American History and Geography. There was one detail that had stuck in my head—Dino said that the servicemen liked to have an audience, especially a female one. They may not have been able to impress Suze, Maria, and Rhona by humiliating their friends, but that didn't mean it didn't work for other women. Like Grace and her friend Josephine.

What if Grace had been there the night this happened? It would certainly give Tom reason to lay low. It was one thing to fight back and lose, but it was another thing to fight back and lose in front of the girl you were hoping to win back. He might've been so humiliated that he took off then and there.

But would Grace have just let him run off without checking to make sure he was all right?

Probably. Especially if she was desperate to get rid of him.

I needed to see Grace. Not at my house, but in her own element at Chapin, where she didn't know she was being watched. I wanted to see how much she'd really changed since I'd left. I wanted to know why she hadn't told me about Tom.

And despite my promise to Pop to stay on the Lower East Side, I was going to do it that afternoon.

15

THERE WAS NO TELLING how quickly Grace would leave Chapin after school, so rather than waiting until the end of the day to go uptown, I decided to skip typing class.

I'd never skipped before and I had no idea what would happen when I did. Would they send a truant officer after me? Call Pop and report the absence? I couldn't take any chances, and so just before the period started, I sought out Pearl and asked for her help.

"I need to leave school," I told her.

"Now?" I nodded. She didn't ask why or where I was going. I think she was so thrilled that I was talking to her that she didn't dare risk rocking the boat.

"Can you snag the attendance records for my typing class and make sure no one knows I'm playing hooky?"

"Sure. Absolutely."

A twinge of guilt passed through me, but I didn't have time to analyze it.

"Thanks," I said.

"What are friends for?"

It was surprisingly easy to walk off campus. I called the house from a pay phone plastered with a sign that warned me to keep my calls brief so our enlisted men could use the lines. Mrs. Mrozenski answered on the third ring, her voice so out of breath that I had to imagine she had been upstairs when she first heard the call.

"Hi, it's Iris," I said.

"Everything is okay?"

"Everything's fine. I had a quick break between classes and wanted to ask if you'd tell Pop that I have to stay after school."

"You have a meeting maybe?" It was like she was feeding me a ready-made excuse because she didn't think my vague reason would be sufficient for Pop.

"Yeah, a meeting." I felt terrible about the lie. Pop and I were supposed to be honest with each other. But the pull was too strong. I needed to see Grace.

"Dinner will be at six," said Mrs. Mrozenski. "You will be back then?"

"Absolutely."

I took a train uptown, feeling like I was breaking a thousand laws along the way. What if Pop—or someone he knew—saw me? That would be it—no more second chances, no hope of one day working by his side, nothing to help me pass my time but school and Pearl.

My travel companions only made me feel worse. Enlisted men in uniforms so new you could still see the pinholes from the tags they'd removed rode the subway with the wide-eyed gaze of tourists. I thought of the men we'd encountered on Friday night and wondered if these boys shared similar thoughts about zoot suits and patriotism. But then they looked at me with such sad expressions in their eyes, like I reminded them of their sister or the girl they'd left behind, and I felt ashamed for thinking they were capable of doing anything wrong.

I got off at 86th and Lexington and walked the familiar streets, taking in the fall smells of the privileged part of the city. As I arrived at Chapin, the doors burst open and the first of the girls piled out of the main building. They weren't headed home. Chapin didn't end with its last class. Now was the time for the various sports and clubs the girls participated in to kick off their meetings and practices. In groups of twos and threes, the identically clad girls headed for Drama, Dance, Orchestra, Yearbook, Student Government, Newspaper, or the dozens of other activities they could sign up for. If I were still there, who knew what I'd be doing?

It didn't matter, I told myself. I was gone now. There would be no opportunity to excel at playing the handbells or writing poetry for the literary magazine.

Girls continued streaming out of the building, Grace among them. In her company was someone I didn't recognize. She had a mane of bright red hair that looked like it would frizz out if it wasn't tamed into the victory rolls she currently wore. This had to be Josephine.

Neither of them wore their uniform. Clad in street clothes, their faces made up with a heavy hand, their saddle shoes exchanged for pumps, they obviously weren't headed to a club meeting, rehearsal, or lacrosse match. They exited the gates and I counted to twenty and followed after them, keeping enough distance that I'd have time to react and hide just in case they suddenly turned around.

Josephine's voice was low and musical, though she made no effort to keep it quiet. "How about if we try the Wall?" she said to Grace. She meant Horn & Hardart, the automat we used to frequent after school.

Grace bowed her head in supplication. She seemed to be fighting to keep pace with her friend. "There weren't that many last time—"

"Last time we went too early."

"I suppose it's worth a try."

A group of sailors approached from the opposite direction. Josephine slowed her pace, forcing Grace to do the same. I responded accordingly, ducking to the right so I didn't walk into anyone.

"How's my hair?" asked Josephine.

"Good," said Grace.

"Lipstick?" She bared her teeth, momentarily looking like a wolf.

Grace scraped at one of her own incisors to indicate where Josephine should devote her attention. "You got a little lip cream there."

"The tall one's cute, don't you think?" As she asked the question, she waved at the sailors, fluttering her fingers like some movie coquette.

"He's zazz all right," said Grace.

"Where are you headed to, girls?" asked the sailor Josephine had just described as cute.

"Wouldn't you like to know?" she said back.

"I don't suppose you have time to show some boys from out of town where they can get a good cheap meal."

"Depends on how cheap you want it," said Josephine. "Girls like us have standards."

The boys stopped, bringing Josephine and Grace to a standstill. The crowd parted around them, me included, and continued on its way. I put a scarf over my hair and pulled up the collar of my jacket, hoping it would hide my face. I walked ten steps, then doubled back, pausing at a newsstand where I pretended to be absorbed by that day's headlines.

"What do you say, fellows?" said the tall sailor. "Would a little company make you willing to stretch your budgets?"

"How old are you?" asked one of his friends, a short boy with a nose like a beak.

Now it was Grace's turn to pipe up. She shifted her body, sticking out her chest while arching her back. "How old do you think we are?"

He stared at her for a moment. "I'm guessing you two are still in high school."

"Then you'd be guessing wrong," said Jo.

He cocked his head toward Grace. "That so?"

"Would I lie to you?" said Grace.

"No, I don't think you would."

A wind blew past, bringing with it the first hint of the approaching winter. Even though Josephine was wearing a coat, she shivered and rubbed her hands together like we'd just been hit by an arctic blast.

"You cold?" asked the tall sailor.

"Freezing. Mind if I put my hand in your pocket?" She fluttered her lashes like she was a Southern belle.

He pulled his peacoat from his body. "You go right ahead." She slid her hands into the navy wool jacket, keeping enough of a distance from the boy that her behavior didn't seem overtly improper. "So where are we taking you two for dinner?" asked the sailor.

"There's an automat a few blocks from here," said Josephine. "How 'bout we meet you there in an hour?"

"Why not walk there with us now?"

"Because I can't keep my hands in your pocket all night. I need to pop by my house and get a hat and gloves."

"How do we know you and your friend won't stand us up?"

"You don't," said Josephine. She removed her hands from his jacket. "Ta-ta." She waved goodbye to them, looped her arm in Grace's, and then continued on her way.

I stepped into place behind them as they passed the newspaper kiosk. The sailors watched them leave and then headed in the opposite direction. Josephine was silent for half a block, then tossed a look over her shoulder to verify that the sailors were gone. Once she was sure they were, she removed a wallet from her jacket and flipped through its contents.

"Fifty dollars," she told Grace. "Not bad."

"I thought we were going to get dinner with them," said Grace. She sounded irritated, though I don't think it was the fact of Jo's crime that bothered her so much as the change in plans it represented.

"I didn't like the looks of them up close. All that talk about a cheap dinner. And how dare they ask our age."

Grace pouted. "I can't believe you stole from him."

"I'm cutting out the middleman," said Josephine. "Why go through the trouble of listening to their boring war stories for a free meal when we can just take the cash and run?" Josephine removed a pack of cigarettes from her other pocket. She tapped out two, put both to her mouth, and lit them like she was Humphrey Bogart. Once both had ignited, she passed one to Grace, who greedily sucked at the slim white tube.

"It's probably his money for a month," said Grace.

"If you feel so bad about it, why don't you track him down and give him your take?" Jo removed a hunk of bills from the wallet and passed them Grace's way.

"Don't be stupid," said Grace. But she took the money.

"You're the one who's being unpleasant. I'm just trying to have a little fun." Josephine snapped her fingers as an idea occurred to her. "Speaking of fun, how about if we show up at the automat and rescue him by paying for his meal with his own money? Wouldn't that be a scream?"

"Not really. Ten to one the minute he realizes his wallet is gone he'll figure out who took it. I'm not in the mood to get arrested."

Josephine rolled her eyes. "Fine. Then what do you want to do?"

"Meet someone to take us for dinner and dancing. Like we planned."

They paused at an intersection.

I took a step backward and bent down to tie my shoe, worried that I was getting too close to them. As much as I wanted to hear how this argument played out, the last thing I wanted was to get caught.

"Iris?" Behind me, a familiar voice rang out. Two of them, actually—it was Bea and Bev.

I looked back toward Josephine and Grace. They hadn't

heard my name. They were too caught up in their own drama to pay attention to anything else going on around them. I spun around and smiled at the twins.

"Oh my gosh," said Bev. "It is you. Are you visiting your aunt again?"

"Yes," I said. So much for my disguise. I stood up, pulled the scarf from my hair and shoved it in my pocket.

"Grace said she saw you on Saturday."

"She sure did," I said. I tried to echo their polished enthusiasm even as I wondered what was fueling it. What had Grace told them about our time together?

"Are you looking for Grace?" asked Bea.

Grace and Josephine crossed the street. Their pace had picked up. Had they reached a decision about how they were going to spend their evening, or were they still arguing?

"No, I'm actually on my way home," I told Bea. I was even less comfortable seeing them now than I had been during my first stakeout. Were Bea and Bev privy to the rumors about Mama? If they were, thankfully they were too well bred to drag my scandal into broad daylight. Which wasn't to say that they didn't regularly discuss me in the hallowed halls of Chapin.

"Grace said you're going to get together again," said Bev.

"Maybe. I mean, it depends on our schedules and stuff."

"Believe me, it would be good for Grace," said Bea. "We were so glad when she told us she saw you. I'm sure she told you about you know who?"

Who was *you know who*? Tom?

I shrugged to indicate that I didn't know what they were talking about.

"Josephine O'Hara," said Bev.

"Oh, right. Yeah, she mentioned her a time or twelve. I'm surprised those two get on so well," I said. "Jo's an upperclassman, right?"

"I think that's why she likes Grace," said Bev. "She figured out she was top dog of the underclassmen and made a beeline straight for her."

"So I take it you two aren't in her band of admirers?"

"Please," said Bev with an eye roll. "She's a scholarship student." She made the word *scholarship* sound like a terrible disease, like polio. Being on aid was usually the kiss of death at Chapin. When we first discovered that Mama's money had run out, Pop offered to look for funding to pay for my schooling. I nixed the idea. I knew word would get out that my family could no longer afford the school and along with it would come the cooed remarks that everyone liked me just the same and don't worry, my secret would never get out.

Except it always did. Those girls whose families had experienced reversals of fortune became social outcasts. At least the girls who'd always been on scholarship knew they were different and didn't expect to fit in. For the rest of us, there were constant digs that the only reason you were there was because everyone else's parents could afford to pay for them and by golly you better be grateful for that.

There was no way I would have let them do that to me.

"Does Grace know that?" I asked.

"She just found out," said Bea. "Can you imagine? Josephine takes the subway to campus each day. The *subway.*"

Did she mean that thing I was getting ready to board to go back to the Lower East Side? How shocking.

"So have you met any cute boys this year?" I asked.

"Not really," said Beatrice. "Besides, who has time? Between studying and extracurriculars, we hardly have a moment to eat."

And they certainly didn't have time to travel across town to visit their aunt, she seemed to be saying. I decided to take a shot in the dark. "Grace seems to have made the time," I said.

"Don't tell me that's still going on," said Bev.

"I heard she dumped him," said Bea. "After the *incident.*"

"Thank God," said Bev. "I would've died of embarrassment if I were her."

"Do tell," I said.

Bea stepped toward me and lowered her voice. "She was going with this boy from one of the public schools. Or at least *he* thought so, anyway. One day he showed up at Chapin wanting to talk to her. And the way he was dressed—"

"In a bright red suit," said Bev. "Like he was a colored boy. And he had those flowers."

241

"Carnations," said Bea. Couldn't he afford nicer flowers with the money he'd made from the locker thefts? Or had that money been used for something else? "She tried to breeze past him, but he kept calling out her name in that accent of his. It was just awful. I mean, it's one thing to be attracted to a boy like that, but to be seen in public . . ."

"Oh, come on—it was kind of sweet," said Bea.

"Are you off your nut?"

"Remember what the note said."

"There was a note?" I asked.

"He dropped it," said Bea. "It was a love letter. Diana Fox found it and by the next morning there were copies all over the school."

"And what did it say?"

Bev fluttered her lashes, obviously not seeing the romance her sister did. " 'I can't live without you. I'll do anything for you. You're Juliet to my Romeo.' It just went on and on. The most notable thing about it was that he actually spelled everything correctly, though I'm sure someone helped him with that. I really thought it was going to ruin her for life. Girls were quoting it for weeks."

"When did this happen?" I asked.

"About a month ago," said Bea. "Of course, eventually everyone stopped talking about it, Grace being Grace."

"The gossip may be gone, but the relationship could still be on if Grace told Iris about him," said Bev.

"She barely mentioned it," I said. "I'm sure the only

reason she said anything to me is because Tom and I go to school together. She probably wanted to warn me that he was bad news."

"Lord and butler," said Bev. "You go to school with him? You poor thing."

"He's not so bad."

They exchanged another look. Judgment had been rendered: Grace may have been able to resurrect her reputation, but I was a lost cause.

"How'd she meet him, anyhow?" I asked. "She never told me."

"Who knows?" said Bea. "I'm sure Josephine had something to do with it. She's always dragging Grace to unsavory places. I've heard they've even gone to USO dances in Brooklyn."

I was half tempted to tell them about my night in Harlem just to see them faint. "I'm surprised Tom gave up on her so easily. He's pretty persistent from what I've heard. There was a girl he dated in public school who practically had to get the police to step in to get him to leave her alone." Poor Tom. It was bad enough that they were dragging his name through the mud; did I have to invent stories about him now, too?

Bea shrugged. "All I know is one day he's showing up at Chapin, and the next day Grace is gushing over how she won't have to worry about ever seeing him again."

A chill passed through me. Was her choice of words

standard sub-deb exaggeration, or was it a clue that what-ever happened to Tom Barney was more permanent?

"I better go," I told Bea and Bev. "My pop busts a gut if I'm late for supper."

"We should get together sometime," said Bev. "We miss you."

"That would be swell," I said. "Anytime either of you want to come to the Lower East Side, give me a buzz. Grace knows the number."

They told me that they'd be in touch, but I knew better than to hold my breath. The Lower East Side was Mars, and I was now a Martian as far as they were concerned.

16

I WAS LATE TO DINNER, but fortunately so was Pop. Mrs. Mrozenski sat by herself at the table, smoking a cigarette in front of a full plate of something that had been wrapped in cabbage and then cooked for hours in tomato sauce. "Sorry," I said as I came in. "Things went longer than I expected."

She wasn't mad. Mrs. M rarely ever got mad. But I could see worry creasing her face. I wasn't sure if it was fear that something had happened to me or concern about what punishment I'd face if I hadn't gotten home before Pop had. And I knew she'd never tell me unless I asked her flat out. As nice as she was to me, she was an intensely private person. And while I appreciated that most of the time, there were moments when I wished there was at least one person in this house who didn't keep their worries bottled up inside.

Her face seemed long and sorrowful. Had something

happened to her son? Letters arrived regularly from him, snatched from the postman's hand and whisked away to her room upstairs, where I imagine she read them in privacy. She never shared their contents, though I often saw a piece of V-mail sticking out of her apron pocket, and more than once I'd caught her rereading his missives like a page of Scripture you toted around and turned to when you needed reassurance.

She did so much for us: cooking, cleaning, putting up with delayed rent. And yet I never thought to ask her about her own life. "Are you all right?" I asked her.

She cocked her head to the right, as though she was trying to prevent her surprise at being asked the question from leaking out the other side. "They released new casualty numbers today for the Navy and the Marines." She passed the newspaper my way. It was folded so that the article in question appeared on top: "14,466 Casualties in Sea Service."

Not even a year had passed yet and we'd topped five figures, and that was for only a portion of the armed forces.

Surely the new, lowered draft age would pass now. And if that happened, every boy in the senior class could be gone in one fell swoop. Including Benny.

I pushed the paper away. "It'll end soon," I said.

"This I pray for every night."

I dug into the meal with as much excitement as I could muster and was pleasantly surprised to find the cabbage full of meat and rice, delicately seasoned to better meet Pop's and my unadventurous taste buds. "This is delicious," I told her, hoping my enthusiasm seemed genuine.

"Is halupki. From my mother's recipe."

I cleaned my plate and dug into a second helping. Rather than letting my mind linger on how massive a number fifteen thousand really was, I forced myself to mull over my conversation with Bea and Bev. I could almost guarantee that the last thing those two were thinking about was the war.

"You are awfully quiet," said Mrs. Mrozenski.

"I'm just tired." I thought about talking it over with her, but given the enormity of what weighed on her mind, my problems seemed ridiculously lightweight in comparison. So Grace didn't tell me about Tom. So what? It's not like she valued my opinion anymore. But it was strange that everyone at Chapin knew about him and she didn't say one word to me. Could it be that she wanted to keep up the illusion that she was superior to me and wouldn't lower herself to trawl the Lower East Side for a boyfriend? Or had she figured out that Tom and I went to the same school and decided it would be wiser not to mention him to me?

But why would it matter if I knew they were connected . . . unless she was somehow responsible for his disappearance. I shook the thought out of my head. As much as Grace had changed—and I had to face that she was now a shadow of the girl I once knew—there was no way that I could believe she would physically harm someone.

We finished dinner, and still no Pop. Was he following a lead in the Barney case, or was there some new job demanding his attention? I went to my room to tackle my homework, which would take all of five minutes if I extended any kind of effort at all. I wondered how much work Bea and Bev were facing. The workload at Chapin was legendary, especially for upperclassmen. They wanted to prepare you for college. Chapin girls didn't just go to university to meet men. They actually went to get degrees.

And me? What would I be doing in four years? Working for Pop, tending my own family, or spending my days as a secretary in some dingy Lower East Side office?

The phone rang, causing me to jump.

"Iris?" Mrs. Mrozenski called up the stairs. "Is for you."

Who would be calling for *me*? I took the steps two at a time, my heartbeat matching the pace of my feet.

Maybe it was Benny. That would explain Mrs. Mrozenski's smile as she handed me the receiver. A boy calling the house for me would be a historic event.

"Hello?" I said.

"Hello, Iris," said a decidedly female voice. "It's Grace."

My heartbeat picked back up. Had she seen me tailing Josephine and her that afternoon?

"Hi," I said. "Is everything all right?"

"Oh, it's fine. I was just thinking about how nice it was to see you on Saturday."

There was something pulled and strained about her voice. Clearly she had another reason for calling, but she wasn't willing to own up to it yet.

"How's school?" she asked.

"Fine. How about for you?"

"Oh, marvelous. But I'm absolutely shattered. You know what a chore Chapin can be."

We both paused and listened to the hum of the line.

"I'm curious about something," she said when the silence began to approach awkwardness. "It occurred to me that I might know someone you go to school with. His name's Tom Barney?"

"Tom Barney?" I repeated, hoping to buy myself some time. What was the best way to proceed? Admit that he had disappeared and garner her reaction? Or pretend all was fine and do the same? What would Pop do? "Sure," I said. "I know him. He's kind of hard to miss. In fact, he used to hang out with the group I went to the Savoy with."

"Really? What do you mean 'used to'?"

"It's the strangest thing. He's been missing for almost a month."

Her breathing deepened. Even over the lousy connection, I could hear the tension strangling her.

"So how do you know him?" I asked.

"We went out a time or two."

"Seriously? I mean, don't get me wrong, he's dreamy, but not exactly the kind of fellow I would figure you for. I guess that's why it ended, huh?"

"Sort of." Another pause. I could picture her in her massive apartment, looping the pigtail cord around her arm. "Has anyone said where he might've gone?"

"No. I don't think anyone knows. He's taken a powder before, but he always let people know where he was going. This time he didn't, and it has everyone pretty upset."

"Do they think something happened to him?"

"They seem to be leaning that way."

I thought I heard a tiny gasp escape from her end of the line. "I think I'm in trouble, Iris."

"What kind of trouble?"

"I think I know what happened to Tommy and it's not good."

It took me a moment to regain my composure. Of all the things that I pictured happening that night, Grace confessing to a crime was at the bottom of the list. "What did you do?" I finally said, hoping the anger I was feeling wasn't apparent in my words.

"It wasn't me, I swear. It was that girl I told you about. Josephine."

"What did she do?"

She sighed heavily, so heavily that it almost sounded a bit theatrical, but that might've been the connection.

"She didn't like that I was going out with him. Thought he was beneath me."

"And you didn't?"

"Honestly, I did at first. But the more I got to know him, the less it seemed to matter."

"Did you tell her that?"

"You have to understand Josephine." That imperious sound was back in her voice, the one she'd used when she was at my house, schooling me on the ways of the world. "It wasn't just about my reputation. She wasn't happy with how he was taking me away from her. I thought she'd get over it, but then she gave me an ultimatum. Told me I had to break up with him, or—"

"Or what?"

"Or she'd tell people what we'd been doing. With the enlisted men."

"Right," I said. She was talking about the favors in exchange for nice dinners and little gifts. Those weren't the kinds of things nice Chapin girls did, and while there was a fine line between a girl being friendly and being fast, there was no way anyone wouldn't have thought Grace had crossed it. If word got out, Grace would be marked as a girl who had ruined herself in exchange for goods and services.

"I told her that I didn't care. I was in love with him, but she swore she would tell. I was so scared, Iris." Was she really? It was hard to tell from her voice, but perhaps enough time had passed that she'd managed to quell the emotion

251

the way I could distance myself from the agony of learning about Mama's death. "I stopped returning his calls, told him it was over. But he showed up at school one day, begging me to take him back. I couldn't stand it, how hurt he was. And so that night I told Josephine that if it was really so important to her that I stop seeing him, she would have to break it off for me. And after that I never heard from him again."

So that's what she'd meant when she told Bea and Bev that she didn't have to worry about seeing him again. "Why do you think Jo did anything more than tell Tom to take a hike?"

"Jo was really strange afterward. She refused to talk about what happened with him. Got upset whenever I brought him up. She made me promise that I wouldn't tell anyone that she'd gone to talk to him."

This was new. Why ask someone to make such a promise unless you needed an alibi?

"Honestly, I didn't think anything would keep Tommy away for good. What we had—it wasn't just a puppy-love thing. I really thought we would be together forever. So as the weeks passed and he didn't try to contact me, I started to get worried. And then on Saturday—"

"This past Saturday?"

"Yes. I went to all the places I knew he used to hang out. I even went by his house. And there was no trace of him anywhere." So that was why she'd really come to the Lower East Side—to find out about Tom. I was her cover in case anyone asked her where she'd gone or, God forbid, saw her entering or exiting the subway.

"Did you go to 240 Houston Street?" I asked her. Maybe Grace had left the note Pop had found in Tom's locker.

"Where?"

"It's just a place I heard some of the kids hang out."

"I've never heard of it."

There was nothing in her voice that made me think she was lying. "Do you think Josephine is capable of hurting someone?" I asked.

"I don't know. There have been stories—rumors really—about things that happened at her old school. She's a scholarship student at Chapin. She lives alone with her mother. Her father is supposedly overseas, though I think she made that part up. She told me once that they moved to Manhattan to get away from something that happened where she used to live. This was supposed to be a fresh start for her family. She . . . she's done things before that make me think she's rougher than she wants me to believe."

"With the servicemen?"

"Yes. She's stolen from them. And I've seen her shoplift. She may not be capable of physically hurting someone, but I wouldn't be surprised if she knew someone who could do it for her."

What I'd witnessed that afternoon certainly corroborated that. "What do you want me to do about this, Grace?"

"I don't know. I just wanted someone to know what was going on. I don't like who I'm becoming. I realized that after I left your house on Saturday. I've become this ugly, awful person because of Josephine. I want it to stop, but mostly I want to know that if she did do something to Tom, she'll pay for it."

Who was the real Grace Dunwitty? Was it the girl who was thrilled to see me on Saturday afternoon, or the cool cat who needed me as her alibi on Saturday night? Or could it be this girl, who seemed genuinely scared and remorseful? I wanted to believe the last one was the version of Grace that counted, but she'd mixed me up too much the last few days for me to completely trust her.

And yet— "I should probably tell you something, Grace. My pop has been hired by Tom's parents to try to find him."

"Oh." She was quiet for a beat while she struggled to take this new information in. "His parents must be pretty worried."

"His mother is. His father is more angry than anything. He seems to think Tom's nothing but a big screwup who they should write off."

"That's terrible. So I guess you're going to have to tell your father everything I just told you?"

"I won't if you tell me not to." Why did I say that?

Because I wanted Grace to like me. Because even after her weird behavior this past weekend, I wanted her to be my friend.

"No, I think you should tell him everything. Especially if it will help Tom." She sighed heavily into the line. "Thanks for listening, Iris. I feel so much better getting that off my chest. You're a true friend, you know that?"

I told her I did.

WE SAID OUR FAREWELLS. I hung up the phone and went into the parlor. There I turned on the Philco and listened to the war news while flipping through *Calling All Girls*. I wasn't reading it, though. I was replaying Grace's words in my head. If Josephine was as manipulative as she said, it wouldn't be hard for her to convince some sailor making eyes at her to hurt a small-time thug on her behalf. And if Tom was wearing the zoot on the night it went down, any number of servicemen would've been happy to humiliate him, just like the scores of others who'd done it before. Only this time, maybe Tom fought back too hard and ended up with something a lot worse than his pants around his ankles.

Where was Pop? I desperately wanted to talk to him. It was time for me to come clean before I got in over my head. It wasn't like him to stay out without telling us when he'd be home. Could he have made his own headway on the Barney case? Was he working on something new? If he was on the tail of someone, he wouldn't necessarily have a chance to call home and express his regrets over being late for dinner. But would a stakeout really last this long? He'd been gone since I'd skipped out of school, longer, in fact, since he hadn't been home when I called Mrs. Mrozenski. He couldn't keep up that kind of pace for hours on end. His stump would grow sore, even if he'd been sitting in one place the entire time. And what about his pain pills? He probably hadn't taken any with him, thinking he'd be home before the throbbing demanded another dose.

I fell into a fitful sleep on the sofa, integrating the chilling news of what was happening overseas into my dreams. In my dream Pop is hidden in the shadows of a submarine, trying to keep himself from being spotted in a space no larger than his office closet. His wound is pulsing, his stump tired of being held in the same position. Slowly, it begins to vibrate, the motion worsening the more he tries to still it. His thigh is centimeters from striking a metal support pole whose top screw has come loose and will rattle when set off by the slightest movement. Pop knows that when that happens, his hiding place will be given away and he'll be a dead man . . .

I awoke with a jolt, uncertain where I was, but doubly glad I hadn't had to experience whatever was about to happen in my dream. What woke me? The parlor was cold, the radio had turned to static, and the front door stood closed. Had Pop returned and bypassed me, assuming it was better to leave me asleep than to make me climb upstairs to my room? No. If he had come home, he would've silenced the Philco, extinguished the lamp, tossed the orange-and-brown afghan over my body to keep away the chill.

Maybe it was the radio signing off for the night that roused me. I switched it off and wrapped a blanket around my shoulders, preparing myself for the cold climb to my room.

A sound came from the kitchen—rattling, like someone was at the back door. Was that what I'd heard? There was no way to know for sure. The back door worked on a skeleton key and was always locked from the inside. Pop used it to haul coal inside and Mrs. Mrozenski used it to take the garbage out of the house, but we were forbidden from using it as a main entrance. Pop said it was because Mrs. Mrozenski's mother had been a maid who was always restricted to the rear door of the house, and Mrs. M never wanted to feel like a servant in her own home. I thought it was funny at the time, especially given that she spent her days cooking and cleaning, but I was suddenly grateful for that little nugget of knowledge, because if someone was at that back door, I knew it wasn't someone who was supposed to be.

Maybe what I'd heard was the wind or the vibration a car created as it passed through the alley. I continued up the stairs, convinced it was nothing, when I heard the unmistakable sound of glass breaking. That wasn't the wind. Someone had just broken one of the small rectangular panes at the top of the kitchen door—I was certain of it. It wouldn't do the culprit much good. The key was never left in the lock. It hung from a hook above the stove. He would realize that soon enough and move on to the kitchen window. It, too, would be locked, but if he broke it, it would be large enough for a grown man to pass through.

My mouth was dry. I wanted to call to Mrs. Mrozenski, but her bedroom was suddenly a million miles away. I didn't want to alert the burglar that we were here and vulnerable. I needed to call the police.

With leaden legs, I went into Pop's office, leaving the door open so I could still hear what was happening in the kitchen. I picked up the receiver and told the operator to get me the police. The dispatcher responded to my calm recitation that someone was breaking in by telling me to lock myself in a closet and a patrol car would be there shortly. From the kitchen more glass broke. I wished Mrs. Mrozenski wasn't so conscientious and had, for once in her life, left a sink full of dirty dishes to slow his progress, but I knew there would be no such thing waiting for our robber. Still, it seemed to take an eternity from the time I heard the window break to when any other sounds came from the kitchen. I turned off the lights in the office and slipped into the small closet that Pop used for file storage and client coats, leaving the door cracked open just a sliver. There, among his galoshes and umbrellas, I sat with my knees pulled up to my chest and waited.

Footsteps left the kitchen and entered the parlor. Then, presumably finding nothing of value, he entered the office and clicked on a lamp.

I was certain my heart was thumping so loudly that, like in my dream about Pop, he'd hear it and uncover my hiding place. I desperately wanted to see him with my own eyes, not only so I could identify him later, but to cement for myself once and for all that this wasn't a new scene in the awful dream I'd been having the moment before.

What would you have done if they had a gun? Pop had asked me after I'd taken the photos of Mrs. Wilson. I prayed I wasn't about to find out the answer to that question.

A desk drawer slid open and papers rustled. Another drawer opened, and another one, though it was clear that whatever he was seeking wasn't conveniently showing itself. From the minute space left by the open closet door, I could see that his back was to me. I longed to open the door just a little more, enough to see the color of his trousers or the shape of his shoes, but I was certain that the hinges would creak, giving me away.

He turned and approached the forbidden locked cabinet, where Pop kept his gun. He rattled the lock and found it immovable. Something new was produced—perhaps an object from the desk? He banged it against the cabinet with enough force that I could hear the wood splinter. Just as I was recovering from that jarring noise, a siren wailed outside the house, announcing the police's arrival.

The culprit cursed. I'm not trying to be a goody two-shoes by not repeating what was said. I honestly don't remember which forbidden word it was because the voice caught me so off guard.

Our intruder was a woman.

In a flash, she was out of the office and running toward the kitchen. I pushed out of the closet, confirmed that the cabinet was broken, and took off after her, just in time to see the edge of her skirt as it turned the corner into the kitchen. Someone was pounding on the front door and demanding, "Open up, it's the police," but I didn't have a moment to spare. I made it into the kitchen and found the back door wide open, the skeleton key protruding from the lock. I rushed out the door and found the alley empty.

17

"WHAT TIME DID YOU HEAR the glass break?"

Mrs. Mrozenski and I were seated at the kitchen table along with Officer Dignam, a man with jowls so pronounced he could have been mistaken for a bulldog. "I'm not sure," I told him. Mrs. Mrozenski wrapped her arm around me. In her other hand she clutched a rosary. "Maybe an hour ago?"

He checked his watch and I stole a look at the time. It was one o'clock in the morning.

"And you're certain the perpetrator was female?"

"Absolutely. I heard her curse. And I saw part of her skirt. It was black, wool maybe. A-line, so it flared when she ran."

He seemed to be attempting to write down everything I said, but I'd lost him somewhere around "A-line."

"It means that the skirt can open up really full, so that you can dance in it."

A commotion came from the front of the house, where two other officers had been left to assess what had taken place in the office. A familiar voice rose above their gruff, officious tones—Pop was home.

He rushed into the kitchen, looking like death warmed over. His face was gray, his hair a greasy mess, and his leg, as predicted, had reached a point where he could no longer put weight on it.

"Oh my God—Iris. Are you hurt?"

"I'm fine."

He wasn't just exhausted and sore; there was something else off about him, though I couldn't quite put my finger on it. Despite his obvious physical agony, he launched himself at me and took me in his arms. I took in a whiff of body odor and something else. He was drunk.

So not only had I wasted an evening worrying about him, I also got to confront a burglar all by myself so he could—what? Get sloshed?

"You're Arthur Anderson?" asked Officer Dignam.

Pop struggled to keep the slur out of his words while I tried to keep him a safe distance from the cop. "Yes. I'm Arthur."

"Where were you tonight, sir?"

His mouth worked like a hand puppet's, but no sound came out.

"He was meeting with a client," I said.

"Have you been drinking?"

262

"No," said Pop. "I haven't." His hands remained entangled in my hair, squeezing my head with such force that I worried he might pop it off if he wasn't careful.

Pop had nothing but respect for the police, but I knew it wasn't a two-way street. Private eyes, even properly licensed ones, were viewed as meddlers who took advantage of people who were too impatient to let the law do its job. Uncle Adam used to bribe the officers that worked his beat to keep them on his side, but Pop had made no such effort. If we barely had money for rent, how could we be expected to grease the mitts of local law enforcement?

"You sure about that?" asked Officer Dignam.

He walked toward Pop. Another step and he'd have all the olfactory confirmation he needed. And then what? Having caught Pop in one lie, would he insist that meant there were others to uncover? Probably. And then what had started as a simple break-in investigation would turn into a close examination of Pop's business practices.

"It's his leg," I said.

"What?"

"Go on, Pop. Show him. You must be in awful pain."

From across the room, Mrs. Mrozenski nodded encouragingly. "I'll get your pills, Arthur." While she left to retrieve the vial from his room, I helped Pop wiggle the leg loose. It dropped to the floor with a thud. His thigh was hot to the touch.

"He's a Pearl Harbor vet," I said. "And quite frankly, he doesn't know his limits."

"Now, Iris—"

"Don't *now Iris* me. Ten hours on your feet? And for what? So some fat cat can get proof that his wife is cheating. And now you're going to be bed-bound for a day. It's not worth it."

He waved me off, aware that the less he said, the better.

"Show some respect, young lady," said Officer Dignam.

"Yes, sir," I said. Mrs. Mrozenski returned with the pills and gave Pop a strong cup of Postum to wash them down with.

"It looks like your business office was the focus of the break-in, Mr. Anderson. We'll need you to let us know what, if anything, is missing. Perhaps it would be easier for you to wait until morning?"

"Yes, I'd appreciate that," said Pop.

"She broke into your cabinet, Pop," I said.

"She?"

"Your daughter said the intruder was a woman. What's in this cabinet?"

"Nothing really," said Pop. "Just personal papers and some case files."

My eyebrows went up at that. Since when had he started locking up case files? "People assume if there's a lock, there's a reason," said Officer Dignam. "Your would-be robber probably assumed that's where you stashed your cash."

Pop smiled. "If I had cash to stash, it would be in a bank."

"Still, take a look around when you feel up to it. If something is missing, no matter how small, you'll want to report it, just to be safe."

THEY WERE GONE by two a.m. By then, the Postum had eradicated all signs of Pop's evening activities and I'd cleared the kitchen of every shard of glass I could find. One of the officers helped us secure the broken window and door panes with boards and then left us alone to sort out why this had happened.

"I'm sorry," said Pop when the police had left. "I'll fix the windows."

"Is not your fault," said Mrs. Mrozenski.

"I should've been here."

She clicked off the overhead light, leaving only the fixture above the kitchen sink burning. "Everyone is safe. Is all that matters."

"Thank you," he whispered. She left and Pop and I sat in the near darkness for a while, listening to the kitchen clock count down the minutes until dawn.

"Why were you drinking tonight?" I asked.

"I don't know," he said. But he did know. I could hear it in his voice. And then it dawned on me why he'd chosen tonight of all nights to get soused.

"The Navy casualty numbers are out," I said.

"How do you know that?"

"Mrs. Mrozenski told me."

"That's not something she should be sharing with you." Even as he condemned her for it, I thought I could hear the slightest hint of relief in his voice that I was privy to the same information he was, even if it didn't weigh on me in exactly the same way.

"Fifteen thousand already dead or wounded. That's a lot of men in a short time," I said. He nodded at his drained mug. "You must know some of them, right?"

"The odds are good." Where I saw an enormous figure that might one day eclipse the lives of the boys I went to school with, he saw the individual faces of men he'd served with. How agonizing that had to be. It was one thing to have to commemorate Pearl Harbor every single time you tried to take a step, but to know that you weren't the only one who suffered, but just one of the first ones? I would've gotten drunk, too.

"I'm so sorry, Pop."

He reached out and smoothed a strand of hair out of my face. "God, you're so much like her." It was so rare that he mentioned Mama that it took my breath away. "She would've been proud of you tonight, protecting me like that. Thank you. I promise you, I won't leave you alone like that again." He left the table and hobbled over to the stove to refill his cup. "You must've been terrified."

"It all happened so quickly." Was I really like Mama?

266

"You did everything right: calling the police, hiding."

I had, hadn't I? I might not have had the right instincts when I tailed Mrs. Wilson all those weeks before, but I'd grown wiser since then. And—boy, howdy—Pop had noticed!

"You should get to bed, Iris."

"What about you?"

"I need to check the office."

I told him good night and headed out of the kitchen. Rather than going to my room, though, I lingered at the top of the stairs and watched him limp into the office. He cursed beneath his breath as he surveyed the damage.

I couldn't help myself. I went downstairs and joined him.

"Is something missing, Pop?"

He was looking at the broken cabinet. Some of the papers that had once been inside it had spilled onto the floor, including his notes on the Barney case.

"I'm not sure."

"Do you think it's related to one of your cases?"

"I don't know." He slowly bent to retrieve the scattered pages. "You get to bed. You look exhausted."

I told him I would, though I was certain there was no chance I was going to sleep that night.

I STARED AT THE CEILING, trying to sort through who would've broken into our house. Clearly it had to do with Tom Barney. If nothing was missing, then whoever it was wanted a good look at the case file to see what it contained. And that meant whoever it was had to know Pop was working on the case.

I took in a breath so sharply that it pierced my lungs. Grace had gone into Pop's office when she visited and was looking at what was sitting on his desk. I'd also told her he was investigating the case. She could've come back here, hoping to get a longer look at his files. Or perhaps she'd told Josephine about them and she was the one I'd heard swearing as the police arrived.

I eventually slept, much to my amazement. When I finally awoke, the light coming in my bedroom was so bright I winced in pain. I turned to look at my bedside clock and was shocked to discover it was almost noon.

I threw on a robe and rushed down the stairs. Pop wasn't there, but Mrs. Mrozenski was.

"So you finally wake. What a night we had."

"I'm missing school," I said, just in case the rest of the world had forgotten it was a weekday.

"Your father called the school this morning, said you were sick. He did not think you would be up for classes after last night."

"Oh." I sat on the sofa arm, unable to process having a whole day with nothing to do. I was touched that Pop let me sleep in. Could we finally be turning a corner? "Where is he?"

"He went to get glass to fix windows. He be back soon. I make breakfast. You must be starved."

I admitted that I was and let her ply me with fried eggs and toast. When the meal was done and the dishes washed, I changed into clothes and went into Pop's office. My plan was clear: I wanted to see if anything was missing from Tom Barney's folder. The cabinet was open when I entered the room, the contents gone. Pop had wised up and moved everything while I slept.

AS I WAITED for Pop to return, I tried to decide the best way to come clean to him. I could claim that I'd stumbled into the case, not realizing that the boy I'd met at school and who had gone missing was someone Pop had been hired to find. But how to explain Grace? He would have to know I'd started an investigation on my own. No, maybe instead I should tell him that my dear friend Grace was in trouble and I needed his help before someone got hurt. She was dating this guy I went to school with named Tom Barney . . .

The front door opened and Pop came in. He was toting something large and flat that had been wrapped in brown paper and secured with twine—no doubt glass he'd just had cut at the glazier. "This way," he directed someone traveling behind him. "It goes in the room to your left. Let's put it on the floor of the closet."

Two men entered behind him, weighted down by a

heavy black object it took every ounce of their shared strength to carry.

"You're up," said Pop with a smile directed my way. "Good."

No, I would be totally honest with him. It was time. "What's that?"

"A safe," he said as the men grunted their way into the office. "I think last night proved that we need to be a little more secure around here."

"Can we afford it?"

"We don't have a choice." He leaned the glass against the wall. "There's something that I want to talk to you about."

Had last night proven to him that I could be trusted to help him work on his cases?

"What's the story, morning glory?" I said, aping Suze.

He gave me a funny look. "Where were you yesterday afternoon?"

"What do you mean?"

"I called the school this morning to tell them you were sick, and they said they were glad to hear that since you missed your last class yesterday."

I couldn't have been more surprised if he'd told me that he and Uncle Adam had kissed and made up. By catching me off guard, he gave me no time for a lie, which I'm sure he knew. "I went to Chapin."

"Why?"

"To see Grace."

Mrs. Mrozenski, hearing the fuss caused by the two men with the heavy safe, appeared in the parlor doorway and watched the scene.

"And you had to cut class to do this?" said Pop.

"I was afraid if I waited until after, I'd miss her."

One of the men in the office cursed as the unforgiving steel box landed on his foot. Pop tossed a look their way, then redirected his attention to me.

He took in what I'd said and rolled it about his head. "I thought we agreed you'd stay on the Lower East Side."

Oh no. I'd blown it and for no good reason. After all, Grace had called me and told me everything. There'd been no need for me to follow her and Jo. "I know, but it was important. She got bad news. About her father." I couldn't believe I'd chosen that as my cover story. What was wrong with me? "He's missing in action."

He frowned and I waited for him to point out the holes in my story. How did I hear about Grace's dad? If she was so upset, why was she in school? But he didn't point out any of my inconsistencies. I wish he would've. Maybe then I could stop myself from digging a deeper hole.

"They were having a vigil after school yesterday for him and all the other relatives of students who were missing, injured, or killed. I wanted to show my support."

"Then you ask for permission to do so."

"I tried to. I called before I went. Ask Mrs. Mrozenski."

My eyes flashed toward the older woman and I pleaded with every ounce of my being that she'd confirm my story.

"Did Iris call here yesterday afternoon?" Pop asked.

She left my gaze and latched onto Pop's. "Yes. She ask for you, but you were gone. I tell her it was all right to be late but to be home by supper. When I think you be home, too." There was an undercurrent to her words that Pop couldn't have missed: maybe if you hadn't been out drinking, you could've talked to your daughter and told her this was a bad idea. "She come home, just like she said." Unlike her father, whose expected arrival time had passed with nary a word.

"I'm sorry," I said. "I shouldn't have skipped. That was a stupid decision."

"School comes first," he said.

"You go to the principal," said Mrs. Mrozenski. "You tell them you play hooky."

A thought occurred to me: the only way the office would've known that I was missing was through the attendance records. Pearl hadn't helped me like she'd said she would.

I guess I knew who my real friends were.

"You don't need to do that," said Pop. "I told them you came home sick yesterday. Being new, you didn't realize you were supposed to report to the office before leaving."

"Thanks."

"Mr. Anderson? Is this where you want it?" One of the

272

men stood in the office doorway, pointing toward the open closet.

"It looks great. Thanks."

While they continued talking, I followed Mrs. Mrozenski into the kitchen. "Thank you," I told her.

"I don't lie for you."

"I won't ask you to do it again."

"No, I don't *lie* for you."

It took me a minute to register what she was saying. What she meant was she'd stuck to the letter of the truth in what she'd told Pop. I had called. I had said I'd be late. Fortunately, he'd never asked her if I'd told her why.

"Be a good girl, Iris. Okay?"

I promised her that I would.

18

POP SPENT MOST OF THE AFTERNOON behind the closed office door, presumably shifting what had once been in the cabinet into the safe. I watched the door like a hawk, promising myself that as soon as he opened it, I would tell him the truth about everything: why I'd gone to Chapin, how the break-in might have been my fault, my connection to Tom Barney. But as the afternoon wore on and the door remained shut, my courage dwindled. I finally decided to go to him.

"Can I come in?" I asked him after I knocked.

"Sure." He was behind the desk examining a stack of papers. I couldn't tell if it was Tom's file or someone else's.

"Did you figure out if anything was missing?" I asked.

"No. I should've made an inventory of the file contents. I'll know better next time."

I chewed on my lip as I pondered how to proceed. "Were there a lot of case files in there?"

"No, just one."

Either he was only working on the Barney case or none of his other cases were important enough to keep under lock and key. "Are you close to solving it?" I asked.

"Close to closing it. The clients called and told me they don't want me to proceed any further."

"Why?"

"They're pretty sure the missing person is missing by choice and they don't want to spend any more money tracking him down." That had to be Mr. Barney talking. I couldn't imagine Mrs. Barney agreeing to halt things until Tom was home safe.

"Do you agree?" I asked.

"I might've until the break-in. Now I'm not sure what to think."

"Did you tell them about it?" I asked.

"Yes. They've agreed to give me until Monday. If I come up with something, I get paid for my time; if I don't, we call it a wash."

I couldn't believe Pop had agreed to that. All that work he'd done and he was just going to walk away empty-handed?

"It's a goodwill gesture," he told me. "I'd rather have them happy than telling everyone who will listen that I took their money and left them with nothing to show for it."

"Maybe you'll solve it," I said. I needed to tell him what I knew. And I would tell him, in five, four, three, two—

"This isn't something you need to worry about, Iris. Mrs. Mrozenski isn't going to throw us out on the street. I promise."

He shifted the paperwork in front of him and knocked a second stack of paper with his elbow. It slid off the desk and scattered across the floor.

He cursed beneath his breath and surveyed the mess like a climber facing a mountain.

"Let me help," I said. I kneeled and began cleaning up the mess. As I pushed the paper into a stack, Tom's name leaped out at me. I recognized Pop's notes and the inventory of what had been in the locker. Everything seemed to be present and accounted for . . . except for the note that mentioned 240 Houston Street.

I double-checked the stack and surveyed the floor beneath his desk. The note was definitely missing.

"Thanks," he told me as I returned the files to him.

"Anytime," I replied.

I GOT TO SCHOOL EARLY the next day and immediately went to the newspaper room. Paul was there, but Pearl wasn't. In her place was Denise Halloway, the girl he'd been with at the Jive Hive, struggling to type up hand-scrawled notes with one finger.

"Where's Pearl?" I asked them as I entered the room. Denise shrugged and looked toward Paul. He was going through another batch of photos, a dust pen clenched between his fingers, his tongue darting in and out of his mouth as he readied himself to wet the tip.

"She said she had better things to do than help me. And right before our deadline, too."

"Any idea where she's doing these better things?"

He shrugged and flipped to the next picture. "Your guess is as good as mine."

I shifted my weight from side to side as I debated what to do next. "How's the Jive Hive?"

"Hopping. You thinking about coming out again?"

"Maybe." A theory was bubbling to the surface. Maybe the note in the locker had been from Josephine. Perhaps she had lured Tom to Houston Street to do whatever she had done to him. "I heard about another hangout: 240 Houston Street. You ever been there?"

Paul frowned. "Are you serious?"

Uh-oh. What had I stepped in? "Why?"

"Um, it's not a hangout, Iris. It's a place for girls who are *in trouble.*"

I had no trouble understanding what *in trouble* meant this time.

I stammered an excuse that I must've heard the address wrong and left them to their work. While I mulled over why Tom would have that address in his locker, I prowled the halls, looking for Pearl's short, dumpy form. What classes did she have? I'd never asked her. All I knew was that she worked in the office during her study hall.

I didn't find her. Instead, I went to Personal Hygiene and then to each subsequent subject, staying after class each time to find out what I'd missed the day before and what I needed to do to catch up.

At lunch I looked for Pearl at her usual table, but didn't see her there. She had to be hiding. She must've known I'd be furious about the attendance thing. I was about to give up my search and join the Rainbows at their table when I realized Pearl had been right in front of me the entire time. She was sitting between Suze and Rhona.

How had that happened? Had Suze seen her sitting alone the day before and invited her to join them?

I walked, tentatively, toward the table. I tried to lock eyes with Benny, but he was deep in conversation with Maria. That was okay. I'd talk to him later. "Hi, Pearl," I said to her. She looked up at me with cold, uninterested eyes. That wasn't the only thing that was different about her. She was wearing a sweater that day that turned her soft, overly padded body into gentle, feminine curves. A scarf was knotted at her neck, in the same style that Rhona wore hers.

"Oh, hi," she said, like I was someone she hadn't seen for a while that she didn't immediately recognize.

I turned to Suze and smiled. "Hey, Joe, whaddya know?" She didn't meet my gaze. Her eyes drifted to the scarred tabletop, where one student after another had carved their initials into the wood. "Mind if I join you?"

"You better scat, pussycat," said Rhona. "There's no room for you here."

"Seriously?" I said.

"You either leave, or we make you leave," said Dino.

"Find the door, drizzle puss," said Maria. She tossed a glance Benny's way. His eyes, like Suze's, were locked downward.

"I don't understand. What's going on? Suze? Benny?"

"Don't make me make you leave, little girl," said Rhona. "Dig?"

I was completely taken aback. What had happened in the twenty-four hours since I'd been gone? I wanted to ask, but—boy, howdy—the way Rhona was glaring at me made it clear that if I didn't leave immediately I'd be suffering from a lot more than sore feelings.

I backed away from the table, humiliated. On Monday, everything had been fine. Suze had been concerned about me, about how upset I'd been by Mrs. Dunwitty's gossip, but I'd assured her I'd put all that behind me. Dino had opened up to me about Tommy. Benny had squeezed my hand and asked me how long I was grounded for. And now not one of them wanted anything to do with me.

Pearl. Pearl must've done something. Telling Pop I wasn't with her and then reporting my absence was only the first of the things she planned to do to sabotage me. Rhona was right—she was evil.

The afternoon passed in a bitter haze. I desperately wanted to leave school, go home, and sulk and ponder, but my promise to Pop that I wouldn't skip class hung heavily over my head, especially now that I knew any move I made would be carefully monitored.

Two thousand hours later, four o'clock arrived and with it the final bell of the day. I gathered my books and started the long walk home. To add insult to injury, a cold heavy rain began and I had nothing aside from my light mackintosh to protect me. I thought about ducking underneath an awning to wait it out, but I was so desperate to get home that I slogged through the downpour, willing to face the humiliation of looking like a drowned rat if it meant I could hide out in my bedroom a little sooner. I was only a block away from home when a sound interrupted the torrential rush of water. What I thought was a hiss was actually my name.

I turned and found Pearl running to catch up to me. She'd had the good sense to bring an umbrella to school, and the combination of being dry and better dressed made her look almost pretty.

"There you are," she said as she arrived at my side. "I've been trying to find you since final bell. You're soaked."

You don't say, I almost said, but that would've required my speaking to her.

"Here," she said, stretching the umbrella out so it covered both of us. "It's big enough for two."

"Keep it to yourself. What do you want?"

She looked taken aback, which was pretty funny, considering. "To talk to you. To make sure you're okay. I heard you were sick."

"Just to my stomach. I've got to go." I stepped back into the rain, instantly regretting my decision. Had it gotten colder? At this rate, I really was going to be ill.

"Iris—wait."

"For what?"

"I need to talk to you. About the Rainbows. Can we go someplace dry? Like maybe your house?"

We were almost there. If I didn't give her a chance to say her piece, I'd wonder about it all night. "Fine," I said.

I refused her umbrella's shelter the whole way there. Unfortunately, the rain picked up, not only giving me a thorough soaking, but making it impossible for her to know that I was still giving her the cold shoulder and deliberately choosing not to speak. We arrived at the Orchard Street house and I let us in. As Pearl shook out her umbrella and left it on the stoop, I kicked off my ruined shoes and entered the parlor.

"You should change," said Pearl.

"I'm fine." I slumped onto the sofa and wrapped the afghan around me. A fire crackled in the hearth, setting the room aglow with reds and oranges. "So what did you want to tell me?"

"I messed up." She took a seat in the rocker, and her eyes danced around the room. Unlike Grace, she didn't judge her surroundings. If anything, she seemed delighted in their familiarity. "We have a table just like this," she said, her hand stroking the wooden cocktail table beside her. Her fingers traced the edge of the lace doily at its center like it was a childhood dress she hadn't seen in years.

"You are home, Iris," said Mrs. Mrozenski as she entered the room. She took in the state of my hair and clothes and jumped. "You are soaked."

"I'm fine. The fire and blanket are warming me up. This is Pearl Levine."

Pearl leaped to her feet and offered Mrs. Mrozenski her hand. "Is this your house? It's lovely."

They made small talk that I struggled to ignore. Unlike Grace, Pearl was sincere, her questions genuine inquiries. It turned out Mrs. Mrozenski knew her mother. Her daughter, Betty, had sat for Pearl and Paul when they were small.

"I was so sorry to hear about your brother. Is tragedy. There is no other word."

"Thank you," said Pearl.

Mrs. M left to make us cocoa, a rare treat since rationing had started. Pearl returned to her seat.

"So how did you mess up?" I asked.

"Monday. After school. I ran into Suze. She was looking for you. I told her that you'd left before your last class and she asked me if you'd left because you'd gotten more news about your father."

I could see the writing on the wall: Pearl didn't know

that Suze thought Pop was overseas. And so, innocently, she'd corrected her, not realizing that by doing so she was also branding me a big fat liar.

Pearl acknowledged that this was exactly what had happened. "As soon as I said that your pop was fine, you could see all the blood rushing out of her face. I wanted to fix it, so I said that he *had* been injured in the war, he'd lost his leg at Pearl Harbor, but that just made things worse."

"Oh God."

Her face was bright red with excitement and fear. She'd had to wait two long days to tell anyone this story. "Rhona and Dino showed up just as I was telling Suze this. And then Rhona asked me your last name." The leg had tipped her off. Who knew Rhona was that observant? "I told them—I didn't think it was a big deal—and Rhona tells Suze that it's the same surname the detective with the bum leg had. They asked me if your dad was a cop. I said I didn't know, and right then Paul shows up, wanting to know if I was coming to the journalism office . . ."

I was going to throw up. "He told them, didn't he?"

"I know my brother's a drip, but he honestly didn't know what was going on. And by then they were laying it all out, all the questions you'd asked about Tommy—they would've put it together eventually, Iris."

It was worse than I could've imagined. Not only did they know I'd lied about Pop, but now they knew I was the detective's daughter. There was no coming back from this. My cover was blown and so was any hope I might have had of being friends with Suze and anything more with Benny.

"I didn't know what to do, Iris. I was really afraid they'd hurt you. Not Suze, but Rhona was so angry. I needed to distract them and so I decided then and there to become a double agent."

I didn't think I'd heard her right. Had she snapped? Gone goofy? Was her grief over her dead brother so pronounced that she thought she was living in a Humphrey Bogart film? "What are you talking about?"

"I knew I'd messed things up for you, that you weren't going to find out anything else about Tommy from them, so I thought I would try to become their friend and maybe they'd tell me." Her voice droned on. As soon as Paul left, Pearl told Rhona and Suze that I'd been using her to get information from the attendance office and that I'd pretended I was her best friend until other people began talking. "I cried," said Pearl. "I just stood there in the hall and bawled about how you were the first friend I'd had since my brother died and how much it hurt to find out you were using me. Suze invited me out then and there—we went for milk shakes at Normandie's. And then yesterday Rhona took me shopping and helped me pick out this." She plucked at her sweater. "I felt so bad at lunch today. I wanted to warn you, but there was no way I could without them seeing me talk to you."

I was shocked Pearl had it in her. Who knew she could be so duplicitous? "What about Rhona?" I asked.

"I apologized to her."

So Pearl *had* started the rumor? At least that question was answered once and for all. "So why didn't you fix my attendance record on Monday?" I asked.

"They told me not to. They said I had to stop letting you use me."

The funny thing was, they were right.

Since the beginning, I had been taking advantage of Pearl, seeing her first as a way to stop being thought of as the strange, friendless new girl and later relying on her access to information to get me what I wanted. Yet for all my selfishness, I don't think Pearl saw things that way. Even as she cried to Rhona and Suze about the way I'd mistreated her, I had no doubt she really believed she was inventing my misbehavior.

Mrs. Mrozenski appeared with twin cups of hot chocolate and a plate of cookies and disappeared just as quickly. I wrapped my hands around the hot mug and finally felt the chill start to leave my body.

"Did you get in trouble?" asked Pearl.

"No," I said. "It's fine. It wasn't fair of me to ask you to do that to begin with."

"Why didn't you come to school yesterday?"

I told her about the break-in. I didn't stop there. I also told her about my visit to Chapin on Monday, about my old friend Grace Dunwitty and her new pal Josephine O'Hara. She listened intently, picking at the cookies with enormous restraint.

"Wow," she said when I'd paused in my recitation. She honestly didn't know what to tackle first. "You don't really think he's dead, do you?" Her eyes started to water.

Dead? Hearing the word said out loud shocked me. But it was what I was thinking, wasn't it? It was the only explanation for his absence that made any sense.

"I don't know what to think," I told Pearl. "It doesn't make sense that he would've stayed away this long unless something is keeping him from returning."

"Bu . . . but there must be loads of other reasons for that." *Like what*, I wanted to ask, but it was clear that wouldn't help things. "What does your pop think?"

If Pearl and I were going to be friends, I needed to be honest with her. About everything. "I don't know. Look, I kind of lied before. I'm not working with my pop. He won't let me. Everything I've been doing I've been doing on my own. We're broke, Pearl. I don't know what's going to happen if Pop doesn't solve this case." That wasn't all I told her. I also told her about Mama, about the rumors of the affair, and what Suze had said to calm me down.

"I'm so sorry, Iris. I think Suze is right, though. People make up awful stories for the dumbest reasons." I could tell she was itching to say more, but wanted to hold back for my sake. "Do you think Josephine and the break-in at your pop's office are related?"

"Definitely."

"So what are you going to do about Josephine?"

I checked to make sure Mrs. Mrozenski wasn't about to appear in the room. "I don't know yet. For Pop to convince the Barneys that Tom didn't run away, I need proof, which means I need her to confess. The question is—how?"

Pearl thumped her forefinger against her cocoa mug as she pondered the problem. "If she's as awful as Grace claims, do you know who I'd love to see her get cornered by? Rhona."

"That'd be a scream."

"Think about it—Rhona's not scared of anyone. She's tough. She could be Josephine's match."

The more I thought about it, the less absurd the idea seemed. If we somehow let on to Rhona that Josephine was the last person to see Tom alive, she might be able to force a confession out of her.

"But how would we ever get those two together?"

"Josephine likes dangerous places, right? What if you invited Grace and her to go with you to the Savoy Ballroom?"

There would be a lot of witnesses at the Savoy—not just Rhona and Suze, but a whole dance floor of people who could observe what was being said. "But if Rhona and Suze see me there, they'll know something's up."

"So we make sure they don't see you."

"We?"

"I could get Suze and Rhona to take me to the Savoy. We synchronize things to make sure your friends and mine run into each other." *Her* friends. Would Benny be there, too? Would he dance with Pearl and kiss her right before the evening ended? "Rhona knows what Grace looks like, right? And that she used to be your friend?"

"Yeah. So she said. But how are you going to get them to take you to Harlem?"

Pearl shrugged. "I got them to invite me to lunch, and I never thought that would happen. How hard could it be to wrangle an invitation to go dancing?"

19

I USED THE TIME before Pop got home to call Grace. I told her Pop couldn't do a thing without more evidence and then explained how I proposed to get that evidence. She didn't seem thrilled with the plan, but when I explained it was the only way I could think of to convince the Barneys to go after Josephine, she gave in.

The next afternoon I met up with Pearl at my house, far from prying eyes, and reviewed her progress on getting an invite. She was being very careful with how she played things, making sure not to drop hints that would be too obvious (I was impressed that she was aware that she had a habit of doing this). Unfortunately, that gave Rhona and Suze no reason to even make the offer. By Friday we were in a panic: the weekend was upon us and no invitation was in sight. I decided I was going to have to do something to force their hand.

During lunch, which I now ate alone, I approached their

table. I lingered on the sidelines for a little while, listening as Pearl laughed at their jokes. My heart ached at how easily she fit in with them. It was so strange how she could go from being the girl they all made fun of to being one of them. Sure, I had made the transition just as swiftly, but until I left Chapin, I'd always had oodles of friends. This was a new experience for Pearl and as badly as I envied her, I admired her, too. I didn't want her to have to go back to the way things were once we got the information we needed. Pearl deserved this. Even if it meant I was alone and friendless from here on out.

"You need something, girl detective?" asked Rhona, snapping me out of my reverie.

"I wanted to talk to Pearl."

"So go on and beat your gums," said Maria.

Everyone at the table stared at me, waiting for me to make the next move. Everyone, that is, except Benny.

"I was hoping I could talk to her alone."

"And I was hoping to be a natural blonde," said Rhona. "Looks like neither one of us is going to have our wishes come true."

"What do you want?" asked Pearl. Her voice contained a snappishness that sent me off balance. Even though I knew she was acting, it still hurt.

I shuffled my feet, making it clear exactly how uncomfortable it was to have to talk to her in front of everyone.

"I was wondering what you were doing this weekend. I thought maybe you could come and stay at my house."

Pearl rolled her eyes. "And what made you think I would want to do that?"

"Because we talked about it last week."

"Last week was last week. Seems to me a lot's changed since then."

She was good at this. Too good. "So what are you doing?" I asked.

"I'm going to the Jive Hive tonight."

"So you're free on Saturday?" I asked.

Pearl's mouth dropped open, but no sound came out. She had rehearsed this nicely. Her tough exterior melted away as she came to realize that in fact she had no plans.

Suze picked up on it immediately. "As a matter of fact, Pearl's going out with us tomorrow," she said. I wished it were Rhona who was speaking up. Having Rhona and Maria be mad at me was nothing new, but knowing how hurt and sore Suze was made me sick to my stomach.

"I am?" said Pearl.

"Of course you are," said Rhona. "You're coming to Harlem with us, remember?"

"I'm going to teach you how to jitterbug," said Dino.

At least it wasn't Benny who'd made the offer. I had that to be grateful for.

"All right," I said. I backed away slowly, like I was hoping they'd change their mind and invite me along, too. And the sad thing was, I really was hoping that. I would much rather spend the evening with them than trying to worm a confession out of Josephine. "Have fun," I told Pearl. "If you change your mind, you know where to find me."

I increased my speed, but I wasn't fast enough to make it out of the cafeteria before they started laughing at me.

GRACE CALLED ME that night to make plans. We would meet at her house at seven to get ready for the Savoy. It would be a whole lot easier to sneak out of her house than to try to justify to Pop why we were leaving mine so late.

I just needed to convince Pop that me going anywhere was a good idea.

"Is it all right if I stay over at Pearl Levine's tomorrow night?" I asked him that evening.

"Will you really be staying at Pearl's this time?" he asked.

"Yes." And I would, too. As soon as everything was over in Harlem, I'd go home with Pearl to her house. So it wasn't really a lie.

"It's Halloween, Iris. I don't know if that's such a good idea. Who knows what sort of mischief will be going on?" Mayor La Guardia had appealed by paper and radio for people to keep the peace that weekend. There was enough blood and gore happening abroad; we didn't need even the pretend stuff cluttering our streets.

"We're not doing anything. We'll just be at her house."

He pondered this. I should have said we were going to a movie, just in case he tried to check on me again. "I want to talk to her parents," Pop said.

"Seriously?"

"Yes, seriously. You've been making some bad decisions lately, and I think it's my right. It's either that or an automatic no."

I was close to laying into him for that, but I knew it would get me nowhere. "All right," I said. "I'll have her mother call you tomorrow."

"Then you'll have your answer tomorrow."

I obviously couldn't get Pearl's mother to call him. My only option was to take a page out of Rhona's book and have someone impersonate Pearl's mother. I didn't feel comfortable asking Pearl to do it, not after everything else she'd done for me. Instead, I turned to someone who was bound to be much less conflicted about lying to an adult: Grace.

She called Pop late Saturday morning, posing as Mrs. Levine. She apparently has quite a future as an actress, because when he hung up with her he didn't hesitate to give me permission to spend the night.

Pearl came to our house after lunch to talk about what she should wear to the Savoy. Pop greeted her at the door and told her how much he'd enjoyed talking to her mother. Pearl played along with the same cool conviction she'd shown me when she was sitting with the Rainbows.

"Sorry about that," I told her when we were safely in my room, away from Pop's prying ears.

"You should've had me call him," said Pearl. "I do a great imitation of my mother."

"I didn't want to make you lie for me."

She frowned. "But you just did."

I hadn't thought about that.

"Should I drink?" asked Pearl.

"At the Savoy? It's your choice, but I wouldn't if I were you. In the first place, it's not like you think it's going to be."

She lifted her head, as though to reinforce that she was more mature than I was giving her credit for. "I've had Manischewitz at Passover before."

The overly sweet kosher wine had nothing in common with the hooch Rhona toted around. "Then you're definitely not ready for real booze." The truth was, we had no idea how alcohol would affect Pearl and I wanted her at her most present that night, just in case something went terribly wrong.

"What do I do if someone asks me to dance?"

"It's a ballroom, Pearl. Not a bond drive. You're going to have to dance."

"But I don't know how."

To reassure her, I put a Glenn Miller platter on the phonograph and showed her the basic moves that I remembered from my trip to the Savoy. I imagine it was a bit like watching Pop dance—stiff, awkward, and more basic than a loaf of white bread—but seeing things broken down into simple steps was what Pearl needed. She'd learn soon enough how complicated dancing could be when people who could really hoof it shared the floor.

At five o'clock we said our farewells to Pop and set out for Pearl's house. I lugged an overnight bag packed with the skirt and shoes I hadn't returned to Suze, cosmetics I'd borrowed from Mrs. Mrozenski, and a comic book to keep me occupied on the subway. Once we turned the corner, we parted ways, and I headed to the station. By five-forty-five I was uptown and en route to Grace's apartment. Fear made me walk too fast and I ended up in front of her building earlier than I wanted to be. I decided to walk around the block to calm myself down. As I passed the park, someone called out my name. I slowed and glanced over my shoulder, dreading which person from my former life I was about to run into. It was Aunt Miriam.

"Iris, is that you?"

It was too late to deny it. I stopped walking and tried to match her smile for smile. "What are you doing here?" I asked. While Uncle Adam and Aunt Miriam lived uptown, their apartment was nowhere near where Grace lived.

"I came with friends to their temple for services. Now I'm bound for home." And it was still the Sabbath, at least according to the strict laws Miriam followed. That meant no cabs and no subway. She either legged it home or waited until three stars appeared in the sky, lifting the ban on work. I felt guilty for my own easy trip uptown. While she never criticized how Mama and Pop lived, she couldn't have been happy with how completely they'd abandoned their religion. "The question is, what are you doing here? Is your father with you?"

"I'm staying at a friend's tonight. Pop's at home."

"A Chapin friend?"

I answered right away, such was the power Aunt Miriam still wielded over me. "Yes, Grace Dunwitty."

"Good for you, Iris. I always liked Grace. You need to keep up with girls like that. That's where you belong."

That's where I belonged? Among thieves and murderers? If only she knew. "I better go. She's expecting me." I turned, hoping that was the end of it, but she caught me on the shoulder and wouldn't let me leave.

"We miss you, you know. You're always welcome in our home."

"Thanks," I said. "I miss you, too. We both do." I liked Aunt Miriam and I knew deep down Pop did, too. I didn't want her to take Pop's decision to cut off from Uncle Adam as a personal slight.

"Your father talks about us?" she asked.

"Sometimes."

She smiled. The relief was evident in her eyes. "What's happened between your uncle and your father, it doesn't have to change things between us. This is your father's choice, but it doesn't have to be yours." She spoke slowly and deliberately, nodding when she completed her sentence, as though she needed my acknowledgment that I'd understood her.

"I know," I said. I felt guilty, for some reason. It was like we were criticizing Pop, and how was that fair?

"Your father's business is good?"

I felt like I needed to stick up for Pop in some way, even if I hadn't exactly betrayed him. "Very good."

"He's able to handle the work with his leg?"

"Most of it. When he needs help, he asks for it."

"From whom?"

I don't know why I lied. I guess I wanted to prove that Pop and I were a team. "Me."

She frowned. "You help him in the business?"

I nodded.

She took both of my hands in hers and smiled. "You be a good girl, Iris. Come to see us. Please."

I promised I would, if only because it meant I could escape her hold and hurry on my way.

I was ten minutes late to Grace's house. The same doorman who'd been on duty on my last visit greeted me, though his demeanor was considerably warmer this time. I expected him to remark on the present I'd left in the plants outside the elevator, but he'd either forgotten about my mountain of upchuck or decided that since I was an invited guest, I deserved a little discretion. I arrived at Grace's floor, hoping to find her waiting for me, but it was Mrs. Dunwitty who stood at attention as the elevator doors slid open.

"Iris. I'm glad you were able to come. I was so excited when Grace said she'd invited you over."

I couldn't meet her eyes. The wound was still too fresh. Her voice instantly conjured that other conversation, the one in which my mother had been having an affair.

But that wasn't true. It was just gossip.

"I was hoping I could have a word with you before you go inside," said Mrs. Dunwitty. Was she going to throw me out? Repeat her tale and explain why it was the truth?

"All right."

She fixed a grin on her face, as carefully considered as the twinset she wore with pearls. "I understand you may have overheard some things last weekend. Please forgive me for anything inappropriate I may have said. I want you to always feel welcome in our home. Of course, what you overheard was just that: a private conversation that I certainly wouldn't have chosen to make public to you or to anyone else."

There was an air of blame in her voice that I couldn't miss: it was my fault for eavesdropping, not her fault for saying these things. Grace had made her apologize and she was following the letter of the law without really accepting any blame for what had occurred.

"Your mother was a lovely woman. We all miss her terribly."

"Thank you," I muttered. "I should probably get inside."

I pushed past her before she had a chance to say anything else.

Grace was seated at the vanity in her bedroom. She was alone.

"Oh, you're here! Thank goodness—I was starting to worry. Did Mother apologize to you?"

I nodded, not having the strength to repeat what she'd said. "Where's Josephine?"

"She'll be along shortly, once Mother leaves. Those two are oil and water, so Jo tries to time her entrances and exits accordingly."

She may have been a thief and potentially a murderer, but Josephine was also a good judge of character.

Grace took me in with her eyes for the first time. "You look beat up. Everything all right?"

I tried the truth on for size. "I ran into my aunt on the way here. And then that scene just now with your mother."

"Hell's bells. Grownups can be so taxing, can't they? I do hope Mother didn't say anything else to upset you." She fluffed her hair in the mirror. I got the feeling that if I did own up to Mrs. Dunwitty's apology being light on sincerity, Grace would make a big stink out of it, and I didn't have the energy to face that on top of everything else.

I needn't have worried. Grace quickly forgot what we were talking about and stood up to model her outfit. She twirled in front of me, showing off the dress she'd bought just for tonight's expedition. From the way she was acting, you would've thought she really was just going out for a night on the town, not hoping to trick her supposed best friend into confessing to her role in a murder. "What do you think?"

"It's swell. You'll fit right in."

"I hope so. There's nothing worse than going someplace new and sticking out like a sore thumb." She took me in top to tail and turned up her lip slightly. "Is that what you're wearing?"

"Only part of it. The rest of it's in here." I patted my overnight case.

"Clever girl—I guess you didn't want to get wrinkled on the subway."

I sat on her bed as she returned to the vanity stool. "I'm surprised you're not nervous," I said.

She concentrated on plucking an errant eyebrow hair. "Oh, I am, but I figure it's out of my hands now. Whatever's going to happen is going to happen, right?"

"You never said how Josephine reacted to tonight's plan."

"Oh, she was thrilled with the idea. She's always wanted to go to Harlem. Especially when I told her there'd be loads of servicemen there." She moved on to the other eyebrow. How had she shaped them so perfectly? My own brows looked like uneven hedgerows.

"Don't you want to hear my plan?" I asked.

"I don't have to do anything, do I?"

"Not exactly, but I think it would be helpful for you to know what to expect. Just in case."

She spun around on the vanity stool and set her hands on her lap. "All right—I'm all ears."

Unfortunately, I never got to tell her. Right then her bedroom door flew open and Josephine O'Hara walked in.

HER EYES, CLOSE UP, were a pale blue-gray. I used to think Rhona had dead eyes, but after seeing Josephine's, I realized Rhona's were simply chilled by her manner. Josephine had peepers that were completely soulless.

"You're early," said Grace.

"My mother was driving me crazy. Another minute with her and I swear I was going to snap. You must be Iris."

"I must be. Nice to meet you," I said from my perch.

"Likewise," said Jo. "So are we ready to cut out?" Her red hair had been tamed into curls, her face painted with a careful hand. Her clothes were expensive and, given her background, most likely paid for with money she'd lifted from soldiers' wallets or coerced them into ponying up after an evening of freebie dinner and dancing. From a distance, she was a dead ringer for Rita Hayworth. But up close she was just another high school girl playing dress up.

It was hard to see her as a killer. But then did anyone with the capacity for such things really look like a murderer?

"It's really up to you two," I said. "There's no point in

getting to Harlem before nine. Not unless you just want to walk the streets and take in the sights."

"That doesn't sound very wise," said Jo. "I say we wait to leave until at least eight-thirty. That okay with you, Gracie?"

She had returned to her vanity and her tweezing. "Sure."

"So Grace says you're in public school now," said Josephine.

While everyone else talked about my descent in euphemisms and soft voices, Josephine made no such allowances. After all, she had been a public school girl herself until recently.

"That I am."

"That must be . . . interesting."

"The school's terrible and the people who go there aren't much better. But I'm stuck."

She lifted her chin slightly and I got the impression that I'd just passed some sort of test. "Grace says you have a fellow there."

Benny. What was he doing right then? Putting on his zoot suit and slicking back his hair? Or had last weekend scared him into donning more conservative rags? Whatever his choice, I hoped for his sake no one bothered him that night.

"Had. I don't think we'll be announcing our engagement anytime soon."

"What happened?" asked Grace.

I thought carefully before I spoke. As much as I hated to think about everything that had happened that week, I could put my loss to good use here. "I wised up. I realized that fixing my wagon to a public school boy wasn't going to do me any favors. I may be trapped at a public school for the next four years, but I don't have to become one of them, you dig?"

"That I do," said Josephine.

"You don't think that sounds snobbish?" I asked. I wanted to get on the topic of her own time in public school, hoping to find out why she'd had to make a clean break before she came to Chapin.

"More like wise," said Josephine. "You tie yourself to the wrong balloon and you might find yourself grounded for the rest of your life."

"You sound like you're speaking from experience."

"I figured out that if I want to go anywhere I've got to put myself first."

It was actually good advice. I wasn't prepared to hear wisdom coming out of her mouth. Did that make me just as vulnerable to her as Grace was?

"Are you seeing anyone now?" I asked.

"Jo prefers a band to a soloist," said Grace with a wink.

"Just because I don't want to be tied to the wrong fellow doesn't mean I don't want to have fun. And the safest way to do that is to make sure your dance card is always full," said Josephine. "And you're one to talk. You get this girl around an Army Air Corps uniform and she'll offer to take back things she didn't steal."

"The hell you say!" Grace tossed a cotton ball her way, intending it to be a reprimand. It fell ineffectually to the ground.

"You know it's true, Grace." She pointed her thumb Grace's way. "She comes off like butter wouldn't melt in her mouth. I even bought her act for a while. But this girl has the devil in her."

Grace pushed her lips into a pronounced pout. "So I like to have fun. So what?"

"My point exactly," said Josephine.

Someone knocked on the bedroom door. "Grace? It's Mother. I'd like to have a word with you before I leave."

Grace excused herself and left Josephine and me alone.

"I like you," said Josephine.

"Thanks."

"When Grace first told me about you, I was worried you were going to be like all those other squares from Delaware."

"I have my moments. Funny how public school changes what you're willing to do, but then you probably know that. Grace said you were at a public school before Chapin."

Josephine fished a brass cigarette case out of her bag and popped it open. With one hand she struck a match, with the other she offered me the contents of the case.

I considered the offer carefully. I might've been betraying Pop in a thousand different ways that night but I wasn't about to add smoking to the list. "No, thanks."

She tweaked her mouth to the left and exhaled a stream of smoke. "Yeah, I did my time."

"How'd you end up at Chapin?"

"Fell in with the wrong crowd. Bunch of bad influences, the lot of them. It was either private school or a reformatory. Fortunately my grades were good, so I got a scholarship instead of a sentence."

"Lucky you. And so now you get to be the bad influence?" I meant it as a joke, but as soon as I said it, I worried she wouldn't take it that way.

She narrowed her eyes. "How much has Grace told you?"

"Not nearly enough, I'm afraid. She clams up if she thinks she'll look bad. She doesn't realize how much I've changed and that I assume she's changed, too."

"That's Grace all right."

It was obvious she wasn't going to tell me anything unless I offered her something first. "She said you two like to play the soldiers you meet. Get a few gifts and a nice meal or two and pay as little as possible in return."

"You think that's bad?" she asked.

"I think it's clever. You can't use someone who doesn't want to be used."

I don't think she knew I was parroting Grace. Only that I was echoing a philosophy she happened to share.

"So are you game?" she asked me.

I hadn't considered the possibility that they might want me to join in on their scheme. "I might be willing to give it a try."

Jo relaxed. "I'm surprised Grace owned up to it. Like you said, she doesn't like to be associated with anything that makes her look bad. So you know she traded in her halo for a pair of devil's horns?"

"I'm not sure she ever had a halo."

Another exhale of smoke, this one aimed right for me. "Funny, I think you and I are the only two people who've figured that out."

I took a chance. "What about Tom Barney?" I said. "Surely he knows."

Surprise flashed through her eyes. "The sad part is, he doesn't. And that means the joke's on him."

Grace appeared in the bedroom door, her face long and serious.

"Is everything all right with your mother?" I asked.

"Fine. She's gone now, thank goodness."

We took turns at the mirror, getting ourselves ready for our evening out. As I slipped on Suze's skirt and pumps, I wondered what she would think of me wearing her clothes. I'd make it up to her somehow.

Josephine whipped out a tube of magnet-red lipstick,

and we took turns putting it on. She then disappeared into the bathroom, leaving Grace and me to finish our preparations by ourselves.

"What did you two talk about while I was gone?" asked Grace once she was sure we were alone.

"You, mostly. She seemed awfully eager to make sure I knew that you were just as bad as she is."

"She knows something's up. That's why she came early and braved Mother. I wouldn't be a bit surprised to find out she was listening outside my door for a half hour before she announced her arrival. She doesn't trust you."

How could that be? She seemed to not only trust me, but to actually *like* me. "How can you tell?"

"Little things. Like how she asked you about the boy you're seeing. I never told her you were seeing anyone. That was a test."

"Of what?"

"I'm not sure, but it's not good. You need to be careful, Iris. She knows she's being played and she's going to do everything possible to turn the tables on you tonight. This could get ugly."

I found it impossible to wrap my head around that. I had been starting to think Josephine wasn't as bad as we'd made her out to be, but if anyone knew the real Josephine, it was Grace. This girl was clever—clever enough to get into private school instead of juvie. Clever enough to make my once straitlaced friend go along with her schemes. And clever enough to make sure Tom Barney disappeared for good. I couldn't afford to let my guard down with her.

Josephine reappeared with her hair carefully pinned into place. She seemed to have matured during her brief time in the bathroom. Or maybe it was just my understanding of her that had changed.

"Let's blow," she said. "I'm in the mood for some dancing."

20

IT WAS EVEN HARDER to find a cabbie on Fifth Avenue willing to take you to Harlem than it had been on Delancey Street. After four failed attempts, Josephine offered to double the driver's rate for the lift. He was still reluctant, but the promise of twice the cash at least gave us the chance to hear about his reluctance on the drive there.

Of course, Josephine didn't actually have the money in hand. She might've pocketed enough from her latest marks, but it seemed her intention all along was to make Grace pony up for the bill. So, in addition to being a manipulator, she was also a moocher. And Grace did exactly as she asked, pulling the crisp bills out of her wallet with absolutely no hesitation. She would do the same when we got to the Savoy, paying for all three of us like it was her obligation.

The Savoy was the same as on my first visit: packed to the gills, the music loud, the hoofing hot. I tried to navigate the place like I was well acquainted with it, and did a pretty good job schooling them on where to wait before the doors opened, and where to go once they did. As we entered the ballroom, I pointed out the sights the way they'd been pointed out to me, using the same lingo Suze had, although I misused half the words and made up new ones to replace the ones I couldn't recall. It was all right, though; it wasn't like Jo and Grace would know any better. Nor did they care. As I rambled on about this band and that dance step, they both took in the amazing world swirling around them. I wanted to stare and gawk, too, but I was too nervous to play tourist. We had a plan I had to follow: at midnight, everyone needed to be in front of the building, where Josephine and Rhona would have their showdown and what happened to Tom would finally come to light.

That was hours away. I had no idea how I was going to occupy myself until then.

Josephine had no such concerns. We weren't in the ballroom five minutes before someone hauled her onto the floor and engaged her in a whiplash-inducing jitterbug. For a girl who was supposedly so calculated, she knew how to let go and give in to the music.

"She really comes on like gangbusters," I said to Grace.

"She knows it, too," she replied. We stood near the wall, a couple of wallflowers waiting to be picked. Grace's eyes danced over the crowd, looking for who knows what. Just when I thought we'd both be stuck there forever, a man grabbed her hand and pulled her onto the floor. I receded further into the wall, torn between wanting to dance and wanting to hide. I combed the crowd, looking for Pearl, but there were far too many people for me to be able to spot her. I stepped away from my hiding spot, hoping to get a better view of the room, when a sailor took my hand and asked me to dance.

I said yes. After all, I might get a better vantage of the ballroom.

It wasn't like dancing with Benny. Oh, my partner was light on his feet, but I was as stiff as a Popsicle stick. I still knew the dance steps I'd been taught the week before (and had taught to Pearl just that afternoon) but the fluidity I'd experienced dancing with Benny had vanished.

"Relax, doll," said the Fred Astaire to my Ginger Rogers.

Maybe it was him. He was nice-looking, but he wasn't Benny. Instead of wearing the zoot, he wore Navy dress blues. His hair wasn't slicked back with Brylcreem, but cut close enough to his scalp that the skin showed pink beneath it. He wasn't the only enlisted man in the club that night. The Savoy was teeming with them. The sea of brightly colored dresses and suits was broken up by a uniformed stream of khaki, blue, and white.

Fortunately, though, the enlisted men were outnumbered by the regular attendees. There would be no humiliating the men wearing zoot suits here. This wasn't their turf.

Josephine caught my eye from across the floor. She pinched her forefinger and thumb into an O to let me know what she thought of my partner. She nudged her head to the left and I followed her line and found Grace in the arms of yet another soldier. Poor Grace with her ballroom lessons and impeccable posture simply couldn't give in to the Lindy Hop. She was the exact opposite of her name.

"You come here a lot?" asked my partner. I thought I smelled alcohol on his breath. Whatever it was, it wasn't pleasant.

"No. I'm only in high school," I said. "How about you?"

"First time in New York. The boys and I decided to do it up right and come here tonight. We ship out Monday."

I tried to relax, but it wasn't working. My reason for being there weighed too heavily. "Do you know where they're sending you?"

"Nope." He slid to the right and tapped his foot. "How old are you?"

If I'd been trying to impress him, I would've lied. "Fifteen. Bet I look like a baby, huh?"

"Want to know a secret?" I nodded, though I didn't, not really. "I'm only sixteen."

"How can that be?" I said. "Don't you have to be eighteen to enlist?"

"That's why it's a secret."

"Why do you want to go off to war? What's the hurry?"

"It's a lot better than wasting away learning about things

that have already happened and memorizing dates and names, right? I'd rather be part of history than spend my time learning about it."

He obviously thought the news would impress me, but I couldn't find it in me to gush over how brave he was. After getting caught in my own deception, I was hardly going to reward someone else for theirs. Besides, weren't rules about what age you had to be to enlist there for a reason? Even under the best of circumstances, people were getting killed. I hated to think we were banking on our freedom being protected by a bunch of boys with guns who were too young to know how to use them.

The dance ended and I exchanged one partner for another, and then still another. No one asked me for a second dance. I might've looked like I could cut a rug, but it only took a measure or two before they figured out my legs were as stiff as the cuffs on their slacks. But the activity made the time pass quickly and gave me a chance to survey the room from one side to another. It wasn't until my last partner pulled me into his arms that I spotted Rhona. She was partnered with Dino, whose bright yellow suit turned into a blur of color as he spun around the dance floor. I almost waved when I saw them, but then I remembered what I was there for. Instead, I tried to lead my partner toward the other side of the room, where I was less likely to be recognized.

"What's the matter?" he asked me.

"Leg cramp," I said. I broke our hold and hobbled away, hoping my lousy acting skills weren't drawing any more attention to me than necessary. As I slinked toward the wall, I saw Suze spinning toward Benny. Both of them were grinning from ear to ear as he tossed her into the air for a hip to hip.

"Iris?"

I turned and found Pearl just over my left shoulder. She waved me over to the wall, where she was cooling herself and drinking out of a flask.

Rhona's flask. Oh no.

She saw my panic as I took in that silver portent of doom and shook her head. "Relax. I dumped it out when she wasn't looking and filled it with water. Want a swig?"

I chugged the container half empty and passed it back to her. "How's it going?"

"Fine so far. I got worried when I couldn't find you."

"Me, too. Having fun?"

She was trying to be calm and collected, but I could feel the excitement that bubbled beneath the surface. "I've danced twice—once with Benny and once with Dino. I thought for sure I'd trip and that would be the end of it, but I actually was able to keep up with them."

"Good for you." Jealousy burned through me the way Rhona's booze had passed down my throat the week before.

"Where's Josephine?"

I gestured toward the other side of the room, where most of the military men were gathered. "Over there somewhere. I'm not sure how useful tonight's going to be. Grace seems to think she's on to us."

"Rhona's in a beastly mood. I say we still let her have at Josephine."

"Suit yourself."

Another hour to kill, and my dogs were barking. I'm not sure how many times I danced, but each time I felt a little less pleasure. Maybe it was the fear of how much closer we were to events coming to pass, or maybe it was simply that the Savoy lost its magic when I wasn't there with the Rainbows.

At ten to twelve, I found Grace, and together we tracked down Josephine. She reeked of booze and a sweet smoke that I learned was from reefer. She'd discarded her shoes and switched to dancing in her bare feet.

"We've got to make tracks," I said.

"But the evening's young," she slurred. "This is Randolph." She clung to the arm of an Army sergeant. "He's talking about buying me a steak dinner."

"Can she get a rain check?" I asked. I pulled her away, strongly enough that her hold on his arm broke.

"Are you kidding?"

"I'm bleeding," I said.

"Then get a bandage and sit the next one out."

"Not that kind of bleeding." I raised an eyebrow, hoping she'd catch my meaning. "I don't mean to be a pill, but I'm dying here and I want to go home."

I was worried she'd just send me on my way to deal with it by myself. In fact, Grace had warned me as much when I'd suggested the strategy to her. But something in my face must've sold my pain as real, and the possibility of my humiliation—and hers and Grace's—was great enough that she gave in.

"Oh, bother. What timing. All right, we'll go."

While she said her farewells to Randolph, we tracked down her pumps. We hit the stairs just as the clock chimed twelve. I hadn't seen Pearl round up her crew, but knowing Suze they were already outside looking to hail a cab. She didn't mess around with her curfew, not when the punishment was a hit to the mouth.

Just as we arrived outside, I spotted them. They were near the wall where we had waited the week before, already analyzing their night while Dino sang the songs everyone else had forgotten. Pearl spotted me. Before anyone else had a chance to eyeball me, I turned back to Josephine and Grace and whispered, "I'll be back. I need to hit the ladies' one more time."

I missed the first five minutes of what came to pass, but Pearl was happy to recap it for me later on.

Right after I left, Pearl turned to a very drunk Rhona

and remarked that Grace looked familiar to her. "Does she go to our school?"

Rhona said no, but immediately recognized that this was the girl Tom had been seeing. The others urged her to leave it alone, but Rhona, as Pearl had warned me, was breathing fire that night. Rather than attacking Grace with words, she walked right up to her and slugged her.

Grace's nose gushed blood and she fell to her knees in shock. Rhona's behavior must've stirred something in Josephine, because she immediately leaped to defend her friend's honor. I came back outside right then, but stayed in the background, hoping no one would notice me.

"What is your problem?" Josephine screamed.

"I want to know where Tommy is," said Rhona.

"I don't know," howled Grace from the ground.

"The hell you don't. You did something to him. You made him go away!"

Grace began to sob in pain. Boy, howdy—I felt terrible. Never in a million years did I think Rhona would hit her. And while Josephine was doing everything she could to make sure Rhona didn't do it again, the one thing she wasn't doing was confessing to a crime.

So I stepped out of the shadows and tried to speed things up.

"Grace had nothing to do with it," I said. I tried to help her to her feet, but she'd gone limp.

"What are you doing here, girl detective?" asked Rhona.

"You want to know what happened to Tom?" I said. "Ask her." I pointed at Jo, who looked at me like the world had just gone topsy-turvy.

"What are you talking about?" she said.

"You're the one who told Tom that Grace didn't want anything to do with him anymore. And you're the last one who saw him before he vanished. Why don't you tell everyone here what exactly you did to make him go away?"

Even in the half light created by the neon sign, her eyes burned bright. "I told him what Grace told me to tell him. That she wasn't interested. That military men were her thing now."

The rest of the Rainbows formed a circle around us. "And then let me guess," I said. "You had one of your boyfriends step in and teach him a lesson."

"Is that what she told you?" asked Josephine.

"Never mind what Grace said or didn't say. It's true, isn't it?"

"You've been had, little girl," said Jo. "I liked Tom Barney. I liked him a hell of a lot more than your pal Grace did. Problem was, he was too good for her. She wanted danger, and he wanted a debutante who wouldn't be embarrassed to take him to the country club. I told him that and everything else I thought he needed to hear to get out from under her. But what I didn't do was force him to break up with her."

"She's lying," said Grace from the ground. "She did

something to him. I know it. Make her tell you where she took him that night."

But I didn't get a chance to. Just then a familiar voice called my name and I spun around in time to see Pop getting out of a taxi.

IT WAS AN UGLY SCENE. It always is when you're caught somewhere you're not supposed to be.

"Get in the cab," said Pop.

He took in the sight of Grace on the ground and the blood still pouring between her hands. He saw the crowd gathered around her, just seconds from becoming an unruly mob. And among all those white faces he saw the residents of Harlem who just wanted to spend Halloween night celebrating with hot jazz and the best hoofing in town.

"Pop—"

"Get. In. The. Cab."

There was no option. I slid into the backseat and joined him for a silent ride home.

CHAPTER

21

POP HAD TRIED TO START the same sentence four times, but the words wouldn't come. I'd never seen him that angry before. Finally, the words made their way out of his mouth.

"What were you thinking? Lying to me like that?"

I desperately wanted to know how Pop had tracked me down, but it was clear it wasn't my turn to ask questions. "I didn't mean to lie."

"And yet you've done it again and again over the last few weeks. Is it so awful here, Iris? Is that it? Are you punishing me for moving us here?"

"No."

He paced the parlor floor as he spoke, his limp growing more prominent with each lap he took around the room. "I can't help that we don't have the money for Chapin."

"I don't care about that."

"Apparently you do. Otherwise, why would you go back there? Why would you lie to your aunt?"

And that's when it dawned on me: Miriam had called him. That's how he'd found out that I wasn't where I was supposed to be.

"Do you have any idea how foolish you made me look? Not only was it clear to your aunt that I had no idea what you were up to, I had to spend ten minutes assuring her that we weren't so bad off that I was asking my child to work for me."

So that was why she'd called. "I wanted her to know you were doing okay."

"By claiming I needed a fifteen-year-old's assistance?"

"Maybe you do. One of those girls was with Tom Barney right before he disappeared. That's why I was there tonight. She knows what happened to him."

All movement in the room stopped. Even the mantel clock ceased its ticking. "What do you know about Tom Barney?"

"I went to school with him, Pop. I know his parents hired you and I know you hit a dead end."

A flash of maroon started at his chin and pooled up his face. "I told you I didn't want you involving yourself in anything having to do with my business."

"I wanted to help. I know you didn't have any other work. You said yourself that if you didn't come up with something fast they weren't going to pay you."

321

"That wasn't an invitation for you to meddle."

"I was careful this time. I got to know his friends—the group who wouldn't talk to you." There was no point in explaining how I'd blown that. "I followed leads. I asked the right questions. And I'm telling you, that girl Josephine knows what happened. If someone did something to him, Pop, shouldn't they pay for that?"

Something in his face changed. Had I struck a chord?

"No one's done anything to Tom," he said.

"How can you say that? I have a witness. Grace was dating Tom. Josephine didn't like that and so she did what she could to get rid of Tom permanently."

"According to Grace?"

I didn't understand why he kept going back to her. Of course it was according to Grace. "Yes."

"That's not proof, Iris. That's one person's imagination."

"I know. That's why I was trying to get Josephine to confess."

He put his fingers to his eyes like Mama used to whenever she was starting to get a headache.

"Something's happened to him, Pop. It's not right. She needs to pay."

"Go to bed, Iris."

"So that's it? You're just going to let his parents believe he ran away when we know otherwise?"

"I know you think I'm not capable of doing this job, but I know what I'm doing." He sighed heavily. "I don't think he just ran away." His voice softened, his anger at me no longer important. "I know Tom's dead."

For the second time the room stood stock-still. Had I heard him right? "Someone found his body?"

"No. Iris, Tom wasn't murdered. He was killed during an Army training exercise."

I didn't understand. Tom Barney had joined the Army? "But he wasn't eighteen."

"He lied to join up. I spoke with a recruiter several days ago who remembered meeting him. After that it wasn't hard to track down where he went."

He'd lied, like the boy I'd danced with at the Savoy. But why? "You knew he joined up a while ago?"

"It was an avenue to pursue, like checking hospitals and morgues. It just so happened this one panned out."

"It can't be true. Grace told me—"

"I know what Grace told you. And I'm sure she believes it's the truth, but nothing nefarious is going on. He was just a boy who made a bad decision and paid for it with his life."

I was going to be sick. All these weeks, all this work, and Tom really was missing by his own hand. And now this: dead because of the war, only not really, since he'd died before ever seeing a battle.

"I'm sorry, Iris."

Grace was going to be devastated. I should've stayed out of it. "So what are you going to do now, Pop?"

"There's nothing to do. I'm going to write up my report and tell his parents what I learned. Then the case is closed."

"But won't they want to know why he joined up?"

"They have a son in jail and one they were pretty sure was fast on his way there. They'll probably assume Tom wised up and wanted to turn his life around. So he enlisted."

I could see why the Barneys might want to believe that, but I just couldn't see Tom leaving everything behind to join the Army. And Grace had been so certain Josephine was behind his disappearance—there had to be a reason for that.

"It's over, Iris," said Pop.

"I know."

But despite the fact that the case was over, I couldn't let it go. I needed to know the end of the story, starting with what happened at the Savoy after I left. Pearl would let me know. And if not her, then Grace.

SUNDAY POP REMAINED locked in his office. Lunch was a silent affair, despite Mrs. Mrozenski's best efforts. At one, Pop left the house. He didn't say where he was going, but I could guess: he was going to see the Barneys.

While he was gone, I performed one last act of disobedience. I headed uptown to Grace's apartment to break the news about Tom. As I walked the forbidden Upper East

Side streets I heard a deep laugh that sounded oddly familiar. I turned toward the sound and saw a woman with her arm intertwined with a soldier's. She laughed again and kicked up one of her scuffed high heels. It was Mrs. Wilson, the woman I'd photographed all those weeks before. But her companion wasn't the man I'd caught her with. This was someone new.

She didn't look any worse for wear. In fact, from the way she was carrying on it seemed like she was having the time of her life. She looked my way and smiled. If she recognized me, it didn't show on her face. I was just another Upper East Side kid, going about my business.

As I made it to Fifth Avenue I couldn't shake the image of her out of my head. She didn't look like a woman who'd been destroyed by my photos. Maybe I'd been incorrect in thinking she was the one being wronged. Like Pop said, sometimes it's not so easy to know who's good and who's bad. We really never know the whole story.

Mrs. Dunwitty greeted me at the door when I arrived. Grace was in her room, resting, I was told. She'd been attacked by a mugger the night before.

I feigned shock and outrage. Wasn't anyplace in the city safe? Then I waited for the inevitable questions about why I hadn't been at Grace's side when she was attacked, but they never came. Grace had already prepared my alibi.

"Is your father better? Grace was so disappointed you had to leave last night. She was so looking forward to spending the evening with you. And of course all this nastiness probably could've been avoided if she'd stayed in as you girls intended. I told her that Josephine was nothing but trouble."

"My pop's going to be fine," I said. "Can I see Grace?"

I was escorted to her room, where I found her sitting up in bed, her face swaddled in white bandages. A lunch tray sat at the end of the bed awaiting retrieval, and the radio was tuned to WEAF for *Parade of Stars*.

We waited until Mrs. Dunwitty left before speaking.

"How are you?" I asked.

"Sore. They set my nose last night, but who knows if it's ever going to be the same. Your pop looked fit to be tied."

"He was. In fact, I can't stay." I knew I needed to break the news about Tom, but given what Grace had already gone through, I wanted to delay it as long as possible. "I really just wanted to get my things and check on you. What happened after I left?"

"Not much. Jo huffed away, calling me a liar. Your friend Pearl got me a cab."

"So no confession?"

She shook her head. "I know it's terribly disappointing. And that was our one chance, too."

There was no point dragging this out any longer. "Actually, I don't think we're going to get anything out of her. They found Tom."

"Really?" Grace's face was a mixture of surprise and

something that I couldn't quite read. Could that be relief? "Where is he?"

I took a deep breath. "He's dead, Grace."

The life drained from her face. "Oh."

"That's what you expected, right?"

Her fingers trembled like keys on a piano. "Of course. I just hoped that it wasn't true. How did you find out?"

"Pop told me."

Her mouth formed a small O. "So then he must be going after Josephine."

I put my hand on hers, hoping to comfort her. "Josephine didn't do it. It turns out he enlisted. He was killed during a training exercise."

"Well, then, she must've convinced him to enlist."

"That's my thought, too. Unfortunately, Pop doesn't think his parents will care. Either way he's dead."

She winced as pain worked through her face.

"Are you all right?"

"I don't know. I need a moment alone. Would you help me to the bathroom?"

I did as she asked, lending my arm for support. I left her there and returned to her room. Poor Grace. Like me, she'd been led to believe that something darker was behind Tom's disappearance. And then, to make matters worse, Tom had done this thing no one understood. Why did he enlist? What motivated him? Had Josephine convinced him to do it? Was there something about him that none of us had been able to uncover, something that made him want to defend his country? Or were his parents right that joining up was his way of making a fresh start?

I moved the dirty dishes to the dresser and fluffed Grace's pillows. Beneath them was a shoebox full of letters—V-mail, I realized, the kind that had come from soldiers overseas. I picked up the box, intending to find its lid and store it. But the topmost note caught my eye. It was signed by Tom.

"Dear Grace," it began. "Basic training is pretty much what you'd expect. The food is awful, the company worse, but thinking about your smiling face is getting me through it. I'm going to make you proud, I promise you that. If you want a soldier, I'll be a soldier."

It was dated almost a month before. And it wasn't the only one. A more recent letter written by a friend in his platoon told the sad tale of his death.

So she knew. All this time she had known exactly what had happened to him.

"What are you doing?" Grace came into the room and launched toward me.

"I was trying to tidy up the room. This was under your pillows."

She grabbed for the box. "Give me that."

I relented. After all, I didn't need the box anymore. "I don't understand—you knew? Why didn't you say something?"

"He asked me not to."

I felt like I was trying to work out a math problem some-one had posted on the chalkboard at Chapin. My brain just wasn't prepared for work that difficult. "So then why say anything to me about him?" She'd been in Pop's office. The Barneys' file had been out in plain sight. She must've sus-pected that Pop had been hired to find him, and her visit to the Lower East Side had been an attempt to confirm that. And then the break-in—that had been her coming back to get a better look at things without my interrupting her. "You knew Pop was looking for him, didn't you? Before I told you?"

She slid the box onto a bookshelf beside a copy of *Little Women*. "I suspected as much when you showed up at my house. The coincidence was too much, especially since we hadn't talked in so long."

"If you knew what Tom was up to, why the big act? Help me out, Grace."

Her eyes blazed beneath the shadows cast by the ban-dages. "There's nothing to help you with. What Tom did, he did on his own."

"Then why this big charade?" She didn't respond. Some-thing still wasn't adding up, and she knew I knew it. "Jose-phine was telling the truth, wasn't she? You were never in love with Tom. You're the one who gave him the ultima-tum, not her. You told him that if he wanted to be with you, he had to put on a uniform and pick up a gun." I was shaking. How could someone who was once so close to me turn out to be such a liar?

Perhaps the same way that I had.

"Why did you break into Mrs. Mrozenski's house? Did Pop find something that tied you to Tom?"

"What are you talking about? I didn't break into your house."

"Still, you hoped he'd go away and that would be the end of it. You made him enlist."

"I didn't make him do anything. If he thought he had to join up to be with me, he reached that decision on his own."

"But you did nothing to stop him."

"Oh, bother! He wouldn't leave me alone. You don't know what it was like with all the calls, the letters, the visits. It was humiliating, Iris. So I told him the only way I would ever be with him was if he enlisted. It was his choice to follow through on it."

I stared at her—I couldn't help it. Who was she? The Grace I'd known had never been this self-absorbed. Or maybe she had been, but I'd been too self-absorbed myself to notice. "He's dead, Grace. Don't you feel anything?"

"Of course I'm sorry about that, but it's not like I killed him. Half those boys I danced with last night are going to die in this war. That's what war is. It's sad and awful but it's not my fault."

She was right. No matter how much I wanted to blame

her for Tom's death, she wasn't the only cause. Even if he hadn't gone, there was no guarantee that when he turned eighteen his number wouldn't have come up in the draft. Maybe it wouldn't have been a training accident then, but he could've been killed all the same.

"Why would you try to blame Josephine? I thought she was your friend?"

She rolled her eyes. "Hardly. She's a scholarship student."

"So?"

She crossed her arms. "So I didn't know that when I first met her. She should've told me from the get-go. You know what Chapin's like."

I was wrong that Rhona and Josephine were cold. In that moment I'd never seen anyone colder than Grace Dunwitty.

"Who are you?" I said.

A smile bloomed across her face. "The same girl I've always been. You're the one who's changed."

I WAS SO DISTURBED by my meeting with Grace that I went straight to the Barneys' house, hoping to find Pop. He was still inside as I arrived, his familiar silhouette seated in the parlor with Mr. and Mrs. Barney. I remained outside sitting on the curb until he was done.

"What are you doing here, Iris? Is everything all right?"

I stood and went to him. This wasn't the kind of thing to

talk about on the street and yet I knew if I waited a moment longer to get it out, I'd explode. "Grace made him do it."

"Made who do what?"

"She made Tom enlist. She said she wouldn't continue dating him if he didn't."

He took my arm and pulled me away from the house. "Are you sure?"

"Positive. She has letters from him where it's clear he's doing it for her."

He lowered his voice and seemed to be imploring me to do the same. "How do you know this? Did you go see her?"

I could see what was coming: another lecture about how disobedient I was. "Damn it, Pop—this isn't about me." I shocked him with the profanity, I could see that. "Yes, I went there. I thought I owed it to her to tell her what really happened to Tom. I was going to console a friend who was about to find out the boy she loved was dead. And if that makes me a bad kid in your eyes, then I guess that's what I am." I shook free of his grip and started up the Barneys' walk.

"Where are you going?"

"I have to tell the Barneys."

He gently took my hand in his. "No, Iris. They don't need to know the why behind this."

"But he'd be alive if she hadn't manipulated him."

His other hand found mine and squeezed. "And she's

going to have to live with that. But as awful as what she did was, it's not a crime."

"But still—"

"Honey, right now they think their son was trying to turn his life around. Whether they know the truth or not, the outcome is still the same. He's still dead. Understand?"

I nodded. He was right. What good could come from letting them know that Tom did what he did to please a spoiled rich girl? All it would do would increase the sense that his loss was absolutely pointless.

I let Pop pull me toward the street. As we started home, I thought about Mr. Barney, about how easily he'd given up on his own flesh and blood. Tom wasn't perfect, but he was hardly the terrible boy he made him out to be. And while no crime may have been committed, beyond Tom's insatiable need to please people who didn't deserve the effort, I had to wonder if Tom's desire to make Grace happy wasn't rooted in some similar desire to please his pop.

"Have you given up on me?" I asked Pop.

"Why would you ask that?"

I shrugged, unable to put what I was thinking into words.

"I wish you were more cautious, Iris. But I can't say I'm surprised that you're not, given who your mother was." He winked at me. "When we first met she took me to a York-ville dance hall. It was supposed to be for Germans only, but she paraded me inside with a look on her face that dared anyone who had a problem with me being there to challenge her. No one did. I asked her later why she took me there and she told me that she figured if she could get me into someplace restricted to Germans, it would be a lot easier to get people to accept that she was marrying me when the time came."

I'd never heard the story before, but it didn't surprise me. Mama claimed she knew she wanted to be Pop's wife from the first second she saw him. "If you understand that I'm like Mama, why can't you let me help you?"

He didn't answer me.

"I'm going to keep at it, Pop. I can keep doing it behind your back and making mistakes, or you can teach me how to be safe. The choice is yours."

He was silent for half a block. Just as I was starting to think that he was never going to respond, he paused before a row house with a low wrought-iron fence. "If I agree to this, will you follow my rules and only do exactly what I tell you to?"

"Absolutely."

He rubbed his chin, where that day's beard growth peeked through the smooth skin, adding contour and dimension to his face. He may not have known me, but I was kidding myself if I thought I knew him. "Maybe we can give it a try. But you play by my rules. No more lies and no more secrets. I can't work with you if I can't trust you."

"All right," I said.

"And I need you to trust me. I promise you we won't

starve to death or end up on the streets. Things are hard right now, but they're not desperate." That was good to know. "I don't pretend to know what it's been like for you, Iris. I know it's been hard. I know I'm not the parent you would've chosen if it had been left up to you."

I didn't argue with him. After all, I'd made a pledge to be honest. "Why did she do it, Pop?"

"I wish I could tell you. I don't think we'll ever know, and that's the worst part, isn't it? That she could do something so terrible and not even leave us understanding why."

Tears squeezed past my nose and landed on the sidewalk in front of me. "Do you think I did something that upset her?"

"No. Absolutely not. This had nothing to do with you, I'm certain of that."

"I've heard things—"

He fished a handkerchief out of his pocket. "Idle gossip, Iris. That's all. Everyone wants a reason, and sometimes they come up with the worst explanations possible, even when there's no basis for it. To them, any answer is better than no answer."

I mopped at my eyes and wiped my nose. "I don't think I can forgive her if I don't know why she did it."

"That'll change," he said. "You'll see."

"I dream about her," I said. "In my dreams she's always alive."

He nodded. "Mine, too."

I was surprised. I had no doubt that Pop missed her, but it never occurred to me that he dreamed about her, too.

He put his hand on my head and ruffled my hair. "You know how when you dream Mama is still alive and then you wake up, you have to suffer her loss all over again? In my dreams I'm running. And then when I wake up—"

He didn't finish the sentence. He didn't have to.

22

I CALLED PEARL and let her know the ugly end to the story of Tom Barney. She cried at the news. Like me, she didn't want to believe something tragic could happen to someone our own age. Just because it was the war that had done it, or the desire to be part of it at least, didn't make Tom's end any easier. Just more inexplicable.

There were more people I had to talk to.

I found Rhona at Normandie's after school. She sat at the counter drinking an egg cream while Suze divided her time between her and a booth filled with other customers. Rhona started when she saw me, but quickly recovered, setting her jaw in a way that made it clear she wasn't going to let me ruffle her. "Well, if it isn't the girl detective."

"I need to talk to Suze and you," I said.

"Suze is busy. And I'm not in the mood for your off-time jive."

On cue, Suze eyeballed me and darted into the restroom.

Boy, howdy—they weren't going to make this easy. "I thought you might want to know about Tom."

Rhona squared her shoulders. "Go on."

"He's dead, Rhona."

The tough-girl act vanished. "Was it that girl Josephine?"

I shook my head. "He enlisted in the Army. He was killed during a training exercise."

Her eyes looked wet. Anger flashed behind the tears. "Tommy enlisted? Why?"

I searched my pockets for a handkerchief, as Pop had done for me. "He did it for Grace. She convinced him it was the only way she'd continue seeing him."

She took the handkerchief, but didn't use it. Instead, she mashed it in her hands and twisted it until I expected the fabric to tear in half. Grace would get hers. Rhona would make sure of it.

"Thanks for telling me," she whispered. It was obvious she wanted me to leave so she could be alone with her thoughts, but I wasn't done yet.

"I've been trying to figure something out," I said. "How did you put together who my pop was?"

"Your friend Pearl Harbor told me."

"But see, I think you knew before then and she only confirmed it. You were at my house, weren't you?"

Her expression said it all. She'd been there all right, going through Pop's files.

"You came to get the note. The one you'd written the

doctor's address on. 240 Houston Street." It was the i's dotted with circles that had given it away. The same i's that had been in the notes to Principal Deluca that Rhona had forged for Tom.

She stared at me and I could see how surprised she was that I'd put it together.

"You were pregnant," I whispered. "Not last year when Pearl started the rumor, but this fall, right before Tommy started breaking into lockers. He'd never done anything outright illegal until then. He did that for you, didn't he? He wanted to get money to help you. And then you dumped him."

"I didn't want him tied to a girl like me. I'm nothing. I'm always going to be nothing. He was better than that, even if he didn't know it yet."

It was funny how a girl everyone thought was bad news saw the potential in Tom, while someone like Grace couldn't wait to tear him down.

"So why did you steal the note?" I asked.

"I was worried your pop would put it together and word would get back to Tom's old man. If he did come back, I didn't want that hanging over him." What was it like to fear the people you were supposed to love? I hoped I never found out. "So I guess you're going to tell everyone."

Did she really think I was that kind of person? "You already suffered plenty of humiliation last year. I won't put you through that again." I started to leave, then stopped myself. "Of course, I could go to the police about the break-in."

The little weakness I'd seen in her disappeared. "What do you want from me?" she hissed.

"I want you to make Suze forgive me."

"Oh, little girl—I'm afraid you're going to have to do that on your own."

I WAITED UNTIL SUZE was off work to talk to her. As she exited Normandie's and started for home, I rushed to catch up with her. She didn't seem surprised to see me. Or happy about it.

"Rhona already broke the news," she told me.

That was good. At least I was spared from having to do it twice. "Could I talk to you for a second?"

"If you make it fast. I'm meeting Maria." Her pace slowed slightly. I no longer had to jog to keep up with her.

"I'm so sorry. About Tommy. About everything." I had no idea what else to say. "Here." I passed her a bag with her skirt, shoes, and jewelry in it. She checked the contents and then tucked the sack under her arm.

"I bet you got it good when your pop found you in Harlem."

"It wasn't pretty."

"How'd he find out where you were?"

"My aunt told him."

She raised an eyebrow.

"My real aunt," I said. "I ran into her near Grace's apartment. She called him and he realized I wasn't where I told him I'd be. I guess once he realized I lied about that, he figured he better check all the places I'd been lately without permission, including the Savoy."

"So I'm not the only one you lie to?"

That hurt. Not that it wasn't true. "I didn't mean to lie about my pop. That first day I was so desperate to make a friend, and so when you assumed my pop was at war, I just let you. And by the time Tom disappeared and Pop got involved, it was too late for me to make things right."

She lit a cigarette. "And what about your mother?"

"That was true. Every word of it. I know you don't trust me, and you have every reason not to, but please believe me when I say I didn't mean to hurt you. I like you, Suze. I liked all of you." I felt naked standing there on the sidewalk with her.

She tweaked her mouth to the left and exhaled. "I like you, too, baby girl."

"You coming, Suze?" Maria appeared up the street. In the shadows behind her I could see Benny and Dino.

"I'm on my way," said Suze. "You better head home while the sun's still up," she told me. "You don't want your pop to blow another gasket."

"Will do."

She took two steps and turned back to me. "And remember, baby girl—be good."

I watched them walk away and then headed toward the Orchard Street house. The local businesses were winding down for the evening. Signs in English and Hebrew lured passersby to stop and buy day-old loaves of pumpernickel bread, hand-rolled cigars, and fish piled into barrels. Women called out to one another from the line outside Kamiskey's butcher shop, wishing each other a good evening and asking after their families. The sun started its descent and the air filled with the sounds of children finishing their last games of hopscotch and kick the can before their mothers called them inside. As I rounded the corner, my stomach growled in hunger. With any luck, dinner would be waiting for me and so would Pop and Mrs. Mrozenski. There would probably be a fire burning in the parlor and the radio would be tuned to the evening news.

I quickened my pace, eager to reach home.

THE GIRL IS MURDER
GLOSSARY

aquarium: apartment

beat to the socks: tired

beat your gums: talk

beat your gums off time: talk out of turn

black and tan: dark- and light-colored folks congregating in one place

blow: leave

bringdown: something that is depressing, sad

BTO: big-time operator

bust a button: get upset

bust loose: let loose, have fun

cave: house

clutch your pearls: implies you have heard something so shocking that it will cause you to grab your imaginary pearl necklace

coffee and doughnuts: something cheap or of little value

cold cut: dork

copacetic: fine, okay

cream puff: effeminate man

cubby: house

cut a rug: dance

dago: a derogatory term for a person of Italian descent

dig: understand

dogs: feet

drizzle puss: a drip, a tedious person

early bright: morning

evil: mean

five ticks: five minutes

fraughty: very sad, a deplorable state of affairs

frisking the whiskers: musicians warming up

gangbusters: doing something in a terrific manner, par excellence in any department

gasper: cigarette

got your glasses on: putting on airs

gravel: gossip

hardware: jewelry

hep cat: a guy who knows all the answers, understands jive

Hey Joe, what do you know?: What's going on?

hoofers: dancers

hotsy totsy: someone who thinks they are "hot stuff"

I've got my boots on: I wasn't born yesterday

The joint is jumping: The place is lively, the club is leaping with fun

land o' darkness: Harlem

lord and butler: an exclamation like "oh my goodness"

make tracks: leave

meat: someone new to school

murder: marvelous

off your nut: crazy

oolie droolie: someone very attractive, worth drooling over

pantsed: having one's pants pulled down

Q.T.: quiet

scobo queen: a beautiful African American woman

signifying: to declare yourself, to brag, to boast

Slimey and Atrocious Torture: the SAT test

snood: a hood-like hat

spic: a derogatory term for a person of Mexican descent

square: an unhip person

square from Delaware: an unpopular person from an unhip place

sub-debs: debutantes

take a powder: disappear, leave

Tell me another while that's still warm: Tell me another lie after the one you just told

tipple: to drink

togged to the bricks: dressed to kill, from head to toe

trilly: to leave, depart

trucking: a dance introduced at the Cotton Club in 1933

What's the story, morning glory?: What's going on? What do you have to say for yourself?

What's tickin', chicken?: What's going on?

zazz: special, marvelous

GOFISH

QUESTIONS FOR THE AUTHOR

KATHRYN MILLER HAINES

What did you want to be when you grew up?
I vacillated a bit between jobs, but writing was always in the mix. Sometimes I was an actor/writer, sometimes a lawyer/writer, sometimes a veterinarian/writer. (I guess I was wise enough to know that being a writer alone probably wouldn't support me!)

Were you a reader or a non-reader growing up?
Total reader. To this day, I bring a book everywhere I go because you never know when you're going to miss your bus or undergo some other time-wasting calamity.

When did you realize you wanted to be a writer?
Probably when I was about seven or eight. That's when I played "publisher" in my bedroom, setting up different stations for working on a book (the illustration station, the writing nook, even the sales floor).

What's your most embarrassing childhood memory?
Leaving a note confessing my feelings to my childhood crush. I don't know to this day what I was thinking, but, needless to say,

I got no response. Worse yet, we ended up going to the same college, majoring in the same department, and I lived in fear that he would one day bring up my utterly humiliating attempt to woo him to the friends we had in common. If he did, I never heard about it.

What's your favorite childhood memory?
Gosh, there are so many of them. Holidays for sure—the food, the board games, the lazy afternoons watching movies. Road trips with my mom and sister. That sense of safety and security that allowed you as a little kid to fall asleep in the backseat of a car without ever thinking for a moment that you were in any danger.

As a young person, whom did you look up to most?
My mom, definitely. She was and remains my hero.

What was your favorite thing about school?
English class. And lunch.

What was your least favorite thing about school?
Having to remember a locker combination and P.E. I was never particularly athletic, and being compared to other kids based on how fast I did something was agonizing. Oh, and cliques. I was so incredibly insecure and I hated feeling like I was always being scrutinized. I never felt like I completely belonged to one group.

What were your hobbies as a kid? What are your hobbies now?
Reading, dance, and acting were my hobbies. Now it's reading, running, and acting (plus writing of course).

What was your first job, and what was your "worst" job?

My first job was working at a snack stand at our swimming pool/tennis club during the summer. I was only twelve or so and master of making a grilled cheese. My worst job was probably working at McDonald's when I was sixteen. I had to get the job to pay for the damages after wrecking my car, and every single day I was there just reminded me of how stupid and irresponsible I'd been. Plus I always smelled like grease.

How did you celebrate publishing your first book?

We had a big 1940s-themed party at my husband's recording studio. Everyone wore vintage clothes, drank martinis, and listened to big band music.

Where do you write your books?

Wherever I can. If it's not too jam-packed, I write on the bus going to and from my day job. I have a number of spots in my house that I like to curl up and work in (not at a desk—I prefer to sit somewhere with my feet up). And I love to write outside.

What sparked your imagination for *The Girl Is Murder*?

I was just really drawn to the question of, What would a high school girl's life be like if her mother had committed suicide and her father had come home injured from the war AND she had to start attending public school for the first time? It just seemed like an incredible pile of crap to drop on someone, and I really wanted to know how a character might survive all of that while dealing with the usual agony of adolescence.

Why did you choose to set the story in the 1940s?

I'm so intrigued by how things changed during World War II, especially for women. I'd already written an adult mystery series set during that time period, and I wanted to explore what the war was like for the younger people, since so many of them were the ones who would end up having to fight. How would your feelings change about a "good" war if your friends were the ones dying in it?

What challenges do you face in the writing process, and how do you overcome them?

Every time I finish a book I'm convinced I'll never, ever be able to write another one. I'm also fairly certain that I'm not smart enough to write whatever it is I want to write. I'm not sure how I overcome either of those issues—I suppose my stubbornness wins out—but it's always a long haul, and I don't feel either of those sensations cease until the first draft is complete.

Which of your characters is most like you?

I think I'm probably a hybrid of Iris and Pearl, depending on the day of the week.

What makes you laugh out loud?

A lot. A really well-crafted zinger. My toddler son shoving his toys in the toilet. Realizing I just did something particularly lame-brained like locking my keys in the car. My husband. The man can make me laugh at the oddest times.

What do you do on a rainy day?

Read and write. It's the perfect excuse to not do anything else. And nap. I love taking naps while the rain thumps overhead.

What's your idea of fun?

Eating a heavy, homemade Italian meal, followed by watching anything involving the undead.

What's your favorite song?
That's a tough question, and one that varies based on the day of the week. Today I'd probably say Andrew Byrd's "11:11."

Who is your favorite fictional character?
That's a tough one. I love Daphne du Maurier's unnamed narrator in *Rebecca*. And I found tough-as-nails Ree Dolly in *Winter's Bone* both amazing and heartbreaking. And I've always been a sucker for Jane Eyre. As you can see, I have a thing for strong, solitary women.

What was your favorite book when you were a kid? Do you have a favorite book now?
My favorite books were probably Beverly Cleary's Ramona books. I was a little sister, so I completely related. I'm not sure I have a favorite book right now. There are so many incredible writers out there that, more often than not, whatever I'm reading right now is my favorite.

What's your favorite TV show or movie?
For TV, *Arrested Development* or *Veronica Mars*. For movies, *All About Eve* or *The Philadelphia Story*.

If you were stranded on a desert island, who would you want for company?
My husband. Not only does he make me laugh, he's pretty handy in a MacGyvery kinda way.

If you could travel anywhere in the world, where would you go and what would you do?
Probably go to the UK to visit my sister, niece, and nephew.

If you could travel in time, where would you go and what would you do?
If I had a guarantee that I could leave at any moment I wanted to, I would probably visit the 1940s, just so I could experience life then firsthand, and because I would love the opportunity to meet my grandparents when they were young. But I'm not sure I could handle the blatant racism and sexism for very long.

What's the best advice you have ever received about writing?
Don't give up. No matter how often you're rejected, no matter how harsh the critiques are, keep writing. I think there are two elements that lead to a successful writing career: talent, which you can grow, and persistence.

What advice do you wish someone had given you when you were younger?
It gets better. I wish I could go back and smack my sixteen-year-old self, obsessing over all the little dramas and slights that come with adolescence, and show her how awesome her life was going to turn out if she just waited a few more years.

Do you ever get writer's block? What do you do to get back on track?
All the time. I force myself to write. It's really the only way to push through the block. It's a bit like trying to reach a runner's high—the first few minutes are pain, but once you get into your groove, you feel like you could run forever.

What do you want readers to remember about your books?
That we have so much in common with the people who came before us, and that our ancestors aren't just names on

tombstones—they were real people with real hopes and dreams.

What would you do if you ever stopped writing?
Gosh, that's a tough one. I honestly don't know what I would do. Not to sound too overly dramatic, but I've been doing it for so long that to stop doing it would feel completely unnatural. I can't imagine my life without it.

What should people know about you?
I was rejected. A lot.

What do you like best about yourself?
My ability to persevere. It's rare that I give up on something.

Do you have any strange or funny habits? Did you when you were a kid?
I have mild OCD that certainly manifested itself when I was a kid. I had all sorts of rituals I did to ward off bad things happening to my family.

What do you consider to be your greatest accomplishment?
My son. I'm constantly amazed that I created such a happy, funny little human being.

What do you wish you could do better?
Everything. I seriously always feel like I'm not quite good enough at what I do. It sounds sad, but it really keeps me motivated to try harder.

What would your readers be most surprised to learn about you?
History was one of my least favorite subjects in school. It always felt so distant and irrelevant to me.

A YEAR AFTER THE PEARL HARBOR ATTACK, Iris's father is finally letting her get in on the family business. But when Iris uncovers details about her mother's suicide, Iris is suddenly thrown headfirst into her most intense and personal case yet.

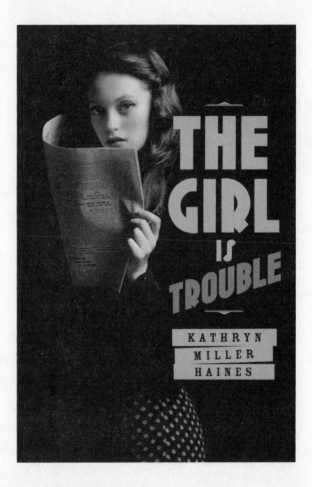

Find out what happens in Kathryn Miller Haines's
THE GIRL IS TROUBLE.

"DO YOU SEE WHERE HE WENT?" asked Pop.

"Not yet," I said. We were uptown, trying hard to blend into the morning crowd. I had no idea it would be so hard to keep my eye on someone while trying not to be seen myself.

"Look harder."

Boy, howdy—did Pop really think I wasn't looking as hard as possible? I focused the camera on Sixth Avenue and scanned the shops on the first floor. I still didn't see where the man we were tailing had gone, but a display that included a red book with a black swastika on the cover caught my attention. Another twist of the dial and the bold yellow text became clear: *Germany Must Perish!* Above the title, words teased emphatically that this was "The Book Hitler Fears the Most."

"Left, Iris. Look left," said Pop.

I swung the camera left, but it was too late: my mark was gone.

Pop elbowed me in the ribs. "There he is, Iris—by the kiosk. Do you see him?"

I trained Pop's Leica on the newspaper vendor. The man in the black overcoat was flipping through a copy of that day's *Times*. "I've got him," I said. "Now what?"

"When he moves, you move. Make sure there are always at least five people between you and him. Got it?"

I nodded, excitement burning through me. This was it: Pop was finally letting me tail someone by myself. "Where will you be?" I asked.

"The Automat. As soon as you get the picture, you join me. You've got fifteen minutes. If you're not back by then—"

"You're calling the cops and my detecting days are over." I rolled my eyes. "I've got it." I slid the camera into my bag. St. Patrick's Cathedral sounded the hour like the world's most expensive starter pistol: ready, aim, follow that man!

Pop splayed his fingers. "Five people, Iris. If you think he's seen you, run in the opposite direction. Got it?"

Another roll of my eyes. The man wasn't going to eyeball me. I'd probably have the picture and be at the Automat before Pop reached it himself.

Pop started across Fifty-sixth Street. He moved about as fast as you'd expect a man with a wooden leg to move. I cringed as a policeman wielding a stop sign halted traffic so Pop could complete his crossing. Once he was out of sight, I started after the man, who had bought his newspaper and now walked east toward Park Avenue. He paused near a mailbox and lit a cigarette. I paused as well, stopping right by the bookshop window. Looking at *Germany Must Perish!* up close made me even more uncomfortable. I'd seen books like it before, only those had proclaimed that it was the Japanese that we needed to eradicate. Once I'd even spied an awful pamphlet that declared that it was Jews who should be erased.

What would Mama think if she could see this? "This man thinks the only good German is a dead German," she would probably say. "He should know better. *Das Kind mit dem Bade ausschütten.* You don't throw the baby out with the water."

But then she was a good German. And a dead one.

The man started moving again. A group of young men in Air Corps uniforms passed by. I silently counted until five of them were in front of me, then continued on my way.

This was easy-peasy. Pop was worrying for nothing.

We traveled two blocks and then the man turned, just like Pop said he would. He discarded the cigarette on the ground, looked at his watch, then tossed a panicked look over his shoulder, like he could sense someone was behind him.

I slowed my pace and let two women carrying packages from Gimbels get in front of me. One of them wore an enormous veiled hat that did a bang-up job of masking me from view.

Apparently satisfied that he was alone, the man continued

walking until he was in front of a brownstone marked number 19. This was the shot the client wanted: capture the mark entering the building, showing his face *and* the address.

He hesitated as though he were debating whether to approach the building. *Come on,* I silently begged. *Get it over and done with before Pop panics and comes looking for me.*

I pulled the camera from my bag and scanned the street for the perfect place to take the picture. Six feet in front of me was a shrub with the last of the fall leaves clinging to its branches. I slowed my pace.

"Little girl," said someone behind me. A finger tapped me on the shoulder. "Little girl?" I tried not to cringe at the "little" part. After all, I was in my Chapin School uniform, and with the plaid skirt, kneesocks, and the two braids I'd woven my hair into, whoever it was had to assume I was younger than fifteen. I turned to find an old woman, bent with age, looking at me. "Your shoe is untied," she said.

"Oh, thank you." I looked back toward number 19. The man was no longer there. Nuts. Had I missed him entering?

"You'd better tie it," she said. "You don't want to risk a fall."

"I will," I said. "But right now I'm kind of in a hurry."

I tried to walk away, but she put a hand on my arm and held me in place. She had milky-gray eyes and an imposing stare that I was willing to bet had served her well during her long career as a prison warden. "That's the problem with you kids today. Always in a hurry. When I was a girl—"

Boy, howdy—was she really going to lecture me?

"You're right," I said. "I'll tie it right now." I returned the camera to my bag, squatted, and wrapped the laces of my saddle shoe into a hasty bow. My skirt was too tight and threatened to bust a button as I crouched. I hadn't worn the uniform in months, not since I'd traded a private school for a public one. "Thanks again," I told her. She narrowed her eyes, but finally seemed satisfied and continued on her way.

I grabbed my bag and attempted to stand back up when a large form cast a shadow over me. It was the man in the black trench coat.

He clamped a hand on my wrist and helped me the rest of the way up. "Why are you following me?" he hissed.

"Excuse me?" I asked. My eyes darted to the left, seeking out the old woman who'd been there moments before. She was apparently faster than Pop, because she'd already managed to move out of my line of sight. In fact, the entire sidewalk seemed to have cleared out, leaving me alone with this man with the very strong grip.

"You've been tailing me since Fifty-sixth Street."

I widened my eyes, hoping that my fear didn't show. Where was Pop? Had fifteen minutes passed yet? "N-n-no," I stuttered. "I'm just looking for my d-d-dog." I reached into my bag and fumbled past the camera until I landed on the object I wanted. Without my eyes ever leaving the man's, I pulled out a leash I'd bought that morning at the five-and-dime.

"Dog?" he echoed.

"H-his name's Skippy." Try as I might, I couldn't make my voice steady. Fear had hold of me and wouldn't let go. "We were on our way to Central Park when he got loose. I chased him down Fifty-sixth Street and thought I saw him turn up this way." My eyes blazed with tears. I pushed them away with my free hand. The man must've thought the emotion was because of my missing dog, not my fear of what he was going to do to me, because he let go and fished a handkerchief from his pocket. "T-t-thanks," I said.

"I'm sorry, little girl. I didn't mean to startle you."

"It's o-o-okay." I mopped my eyes and willed my panicked breathing to slow down. The crowd that had seemed to disperse moments before returned, and I took comfort in knowing that at least we weren't alone. If I screamed for help, surely someone would assist me. I offered him the handkerchief. "Do you want this back?"

"Keep it," he said. "Again, my apologies. I hope you find your dog." He turned and moved back toward number 19. I took a deep breath, gathered my things, and crossed the street. I had failed. Not only had I not taken the picture, I'd gotten caught. The jig was up. No matter what I did now, this guy had my number.

What was Pop going to say?

I couldn't stomach the thought of telling him how wrong things had gone. My working for him was new, his conditions clear: I was fated to do desk work if he didn't think I could handle myself out on the street. I should've been grateful that he was letting me help him at all, but answering phones and making occasional calls wasn't what I had in mind. I wanted to be a real detective.

Instead of heading toward the Automat, I pulled my camera from my bag and trained it on the door to number 19. The man's back was to me, making it impossible to identify who was about to enter the building. I hesitated for only a moment before calling out, "Skippy! There you are." When the man turned to observe our reunion, I got my shot, grabbed my bag, and ran like hell.

I HID IN THE FOYER of a building until I was certain the man in the trench coat wasn't following me. There I freed my hair from its braids, traded my too-small plaid skirt for a longer dirndl one, and pushed my kneesocks into a fashionable slouch. I met Pop outside the Automat two blocks away. It was clear he was on his way to look for me. I guess I should've been grateful—he'd at least waited longer than the allotted fifteen minutes.

"Where have you been?" he asked in a hushed tone designed not to draw any attention to us.

"He saw me," I said. I'd made a pact with Pop not to lie to him anymore, and I kept my word. Sort of. Sometimes I stretched the truth slightly, but kept the basic facts the same. "But I got the shot," I said.

He led me inside the restaurant. The place was packed

with servicemen who wanted to see for themselves a restaurant where machines delivered the food instead of people. Of course, it wasn't really like that. While sandwiches and slices of pie waited behind windows for you to drop your coins into a slot and make your selection, women behind the scenes prepared the food just like at any other restaurant.

"I thought I'd better lie low for a while," I told him as I joined him at the chrome-edged table. "But don't worry—everything's aces."

"Did he touch you?" That was Pop's biggest fear and the reason I couldn't be completely honest if I wanted to work on the street again. He couldn't stand the thought of putting me in danger.

"Nope—he asked me why I was following him and I told him he must be mistaken. I was looking for Skippy." Pop's brow creased with confusion, so I produced the leash. The prop had been my idea. If nothing else, the movies had taught me that the only thing a grown man finds more innocent than a little girl is a little girl with a puppy.

"And he bought it?"

"Hook, line, and sinker." And so, judging from his expression, had Pop. If only I felt as confident as I tried to sound. "He even apologized for accusing me of any wrongdoing."

Pop looked pleased. "So if he saw you, how did you get the shot?"

I should've known he'd ask that. "Somebody across the

street shouted and I guess the noise startled him because he turned toward it. I snapped him right then."

"That was convenient."

Boy, howdy, was it—especially since I was the one doing the shouting.

"What could you have done differently?" asked Pop. It wasn't a criticism. Pop always asked the question, as a reminder that sometimes plans didn't go so smoothly and you had to change things on the fly.

"My exit was abrupt," I admitted. "I was pretty rattled when he talked to me." I loved these conversations with Pop. They reminded me of how Mama and I used to sit on a park bench, pick a stranger, and challenge each other to make three observations about their lives based only on their appearance.

"What could have helped?" asked Pop.

"I could've told him I saw the dog," I proposed. "Then I could've just rushed off in the opposite direction."

Pop shook his head. "There's a good chance of tipping your hand there. If he really believed your story and felt bad for accusing you of following him, he might have followed you, thinking you wouldn't be able to catch the dog on your own."

He was right—I'd been lucky. That was the thing I had to keep reminding myself: Pop had been doing this a lot longer than I had. Detecting was in his blood. "Maybe I could've pointed to a passerby, said they were my mother, and gone running after them." I should've used the old lady. Surely he'd seen me talking to her.

Pop pondered this for a moment and nodded. "I like that. Safety in numbers. It would've been good if he thought you weren't alone—just in case." A funny little pang squeezed my chest. Creating an imaginary mother made me miss my real one all the more. "I want you to write up a report of everything you saw today, okay? Just like I showed you." Pop was big on keeping written records of every move he made. It wasn't just to let the client know they were getting their money's worth; he also said the information could be invaluable to the investigation. You never knew what details that initially seemed insignificant might prove important later on. "Good job, Iris."

I should've been swelling with pride, but the parts of the story I hadn't told Pop were still playing in my brain. This hadn't been easy. What if I wasn't cut out for detecting? What if the next time something worse happened?

"Is something bothering you?" asked Pop.

I couldn't tell him my doubts. There'd be no hope of his sending me out on my own if I did. And I needed to be out there, because stuck at home, with little to occupy me, sent my mind in other dark directions. "I saw this book," I said. "In one of the shops on Fifty-sixth Street. The author says we should get rid of all Germans and make it impossible for more to be born."

"And what does he consider a German?"

"Anyone with a drop of German blood."

"That's a rather extremist view," said Pop. "What do you think?" That was Pop for you—he rarely shared his opinions about the war, even when the perfect opportunity presented itself.

If it took only one drop of blood to make you German, that meant Mama wouldn't have been the only one eradicated—I would've been on the list as well. "I think Mama would be mortified."

Pop didn't say anything. He rarely mentioned Mama. I knew he missed her—he'd owned up to that weeks before— but ever since then he'd seemed determined to try to put her out of his mind. I couldn't do that. If I was going to forgive her for what she did, I had to remember the good things about her; otherwise, the way she died eclipsed everything.

"How can someone think every single German is evil?" I asked.

Pop fished change from his pocket. We both approached the enormous glass-fronted Automat machine and lingered in front of the sandwich section as we took in our options for lunch. Pop deposited his money and pushed the button beside the tuna on rye. The door lifted up and he removed his selection, plate and all, while another one slid into place behind it. "I haven't seen the book, Iris, but there is an idea in war that you must paint the enemy with a broad brush. Otherwise, you'll spend so much time worried about whether the person standing before you is the exception to the rule that you'll never fire your gun. That hesitation can cost you your life."

"But he wasn't just talking about soldiers. He was talking about *everyone*."

He passed a dime and two nickels my way. "Sometimes, the enemy doesn't wear a uniform."

I wanted to believe he was wrong, that it was easy to separate good from evil, but experience had already taught me that the people you thought you could trust were the ones you needed to be the most afraid of. Even still, I never imagined in a million years that the person I would come to fear would be my own mother.